ARKHAM HORROR

It is the height of the Roaring Twenties – a fresh enthusiasm for the arts, science, and exploration of the past have opened doors to a wider world, and beyond…

In the emptiness beyond time and space alien entities known as Ancient Ones writhe hungrily at the thresholds between worlds.

In Arkham, the people feel in their bones that something is different. Something feels wrong.

A dread tide draws fear and terror along the Miskatonic River, and when it reaches Akham, nothing will ever be the same again.

Only a handful of brave souls with inquisitive minds and the will to act stand against the horrors threatening to tear this world apart.

Will they prevail?

ARKHAM HORROR™

The ARCANE GAMBLE *of* HARVEY WALTERS

The Drowned City, Book Three

ROSEMARY JONES

ACONYTE

First published by Aconyte Books in 2025

ISBN 978 1 83908 354 9

Ebook ISBN 978 1 83908 353 2

Printed in the United States of America and elsewhere.

9 8 7 6 5 4 3 2 1

ACONYTE BOOKS

An imprint of Asmodee North America

Mercury House, North Gate,

Nottingham NG7 7FN, UK

aconytebooks.com

"How know we but that she may be an eleventh sibyl or
a second Cassandra?"
FRANÇOIS RABELAIS, GARGANTUA AND PANTAGRUEL,
19TH CENTURY TRANSLATION OF
16TH CENTURY FRENCH TEXT

"It is not possible to formulate any definite opinion
as to the tactical value of heavy flamethrowers of the
battery type. The portable type was found on occasions
to be more useful than other close range auxiliaries…"
ENCYCLOPEDIA BRITANNICA,
THIRTEENTH EDITION, 1926

"When it thunders and lightnin', and the wind begins
to blow
There's thousands of people, ain't got no place to go."
BESSIE SMITH, "BACKWATER BLUES," 1927

Prologue

The three little girls sat on the horsehair stuffed sofa in a rigid row. Dressed in matching ruffled blouses and skirts, one might expect them to look sweet. Instead, many of the more sensitive in the room felt the trio resembled a set of evil goblins.

Trapped in itchy starched petticoats with heads aching from the application of heated curling tongs to their long brown hair, the Palmer triplets felt malevolent. It did not help that their father was telling his favorite story as loudly as possible to the entire room.

"Yes, all born in a row and all girls. We hadn't considered any girl names," he said to the man standing next to him. "So when the doctor asked what to put on the birth certificate, I said name them Baby A, Baby B, and Baby C. And there they are, my ABC daughters." He roared with laughter as the triplets glared at him. Father never noticed how much they hated his story.

Augusta, Barbara, and Columbia drew a sharp breath together and let it out with a sigh. Being exactly the same age (only a few minutes' difference made Augusta the oldest and Columbia the youngest) and often dressed in identical outfits, the Palmer sisters resented their enforced alikeness. But they were not above using it to extract what revenge eight-year-old girls could enact upon an unsuspecting world made to foil their desires.

"But are you sure this is safe for the girls?" Their mother fluttered in the far corner of the room. The sisters despised her almost as much as they did their father. For she was the source of the starched petticoats, the curling irons, and the insistence on "good manners" above all else.

"Certainly they will be safe," said the man in the pale cream-colored suit. Now he was interesting, thought Augusta. Very few men wore such suits in Arkham. Indeed, all of the other men were dressed in somber outfits, as befitted New England gentlemen in 1872. The only variation being whether they wore a long frock coat buttoned closed or open to show off their equally dour vests.

The gentleman dressed in the pale wool coat and pants also boasted a satin vest embroidered with flamboyant vines and flowers. Augusta noted that nestled among the vest's flowers were symbols stitched in silver and gold, symbols that made her feel slightly dizzy if she stared at them too long. She nudged her sisters. The other two turned their gaze on the vest. Barbara looked away first and Columbia made a little frown like she was feeling ill. The three exchanged glances. They rarely needed to speak to know each other's thoughts. The symbols hid secrets, secrets they longed to understand.

"We are simply conducting a small seance," continued the gentleman. "For scientific purposes. The opportunity to explore the arcane realms with triplets could not be overlooked. When one considers the success of the Fox sisters, the metaphysical possibilities seem extraordinary."

"Debunked!" exclaimed another of the soberly dressed gentlemen. "Parlor tricks. Read it in the newspaper."

The man in the flowered vest frowned and shifted a little closer to where the triplets were seated. "There are always those who refuse to believe in genuine manifestations. Who will go to any length to discredit the truth."

Their father caught his wife's arm and led her away from her daughters. "Now, darling, why don't you go into the parlor and have tea with the other wives? There's no need to worry about the girls. This is all perfectly safe and harmless. I will be right here."

Of course, their mother allowed herself to be soothed and shoved out of the room at the same time. Rather than creating a fuss and making her mother stand up for her children, Augusta whispered to her sisters, "Let's find out what they truly want." For she doubted the tale of a seance. Seances were all the rage but there were more than enough mediums in Arkham if someone needed rapping, tapping, or the manipulation of a ouija board. The sisters had tried a few summonings but found ghosts to be weak, misty things. Much like their parents. What they needed, Augusta decided for them all, was a manifestation with teeth and real power.

Perhaps this meeting would lead to such an outcome, if their father restrained himself from doing anything foolish.

Two gentlemen enticed their father into an alcove, half hidden by a curtain, where several cut glass decanters sat. One of the men poured him a generous drink. Augusta also noted they engaged their gullible father in conversation, pretending to laugh at his jokes, and turning him so he had no view of the room.

In short, she and her sisters were on their own. Which was exactly how they preferred it. She smiled at Barbara and

Columbia. The pair nodded back at her, then turned their concentration on the men remaining in the room.

The group gathered closer to the man in the pale suit.

"I thought we were here" – a youngish man with unfortunate whiskers glanced around the room and dropped his voice – "for the summoning of cosmic entities. Not someone's dead grandmother."

"Of course," said the one that Augusta now recognized as the leader of this group. He fiddled with a gold button on his elaborately embroidered vest. "A small test of the Fitzmaurice manuscript. Just to prove its validity."

"I'm surprised Fitzmaurice let you anywhere near his precious heritage," said another. "He's been downright rude to the university when we asked to examine it."

"I may have made a copy of the spell while he was distracted." The leader smiled and winked.

Augusta leaned a little closer as the gentleman drew a piece of paper out of his pocket and unfolded it. In coordination with their eldest sister, Columbia and Barbara also leaned forward.

"A ritual to unlock a door and let one see," said the man.

"See what, Cartwright?" said one of the older men in a liver-colored coat buttoned tightly closed from waist to neck.

"Power!" rapped Cartwright, flattening the paper on the low table in front of the sofa where the triplets sat. "And these lovely young ladies are going to help us by reciting the poem here." He pointed to a line of text and then paused. "You can read, can't you?"

"We are eight," said Augusta in the same tone that Queen Victoria might have used across the Atlantic to declare that she was not amused. Barbara and Columbia simply glared at the gentleman.

"Yes, then we need you to read this," said Cartwright. "Afterward, you can have dessert with your mother in the parlor. There's a cake." He said the last in the wheedling way that indicated he knew nothing about children but had some vague idea that cake was a sufficient bribe.

"I would rather have your vest," said Augusta, still slightly mesmerized by the symbols hidden among the embroidered vines and flowers.

"What? Of course not," said Cartwright.

Now Cartwright looked at the trio with some puzzlement. Did he really think they were just china dolls to be placed on a sofa and wound up to perform as needed? Augusta almost snorted at his reaction.

"The watch fobs," said Columbia, pointing at the trio of shiny fobs hanging from the chain stretched across the gentleman's middle. Each fob was crafted into a symbol very similar to those embroidered on the vest, including a round eye which particularly attracted Augusta.

"Yes," said Augusta with a nod of approval at her sister. "Give us the fobs. Then we'll read your poem."

Cartwright sputtered but the oldest member of the group, or so Augusta judged him by his long, gray beard, overruled him. "Give the girls the watch fobs. It's a small price to pay."

The gold fobs were tipped off the watch chain and dropped into the outstretched hands of the three girls.

"Little harpies," muttered Cartwright but Augusta smiled serenely at him and pretended not to hear. In a clearer tone, Cartwright said, "Please read the poem in unison, ladies."

Augusta considered telling him that they did not know what "unison" meant but Barbara dug her elbow into her ribs. Teasing adults was amusing but they all wanted to learn what reciting this spell would do. So the three sisters in perfect harmony chanted the nonsense verse laid before them. It sounded a little like Edward Lear but turned upside down and inside out.

"When be thou ready to wake, and to rise with a roar, to drive all of mankind to sorrow's shore? Will thou surface when the stars are perfectly spun? We now summon the nightmares, to bend every mind, to learn what is hidden beneath and sometimes behind."

The world wobbled. Later, as they discussed what happened, Barbara objected to "wobble" but neither Augusta nor Columbia could find a better word to describe the disappearance of the table into the shimmering pool which replaced the floor. For an instant, and only an instant, it felt as if they stood on the banks of the Miskatonic River as the water rushed by. An even more distant memory of a day at the seashore conjured up similar smells of brine and decay. Below it all, far away but clearly perceptible, all three girls sensed an ancient and powerful presence.

Through the veil of the water, the triplets perceived a grotesque shape. When they discussed its appearance, the three sisters could never agree about it. Barbara suggested it resembled a giant squid, large enough to swallow a sailing ship. Columbia favored dragons and krakens, those legendary monsters found in the pages of their fairytale books. But they all agreed that the creature slept, eyes closed and its scaly sides barely moving. While this entity slumbered at their feet, Augusta reached down to touch the dreamer, but it was both impossibly close and certainly far beyond her grasping hands. Then the screams of the men surrounding them shattered the moment.

Apparently, the creature in the deep frightened the men, to judge by their whimpers. Cartwright toppled over in a dead faint. Which was ridiculously silly, thought Augusta, who longed to see the entity closer. Not even Barbara, the softest of the Palmer sisters and the only one who actually objected to drowning kittens, was perturbed by the glimpse of the being beneath and behind. Instead, all the girls sighed as the wobbly window into another world disappeared with an audible pop. Obviously, nothing more strange would happen that day.

The table was simply a wooden table with a piece of paper on its polished top. The carpet beneath it was once again a tightly woven pattern in blues and greens that only suggested water if one squinted very hard. Of the gigantic dreaming creature with the alluring scent of decay and destruction, there was no sign at all.

With disgust, the triplets sat back on the sofa. The stunned gentlemen, pale and sweating, looked with wild terror around the room. Stretched out at their feet was the man in the embroidered vest.

"Is he dead?" said the man with the long, gray beard as one of the young men dropped to his knees and shook Cartwright's shoulder.

The man fumbled at Cartwright's neck and then shook his head. "There's a pulse. He's alive. Cartwright, Cartwright, wake up, man!"

The triplet's father, finally aware that something was going on behind his back, emerged from the alcove and rushed to their side. "What has happened? Girls, are you well?" And then, because he did know his daughters, he added, "What did you do?"

"Nothing, Daddy," said Augusta, sliding off the sofa. Barbara and Columbia followed her as she marched across the room, ignoring the men now arguing among themselves about the best way to wake Cartwright. "May we join the ladies in the parlor now? Mr Cartwright promised us cake."

"Yes, yes," said their distracted father. "You should go to your mother."

So the triplets left the room. Augusta slid the folded up spell into the pocket of her skirt. During all the fussing around the unconscious Cartwright, nobody had seen Barbara snatch the paper from the table and hand it to her. Nor had anyone disputed their right to retain Cartwright's watch fobs. It was a pity that she could not think of a way to acquire his beautifully embroidered vest with its strange symbols. As their mother always said, even good girls never received everything that they wished for and bad girls only got what they deserved. A statement Augusta and her sisters tended to interpret differently than their parents expected.

For decades following the seance, the Palmer triplets worked hard to acquire as much magic as they could. They tried the spell again, several times, but the glimpses of the world beyond and beneath remained brief and unsatisfying. The entity below the waves never seemed to notice them or grant them any wishes at all, despite Augusta's certainty that this was the gigantic power with bloody teeth that they needed. So the Palmer sisters turned to other methods to control their world as they felt they should.

Eventually Augusta's precognition skills led them back to the city of their youth. There Augusta and her sisters waited for the day when the stars finally spun into place as the poem promised.

And the terrifying entity that they had sought arrived in Arkham.

CHAPTER ONE

Harvey Walters snatched a few hours of sleep on an item that Davy Schoffner claimed was a cot. Harvey's back insisted on labeling it an instrument of torture. But at least he'd slept in Schoffner's storeroom, which was more rest than anyone in Rivertown expected as the storm grew worse. Since the Miskatonic River began sending waves over its banks in the chilly hours after midnight, the entire neighborhood had been shifting their belongings to higher floors and, in many cases, evacuating themselves up the road to French Hill and other parts of Arkham.

Harvey followed his nose and the scent of coffee through the crowded aisles of Schoffner's General Store. Although it was barely dawn, the store seemed as busy as midday, perhaps even more so. He caught snatches of conversation from the people sheltering next to the cans of beans and bags of flour. It seemed everyone left in Rivertown had congregated in this one familiar spot, discussing what they should do next.

Harvey's newest friends, an eclectic bunch of dwellers from the nearby Flotsam Street boarding house, were already gone to his own home. He hoped this put them far enough away from the rising river water to keep them safe. As for himself, he did not regret his decision to stay at Schoffner's after the eventful encounter yesterday with the malicious Palmer sisters, Columbia and Barbara.

The pair had been attempting a ritual, possibly a summoning, in the Black Cave, using translations of an occult handbook stolen from Harvey. If it had not been for his newest friend, the brave young April May, the two women might have succeeded in unleashing a malignant force as well as harming numerous dogs and a couple of reporters from the *Arkham Advertiser*.

Harvey remained uncertain about exactly what the Palmers wanted to entice into the Black Cave. Recent stirrings in the Dreamlands proved an ancient entity had risen from its eternal slumber. Another Palmer sister, Augusta, had been caught meddling there, rather like a jackal feeding off the remains of a lion's kill. Only in this case, she seemed to be stealing magical power created by nightmares spun off the Ancient One's awakening. Fortuitously, his longtime friend, Dr Carolyn Fern, helped April disrupt those plans too.

Having been thwarted in the waking and the dream worlds, one could hope that the Palmers would take the hint and leave Arkham. Other troubles were clearly on the horizon. The storm and the rising river were terrible enough, but Harvey's own recent foray in the Dreamlands made it clear that an even greater danger was slouching towards Arkham.

While he might want the evil triplets to retreat at their first defeat, Harvey doubted the Palmers were done with their plots and plans. He had met many practitioners of evil occult arts in his years, but none quite as daunting as those superbly confident women who simply turned and walked away when events did not go exactly as they envisioned.

Having spent a few hours earlier questioning the resident neighborhood experts gathered in Schoffner's, Harvey learned that the Palmers were both new and well known in Arkham. At least, the Palmer triplets had been well known in Arkham during their childhood, apparently terrorizing most of the children and several adults in the Rivertown neighborhood. But their reappearance this month was the first that anyone had heard of them in years. Which made them a new threat at a time when Arkham was already under siege by the weather and a cosmic entity that Harvey felt he could not name out loud.

"Wicked those sisters were," said Mawmaw, who had lived in Rivertown for ninety-three years or "from birth until now." She knew the Palmers, once having worked in their house as a maid. Mawmaw also boasted she successfully faced down the Palmer girls over the drowning of a bag of kittens, an act which led to her dismissal by their less than observant parents.

"Their father couldn't see anything past his own nose and their mother just wanted to believe they were perfect little girls if she dressed them like dolls. Perfect horrors, all three. Thieves, too. They'd steal any shiny thing, just like a jackdaw, even though their daddy was a rich man." According to Mawmaw, the Palmer triplets disappeared from Arkham, along with the rest of their family, many years ago. "If they're back, then it is a sign of evil sure to come," spat Mawmaw at the end of her recitation.

Given that Augusta Palmer had escaped from imprisonment in an asylum, a punishment for her ritual disembowelment of her stepmother with a hatchet, Harvey couldn't disagree with Mawmaw's assessment. While Barbara and Columbia seemed to have led quieter lives, they certainly supported their sister's highly questionable actions in recent days.

As for their half-brother Ira, who had been foisted on Harvey through trickery, it would be a long time before Harvey could forgive his former assistant's rearrangement of his books. It was only through luck and a judiciously applied pipe wrench that Ira had been stopped from performing ghastly ritual magic in Harvey's basement the previous day.

Apparently, the return of the Palmers to Arkham, along with other signs and portents, did indicate a major disaster would occur shortly. After a couple hours of sleep, Harvey's tired brain ticked over a long list of possible allies who might be able to assist him in slowing or even stopping the coming catastrophe from engulfing the city that he loved.

Tracking the smell of coffee to the potbellied stove in the back of the store, Harvey found Mawmaw there. The old woman sucked on her corncob pipe as she contemplated a checkerboard. Although she was two decades older than himself, which put her beyond ancient and into the realm of incomprehensible to his students, Mawmaw's eyes twinkled as she slammed down the checker and crowed "King me!" to her opponent.

Lefty Googe shook his head at her. "You're still the terror of the checkerboard, Mawmaw," said the garbageman. All night long, Lefty had used his truck to haul people to higher ground in Arkham. He'd even shifted eighty dogs rescued from the Black Cave to a safer location than Schoffner's backroom, much to Davy's relief. Although Schoffner offered to help, he hadn't realized how much damage so many dogs could do, especially when confined to a small place. Luckily, several of the Drowned Rats, a gang of young men working in Rivertown, assisted Lefty in loading the dogs into his truck and moving them farther away from the river.

"Did you get any sleep?" asked Harvey as he poured the well-boiled coffee from its tin pot into an enamelware cup.

"A little," returned Lefty. "I stretched out in Pequod's cab for a bit."

Harvey found it amusing that his friend had named his garbage truck after Ahab's fabled whaling ship. Lefty even painted the name on the truck's hood. But then his friend was a man of many interests, a former professional baseball player and voracious reader, who had washed up in Arkham some years ago. Although more than twenty years younger than Harvey, the two always found plenty to discuss on the days that Lefty came to pick up Harvey's garbage. Recently Lefty had brought Harvey's attention to the Palmer sisters through a series of encounters that would take an entire book to tell.

As much as Harvey planned to write his memoirs one day, perhaps when he was truly ancient, today was not a day to be mulling over his memories. Today was a day for making plans on how to deal with the evil that was rapidly descending upon Arkham.

He was just about to open his mouth to say as much when a boom shook Schoffner's General Store. An entire pyramid of canned corn rattled to the floor.

"Jupiter's beard," said Harvey. "What was that?"

The door of Schoffner's burst open. A young man rushed in. Another louder boom sounded through the room.

"What's going on, Sol?" yelled Davy Schoffner as he weaved around his fallen display.

"Dynamite!" said Sol. Like Davy, Sol seemed to be a

natural purveyor of Rivertown news. Everyone began questioning him about the explosions shaking the store.

"They started the dynamiting," Sol told those present.

Lefty rose from his chair, his heavy brow furrowed in concern. As he shouldered his way through the murmuring crowd, Harvey followed in his wake. Behind them, the Rivertown residents exclaimed about the new disaster about to befall their neighborhood.

Another boom, even louder than the first two, sounded through the store.

Davy shook his head. "I never thought they'd do it."

"What is it?" Lefty asked, peering through the gloom toward the river.

Sol was practically dancing in place, jigging up and down in excitement. With only slight irritation, Harvey noticed the young man seemed unaffected by a long night of hauling boats out of the river or, for those too big to move, securing vessels to the docks. Sol led the Drowned Rats, which Lefty explained mostly acted as couriers up and down the river for the local rumrunners. They used canoes and rowboats, crafts small enough to slip unnoticed under larger piers and easy to maneuver into tight spaces.

"Police spend most of their time looking for trucks or ships bringing large deliveries," Lefty explained to Harvey. "They don't look at a box or two stowed under fishing gear on a rowboat. Or what's inside a picnic basket in a canoe. You have enough little boats going up and down the river and you can deliver a warehouse's worth of liquor to the gin joints near to the water."

But over the last night, Harvey had seen Sol use his formidable network to shift boats out of danger as well as help sandbag the neighborhood against the rising

Miskatonic River. Then, when a well-dressed man from City Hall showed up at Schoffner's offering "flood abatement" work before dawn, Sol was the first to volunteer himself and the Drowned Rats. So Harvey couldn't help but like the young man, as much as he might resent Sol's unflagging energy.

"We loaded the explosives," Sol told them. "Crates and crates of dynamite. Even had some *Arkham Advertiser* reporter there asking questions and writing it all up for the newspaper."

"Hope you got paid," Lefty said. "City Hall should be thanking you Rats for everything you've done this night."

"We made out fine," Sol said with a twinkle. "Better than I expected."

Another boom shook the neighborhood. "That sounds too close," Davy muttered. "How far outside of city limits were they going?"

"They planned to dynamite a mile or so past city limits, to lower the banks and spread the water into the fields," Sol said. "But it sounds closer."

"Won't blasting a hole in the banks make the flooding worse in those areas?" Harvey asked. He remembered reading about a similar venture down in New Orleans, and the results nearly wiped out two parishes.

Davy shrugged. "Mayor figures losing a few farmhouses is worth saving the city. If the river backs up, we could have a king-sized lake covering Arkham. If dynamiting drops the water levels, the city might be spared the worst."

"Going to take an awful lot of dynamite," said Lefty, sounding as skeptical as Harvey felt.

"They took enough to blow a mile-long hole in the banks," Sol said. "Thirty crates in a bunch of boats. None of the captains wanted all of it on their boat, so they divided up among them."

"Where did they find thirty crates of dynamite?" Harvey asked, pondering the intersection of dynamite, floods, and, if his calculations were correct, a corporeal manifestation of a cosmic entity. He assumed the mayor was not counting on the latter as City Hall always ignored the supernatural, blaming it on delusions of the populace. In Harvey's opinion, they should have kept a few sticks on hand in Arkham rather than using it all on a riverbank.

Harvey never believed that the mayor's plans solved the true problems of the city. Perhaps the local government was good at certain civic endeavors. But they sadly lacked imagination and ingenuity when it came to occult disturbances. Which was why people like Harvey, with decades of experience in dealing with the diabolical, tended to avoid the local government when planning a response to the latest otherworldly cataclysm.

"Do they amass crates of dynamite in the basement of City Hall for possible emergencies? How did the mayor acquire today's quantity of explosives?" he asked. "And wouldn't TNT be safer?" His own understanding of the contributions of Julius Wilderbrand, Carl Häussermann, and, of course, Alfred Noble to demolition was limited. Just what an educated man might know through his casual perusal of a few scientific texts while waiting for the latest shipment of occult volumes from Sweets and Nephew.

"Dynamite was requisitioned," said Davy. "They put out the call yesterday and took every stick in town from a variety of suppliers. Farmers use it for clearing land, blowing up stumps and such. Just had an order come in recently, so I had some to give them."

"You stock dynamite here?" Harvey said, distracted by this vision of what might be found in a general store. Of course, they stored dynamite at Miskatonic University, purely for academic field work such as polar expeditions, but he never thought about how others might use it. Also, he thought it was more likely to be TNT these days rather than dynamite or black powder. Davy shrugged. "Special orders for certain customers are part of my trade."

Another boom sounded and Sol sighed. "I wish I could have gone with them," he said. "But they had all the crew that they needed."

"You wanted to go in a boat filled with dynamite? In a storm?" said Harvey and immediately knew he had asked a foolish question. What man wouldn't want to make such a ride? If he had known about it earlier, he might have been tempted. Except he had a much more dangerous foe to consider. The Ancient One did not awaken and invade the dreams of an entire city every day. This alone was far more dangerous than a flooding river and dynamite, if only for the cataclysmic ripple of negative energy which must now be swamping all of Arkham.

If he understood Mawmaw's recitation of the many youthful crimes of the Palmer triplets, such occult miasma infecting Arkham would lure them into further misdeeds, much as catnip attracted cats. Also, they might want their umbrella back. Harvey had acquired Barbara's green umbrella from his friend, Carolyn. It most definitely added to his problems, as he knew it was no ordinary bumbershoot. Another boom shook the windows and Davy looked distressed. "If they blow out my glass, I might as well be flooded too." Then he turned and waved to the crowd behind him. "It's all fine, folks. They're just doing what they can to lower the water levels."

"Sounds to me like they are trying to blow up Rivertown," said one belligerent voice from the back ranks. In Harvey's experience, there was always one old coot, often himself, who raised objections to whatever was going on.

"Nothing to worry about!" Davy shouted back. Then, over his shoulder, he said quietly to Sol and Lefty, "Maybe you should go down to the wharf and see how it looks. It might be time to get the rest of them out of here."

Most of the people gathered at Schoffner's were stubbornly holding out hope that the flooding would fail to materialize. A few, like Sol and Lefty, planned to stay until the very last minute as able-bodied men might be needed to rescue others. Others, like Mawmaw, were reluctant to abandon the only home they had ever known. As poor and rundown as Rivertown was, it was their neighborhood, and they hated to leave it. Further, there weren't many places for them to go. Harvey had opened his own doors to as many as he could. The city police said Rivertown, the Arkham Merchant District, and even the woods were unsafe.

"Get as far away from the river as you can," suggested one tired young officer who had been patrolling throughout the night. "There are some stations set up at South Church and Miskatonic University. Even the Palace Movie Theater is taking people in."

But how folks were supposed to get there, he couldn't say. Lefty kept piling people who wanted to leave into Pequod and driving them to safer locations. Most of the city buses and streetcars serving the neighborhood ceased their runs during the night's persistent storm but there was talk of the service starting up again in daylight. Very few in Rivertown owned cars, but those who did volunteered to take people where they needed to go. But even as the gutters overflowed and the lower lying streets held standing water, a number of people continued to wait to see how bad the flooding would be.

"I will go with you to survey the scene," Harvey told Sol. The coffee helped but perhaps a quick stroll down to the river would assist him in formulating his plans.

"I'll come too," Lefty said, and Harvey knew he had acquired a guard dog. Apparently young April had been worried about him and asked Lefty to look after him, which was sweet. But Harvey Walters had been taking care of himself in far more dangerous situations for as long as Lefty had been alive. Still, he had been rather touched when Lefty mentioned this was one of the reasons that he had appeared at Schoffner's earlier.

The sound of the river remained a persistent roar throughout the night. Walking down the street to the nearest pier, it sounded even angrier, like a freight train rushing out of control. Small waves were cresting over the boards as boats tied off along the sides banged against the wharf.

"Be careful, professor," Sol called out as Harvey shifted from the road to the pier, gazing toward the sound of the explosions.

"It's not dangerous," Harvey said as Lefty came up behind him. "I have my stoutest boots on." He shifted a few more feet down the pier, trying to see if there was anything in the water.

"Don't get so close to the edge," said Lefty, which again was kind but truly ridiculous. Harvey could walk on a dock without falling into the river.

"It's perfectly safe," Harvey replied, wishing people wouldn't fuss at him just because he was older than them. He'd climbed mountains! He'd faced off with evil cultists!

He wasn't going to be defeated by a slick pier. He waved his friends back as he sought a better view of the center of the river. He spotted movement out there, a bobbing shape which could be an uprooted tree or overturned boat. Or it could be a creature from another world sporting fins and tentacles. Anything was possible now, Harvey knew. To better understand the situation, he needed to see exactly what was spinning down the Miskatonic River.

At that moment, one of the fishing boats banged into the pier again as a wave of water ran over Harvey's ankles. The pier shook.

"Get away from the edge, Harvey," Lefty yelled. He made a grab at Harvey as if to pull him back, but Harvey dodged with the dexterity of a man used to sidestepping students who wanted to discuss their term papers with him.

"Yes, yes," said Harvey, keeping his eyes on the shape in the center of the water. What was the shadow shifting under the turbulent waters, coming closer to the pier? He had to know. So many possibilities, so little time, and the shouts behind him were an annoying distraction. He moved closer to the end of the pier as the river surged forward.

As the debris-laden water struck the pilings, Harvey felt the entire structure tilt as boards cracked under his feet. Mooring lines snapped and loose ends flailed. A huge black cable reared up from the river, almost like a giant tentacle. The cable or whatever it was smashed down on the fishing boat, sending splinters flying into the air.

A shiny trace of slime trails streaked across the boat. At the same time, the pilings shook as if hit by a crushing force. Freed from its mooring lines, the big fishing boat gyrated strangely in the water. Harvey moved closer, ignoring more shouted warnings from his friends, as he tried to figure out why the boat twirled as if caught in a waterspout. It twisted as if an immense hand was reaching up through the water and spinning it like a toy.

The river roared, or at least sound echoed under the pier, vibrating in the wooden structure. The dock timbers began to crack under his feet.

Retreating from the boat banging into the pier, Harvey Walters, much to his disgust, tipped backward into the Miskatonic River as his friends yelled at him to be careful.

Chapter Two

Lefty Googe lunged for his friend as Harvey fell off the pier into the raging waters of the Miskatonic River. April May would never forgive him if he lost the old man just hours after he promised to protect Harvey. Besides, Harvey was a friend. He was not going to let the river have the professor. Lefty knew that he might not be able to save all of Arkham from the flood, but he could save Harvey. Behind him, he heard Sol shout. Lefty belly-flopped onto the bucking pier and slid halfway off, grabbing at Harvey's flailing arms. The flop hurt much worse than sliding into home plate, but it was twenty years since he'd been the Midwest's answer to Babe Ruth.

Managing to hook one foot around a docking cleat, Lefty stopped his slide just before he joined the old man in the river. He made contact with Harvey and grabbed the first thing he touched. Then he held tight to keep Harvey's head above water.

His grasping hands were locked onto Harvey's necktie. The strangling, sputtering sounds made by his friend as he tried to haul him up caused Lefty to pause and adjust his grip. He got one hand firmly fastened in Harvey's coat collar. Harvey's mouth and nose were now out of the river. The old man blew out a plume of water like a surfacing whale.

Looking down into the river, Lefty glimpsed a pile of debris or perhaps a large fish pass beneath the professor's kicking feet. The river stank like a sewer, an almost unbearable stench rising around them despite the rain sluicing down. Another boom resounded from farther down the river. The shadowy shape below Harvey's feet veered away, speeding unnaturally fast for the far bank.

Harvey gave out a gurgle as a wave washed over him. Lefty hauled on Harvey's jacket collar, but the fabric began to stretch under his hand. Harvey choked again so Lefty loosened his grip slightly.

"I need a rope," Lefty called to Sol.

"Coming," Sol yelled back. Out of the corner of his eye, Lefty saw the young man unwind one of the remaining docking lines and throw it toward him.

Much as he once snatched a baseball from the air with ease, Lefty grabbed the rope tossed by Sol. Passing it down to Harvey, they managed to loop it around Harvey's chest. As soon as he was sure the rope was secure, Lefty gave up his death grip on Harvey's coat and rose to his knees. With both hands on the rope, and with help from Sol, they hauled Harvey onto the pier.

The professor rolled up and over the edge with a series of grunts. A fishing boat kept banging against the side but, so far, the dock held. However, Lefty wanted off it as soon as possible. He pulled Harvey to his feet.

Harvey spat out part of the Miskatonic and groaned. "I need more coffee," he said. "Just to wash the taste out of my mouth."

"You are lucky that the river monster didn't eat you." Sol's excited tone of voice implied both relief that Harvey hadn't been swallowed up by the Miskatonic and a certain disappointment that they hadn't met the river monster.

"River monster?" Harvey visibly brightened, shoving his soaking wet hair out of his eyes.

"Yah," Sol said. "They say it snaked Fast Louis right off this dock. Michael McGlen has been hunting up and down the river for it ever since."

"Fascinating!" Harvey said. "I want to know more about this attack."

"Not now. Let's go," Lefty said, steering Harvey toward the street. Both Harvey and Sol seemed inclined to stop right there and discuss McGlen's fabled monster. Which was a very bad idea! The pier swayed and creaked under the assault of the river, the now freed fishing boat banging into its end, and other debris sweeping underneath into the groaning pilings. Lefty felt the wood shifting under his feet. He was certain they would all be dropped into the river in the next few minutes.

"Wait," gasped Harvey. "I need to see what is down there. I swear I saw an organism moving under my feet." He leaned back over the end of the pier while Lefty and Sol kept a tight grip on the rope tied around Harvey's chest. With a disappointed sigh, Harvey straightened up. "It's gone."

Lefty felt some relief that the shadowy figure glimpsed in the river seemed to have disappeared. He had also heard the stories about Fast Louis disappearing off the dock, although many folks in Rivertown thought the monster tale sounded fishy. Fast Louis and Michael McGlen belonged to the O'Bannion gang. It seemed more likely that Fast Louis had been ambushed by other bootleggers, Lefty thought.

Certainly, McGlen had been having dust-ups with the Sheldons, notorious rivals of the O'Bannions, ever since his partner disappeared.

Another boom sounded. Obviously, the mayor's men were still dynamiting, but Lefty could see no sign that it was doing any good. If anything, it looked like more water was rushing down the river toward them. The mayor's tactic might save them from a bigger flood but it wouldn't keep Rivertown above water.

"Come on!" Lefty said and yanked on the rope, pulling Harvey toward him.

"I feel like a dog on a leash," Harvey complained as he stumbled off the pier and onto dry land.

"Valentino has more sense," Lefty muttered, referring to the poodle puppy that he'd helped rescue earlier in the week. Valentino, along with other friends from Mrs Garcia's boarding house, was now sleeping in a dry bed at Harvey's place. Lefty envied the poodle at the moment. Some parts of him had been dry after a night of driving people out of the flood zone. Now those parts were thoroughly wet too.

As a baseball player in his younger days, Lefty often left the field muddy and battered. Hauling garbage wasn't the cleanest or easiest of jobs either. But he'd never felt so thoroughly banged up as when he slid after Harvey along that pier. Some of the splinters stabbing him were worse than Ty Cobb's spikes.

With a sigh, Lefty acknowledged the day probably wasn't going to get any better. He untangled Harvey from the rope. "What were you looking for, professor?" he asked.

"More of those grotesqueries like the one we encountered in the Black Cave," Harvey said.

Lefty winced. He hated caves. Once, when on a trip from

the orphanage, he'd been left in a dark cave as a dare. By the time he got out of the cave, he promised himself that he'd never go underground again. He wanted to follow his friends into the Black Cave yesterday, but the yawning opening put the shudders in him. His friends convinced him that it would be better if he kept watch from outside, but he regretted letting Harvey and his friend, April, go into the Black Cave without him.

True, they'd had Sol and the Drowned Rats with them, but April had been hurt. That fragile little gal, young enough to be his daughter, shouldn't have had to deal with the creature they'd found in the Black Cave, all bulging eyes and teeth according to Sol. And tentacles, too, if he believed the Drowned Rats. Harvey had called it a "manifestation of broken boundaries" (whatever that meant) summoned by a pair of "malignant manipulators of stolen magic" (that definitely meant the Palmer sisters).

Lefty glimpsed a similarly slimy thing with too many limbs on the day he rescued Valentino. While odd creatures often lurked in the shadowy corners of Arkham, it seemed more were appearing in recent days. Along with the current flood, and the attack of sleeping sickness still filling up the hospital, Arkham's luck had turned unusually bad.

He had always done what he could to keep the neighborhoods clean. Beyond picking up garbage, Lefty often dropped a discreet word here and there. If someone pushed a little too hard on the protection racket or something odd slithered out of the river, there were ways of taking care of folks that didn't involve the cops or other authorities. It was one of the reasons he introduced April to Harvey, and let Harvey know about the Palmer dames, as soon as he could.

But now Lefty wondered if his usual nudges and hints would be enough. Seemed like things were getting worse, and he wasn't sure how to fix it. Lefty's worries were interrupted by a loud crack as the pier broke away from its pilings. Wooden planks dropped into the churning water. The debris swept away, along with the fishing boat. The Miskatonic now crested over the bank and the men withdrew farther up the street.

"I'll tell Davy," said Sol. "It's time for folks to leave."

"Miskatonic University still has room at their student union," Lefty said. "Let's take as many as we can. Load everyone into Pequod. I'll run them there." The university was also on the same side of the river as Schoffner's and not that far. So Lefty decided it was the best destination, far quicker than trying to go across town.

"Excellent idea. I shall come with you," said Harvey. "My colleagues at the university can assist me in identifying the precise nature of a certain umbrella. Gaining such knowledge will help me determine the best course of action over the next few hours."

Lefty eyed the professor. He was damp but Harvey was soaked. River water was running off him and making a new stream down the street.

"Maybe I should run you home first," Lefty suggested. "So you can change into a dry suit."

"Nonsense!" Harvey declared. "This is good stout Scottish tweed. It will dry on its own. We should proceed as quickly as possible to the university."

Shaking his head, Lefty followed Harvey's squelching footsteps as they returned to the general store. Sol kept his mouth shut, but he shot several amused glances at Harvey's straight back as they marched up the street.

"The old boy has some ginger in him," Sol remarked. "Do you think anything slows him down?"

Harvey snorted and shot over his shoulder, "It would take more than a quick splash in the river to decelerate my search for answers concerning the occult nature of the object."

"Well, your lungs seem fine, to say all that after being dropped in the river," Sol said with obvious admiration.

At Schoffner's, they organized the oldest and frailest into the truck, with Mawmaw objecting to both labels loudly. Eventually she consented to be hoisted up into the back of the garbage truck and covered with blankets from the store. Some younger men and women hung back, still arguing it was too early to abandon their neighborhood. The booms of the explosions downriver formed an eerie counterpoint to their objections.

Lefty went back into the store to see if anyone else needed a ride.

A mother and a father, with their young son standing between them, pulled a suitcase down from one of Davy's shelves. They paid for it and went up the street to an apartment building. Sol dashed out after them and then came running back. "They say they need a little more time. Not to wait for them. They'll find another ride to her mother's house later this morning," he reported.

The rain drizzled, feeling more like a low-hanging cloud than a storm, but a strong breeze accompanied it, rattling the windows almost as much as the mayor's dynamite. Davy unearthed a tarp from under a pile of rope and handed it to Lefty and Sol.

Outside, they rigged the tarp over the truck bed to give everyone inside a bit more shelter.

Under her pile of blankets, Mawmaw sniffed. "Feels like tornado weather."

"In New England?" asked the wizened sailor sitting next to her.

Mawmaw didn't answer, just burrowed down in her blankets with a mutter.

Looking around, Lefty saw that Harvey was missing again. He sighed. Keeping track of the professor was proving to be harder than he expected.

"Did he go back to the river?" Lefty asked Sol.

"No." Sol pointed into Schoffner's. "He said he needed the umbrella."

A moment later, Harvey popped out of the store waving a green umbrella that previously belonged to one of the Palmer sisters. Harvey was fascinated by its carved shaft, with intertwining tentacles carved into the pale wood and one giant eye formed from mother-of-pearl. Lefty felt queasy every time he glanced at it, like he was standing on a rocking boat, possibly one loaded with explosives.

"I need to show this to a few people," Harvey said. "We may be able to use it to keep trouble at bay."

In Lefty's opinion, the umbrella was nothing but trouble. But he kept his mouth shut. Harvey was the expert.

"Are you coming?" Lefty asked Sol.

The young man shook his head. "Davy's staying. So are the rest of the Rats. We'll be here if anyone needs help."

"Just don't get trapped yourself," Lefty cautioned him.

"We aren't afraid of a soaking," Sol said with the bravado that he usually displayed. But this time, the bootlegger sounded a little more brittle. "Besides, I have a few more things to store away and a couple of crates to shift."

Lefty didn't ask what Sol was moving, because he knew

the answer would probably be "none of his business" or more likely a delivery for the O'Bannions. Most of Sol's smuggling was for the gang, although Lefty always thought Sol freelanced a bit more than was healthy for the young man.

"I'll come back as soon as I can," promised Lefty. He knew Schoffner would stay until the last possible second. The shopkeeper wanted to save his store. But in the end, a man's life was worth more than canned goods and neighborhood camaraderie. He wanted to believe Davy would be sensible enough to leave when there was nothing left to do, but Lefty knew how stubborn the shopkeeper could be.

Lefty suspected Sol would be just as hard to move out of the neighborhood. The young man had stashes squirreled away throughout the neighborhood, some places more risky than others.

"Don't get stuck," Sol said as he waved them on their way. "Lots of water on the roads now."

"Pequod rides higher than any car," Lefty told him, leaning out of the window for a final word. "Deep puddles won't stop us. You take care of yourself too."

"The river won't harm me," Sol joked. "We are old friends."

Lefty hoped he was right. But the recent storm's intensity and the river's roar seemed unnatural. The day felt uniquely wrong, not including the distant booms of dynamite and the shattering of the pier, but he couldn't quite put his finger on what was so bad. Lefty just knew the wind was blowing the wrong way for them all.

CHAPTER THREE

Minnie Klein scowled at the soggy pages of the *Arkham Advertiser* that she'd snatched up from a chair in the lobby of St Mary's Hospital. The slim special edition consisted of only four pages and detailed the biggest concerns of the week: what to do in case of flood, and how to spot the mysterious sleeping sickness affecting so many in Arkham.

She found nothing wrong with the copy, as she'd contributed to both main stories, phoning in what she knew from St Mary's just as soon as she could. Doyle, or whoever had written up the final copy, had taken many of her statements verbatim. They'd even used her earlier photo of the rain-soaked streets of Arkham right in the center of the front page. But where was her byline? Missing!

Also missing was Rex Murphy's byline and Minnie knew he'd worked on the story about bootleggers brawling in Southside.

As Minnie leafed through the damp newspaper, she decided her editor Doyle Jeffries must have pushed this special edition out the door as quickly as possible. Possibly while she and Rex were still trapped in the Black Cave. As annoying as the lack of bylines was, this special edition probably did some good. At least it contained a clear map of places where people could shelter from the flood.

But Minnie couldn't wait to get back to the office and write for a regular edition of the *Arkham Advertiser*, with more depth and broad coverage of the remarkable events happening. Along with proper accreditation for everyone who worked so hard to put together the newspaper.

The damp newspaper left black ink marks on her hands. With a grimace, Minnie wiped them off on her already grimy skirt. No wonder whoever paid five cents for this special edition had abandoned it in the lobby of St Mary's.

She glanced around. For the first time in what seemed like hours, she was alone and that was a relief. A bigger relief was that her friend Rex was going to be fine, according to the doctor who had examined him. When they had been pulled from the Black Cave at midnight and rushed to the hospital, Rex had been unconscious and even slightly cold to the touch. Minnie never wanted to repeat those awful moments of trying to hold him still on the back seat of the car as the driver lurched around corners. At least the young man who drove like a bootlegger being chased by the cops made good time between Rivertown and the hospital. The nurses and orderlies truly had been wonderful in extracting Rex from the car and rushing him into the hospital as Minnie limped behind.

Now Rex was tucked up in a hospital bed and Minnie needed to decide what to do next. She had already turned down her own hospital bed. She definitely didn't need that. Should she go home or go back to the office?

The limp rag of a newspaper at her feet decided for her. Minnie needed to return to the *Arkham Advertiser*. She couldn't believe that Doyle had forgotten to credit her photograph. It was an awfully good shot. And her grumbles had nothing to do with the small scoreboard that she, Rex, and Darrell Simmons kept marking whenever someone got their name on the front page. Winner of the month's tally bought lunch for the other two and held the bragging rights for a whole thirty or thirty-one days. She was so close to winning this month but any of them could land on the front page with the stories swirling around the city. Almost too many to keep track of.

There were times when the newspaper business made Minnie feel like Archy, the famous cockroach who flung himself upon the typewriter keys to write Don Marquis' newspaper columns. Small, insignificant, and battered by the necessity of pounding out words to feed a hungry press. Today was even worse.

But even Archy earned his byline. Doyle had to remember that reporters needed to see their names in print as well as their words.

"Miss, are you well?" said a nurse to her. "Do you need help?"

"No, no," said Minnie, waving the woman off and trying not to tip herself over at the same time. "I am fine. Just leaving." She'd already said the same thing to a number of doctors and nurses this morning. If the hospital had not been so stuffed with patients, she might have been detained. But given the distinct lack of beds available, and the fact that her injuries truly were minor, they had let her slip away from their examinations with an admonition to go home and get some rest.

As if she would sleep! Minnie had no intention of napping on a day when the news was literally flooding the streets.

The nurse gave her a dubious look, as well she might. Minnie was aware that being kidnapped, tied up in the Black Cave, and then rescued by her friends had left her looking less than pristine. Her stockings were in tatters, her dress bore marks of a sludge that smelled even worse than it looked, and her hair was matted beneath her battered hat. Her once smart wool coat was split completely open down the back. But worst of all, somewhere in Rivertown, she had lost her favorite press camera.

Obviously, she needed to return to the *Arkham Advertiser* offices and retrieve her spare camera from her desk. Remaining at the hospital would be a waste of time when the story of the day, indeed the entire year, was happening on the streets of Arkham. A good enough story might even land her on the front page of an out-of-town newspaper like the *New York World*.

Ignoring the slight wobble in her step caused by the broken heel of one shoe, as well as the dizziness still plaguing her, Minnie left the hospital and immediately wished for an umbrella. The tears in her coat were doing nothing to keep the rain off her. Besides, the wool was soaked through, much like her hat, after lying on the floor of the Black Cave.

Although the rainfall seemed softer, she heard a distant booming like thunder. Minnie scanned the sky for lightning but saw none. She turned around and nearly bumped into Columbia Goadby, the *Arkham Advertiser*'s office manager and her unlikely kidnapper.

"You!" Minnie exclaimed as Columbia made exactly the same statement. "What are you doing here?" they both said at the same time.

For it was Columbia who trapped Minnie and her friend, Rex, in the Black Cave with dozens of dogs. Looking at the woman, old enough to be her grandmother, Minnie could not think how Columbia had managed it. She had a dim memory of a green umbrella, a flash of gold, and then nothing until April was shining a lamp in her face. She remembered April's desperate hands pulling on the ropes wound around Minnie's body, and then a fish with tentacles attacked them. But April drove it off with a baseball bat! Which was the strangest memory of all.

No, her strangest memory was of Columbia spouting threats and waving about an umbrella, which April snatched from her and destroyed. None of it made any sense at all.

In front of the hospital, Columbia appeared as she always did, clad in a neat array of brown and green clothes that practically screamed "sensible" to the skies. Certainly, as the office manager, she organized the *Arkham Advertiser*'s chaotic business files into neat drawers of efficiency. She even managed to keep the stockroom actually stocked with useful items like pencils, pens, and notepads.

But somehow she lured Rex and Minnie into the Black Cave and left them there for nearly a day. Minnie could not remember exactly what happened, but she meant to find out more.

"Stop right there," Minnie said, planting herself directly in front of Columbia on the sidewalk, ignoring the rain sluicing down on both of them. "I have questions!"

"Of course you do," Columbia said in her usual calm manner. "You are one of those nosy reporters who think the world owes you answers."

"Sister, we do not have time for this," said a voice behind them. "Get rid of her."

Minnie turned and blinked. The woman standing there could have been Columbia's twin. Like Columbia, she appeared to be in her early sixties. She also was dressed very conservatively in a well-cut coat of brown and green wool.

"Barbara, I agree we must proceed as Augusta instructed," Columbia said, speaking to the other woman and completely ignoring Minnie, much to Minnie's surprise. People didn't generally talk over her, not when she was asking questions in her best reporter voice. "But what do you expect me to do about this reporter? The nasty child, April, destroyed my wand in the Black Cave."

"You still have your fob," Barbara retorted. "Use it. I will help."

"Oh, very well," Columbia said and for the first time she sounded disgruntled rather than unnaturally calm. "But this would be so much easier if you had not lost your umbrella."

"I did not lose it," Barbara exclaimed, shifting to stand shoulder to shoulder with Columbia.

Really the similarities between the two, from face to voice, were frightening, Minnie thought. As was their rapid clipped speech, their answers to each other almost overlapping as if they shared their thoughts as easily as their words.

"I lent my umbrella to Carolyn Fern to control her. I thought we would find it here at the hospital if it wasn't in her office," Barbara stated. "How should I know she would give it to the vicious old man who attacked Ira?"

"We need it back, Barbara. Augusta is furious and you know how dangerous she can be."

"I am not arguing with you. I want the umbrella too. And Ira awake. It's so inconvenient that he is unconscious."

"Augusta can slap Ira out of his silly coma. But let us take care of this problem first."

Throughout the conversation, the pair had ignored Minnie, who was as close to sputtering with indignation as she ever allowed herself to be. As a reporter, she had faced down politicians and gangsters, and there wasn't a lot of difference between them. But those men had yelled at her or shouted about her questions. They had not held a quick, cold conversation as if she wasn't there.

"Right," Minnie said, wishing she had a notepad or a camera in her hand to convey her authority as a member of the press. "What were you planning to do in the Black Cave last night?"

"Summon power to us," Columbia and Barbara said in unison, raising their hands. Each of them held a gold chain ending in an old-fashioned watch fob. The fobs spun before Minnie's eyes, twirling in a hypnotic way. "Chain the dreams. Pull it close from under the sea."

The rain splashed in a rhythmic downpour around Minnie's feet. Outside her head but also inside it, a woman's voice said, "You want to chase monsters. You need to capture the story. Faster, faster, you must go. Run, run, run away from here."

Minnie glanced up and down the street, searching for the fastest way to return to the *Arkham Advertiser*. Brushing past a pair of nondescript women in their sixties, Minnie spotted a taxi disgorging a pair of nurses. Minnie caught the passenger door handle before the cab could leave and yelled through the window, "Take me to the *Arkham Advertiser*. Quick as you can."

She flung herself into the back of the taxi before the driver could object.

Twisting around in the driver's seat, the cabbie looked at her skeptically. "Have you any money?" he said.

"My boss will pay when we get there. I'm Minnie Klein. I have a story to chase," she said with a spark of her usual confidence. As soon as she collapsed on the back seat of the cab, Minnie felt steadier. Doyle would pay once she reached the office. She also had clean stockings and shoes stashed in her desk.

The cabbie grunted but he didn't ask any more questions, much to Minnie's relief. Usually, she enjoyed chatting with the taxi drivers as they crossed town, but she had too much on her mind already. Staring out the window at the raging river as they crossed the Thomas Ward Bridge, Minnie struggled with an aggravating feeling that she'd forgotten an important fact or two.

Chapter Four

By the time the cab reached the *Arkham Advertiser*, her headache was a little better, but Minnie's nagging sense of a lost clue remained. So much was happening in Arkham, with the flood, and the sleeping sickness, and the rival bootleggers still intent on their turf wars. She'd even promised her friend April to do a story on the recovery of dozens of lost dogs by the Drowned Rats gang, although that one probably should wait for a slower news day.

In the newsroom, Minnie found Doyle, who was shouting at someone on the phone. Her editor waved her off with one hand, but Minnie hissed "Taxi! Money!" at him. Doyle nodded and reached into the desk, retrieving the old-fashioned coin purse that he kept for such expenses. He tossed it to Minnie, who took it outside to pay the waiting cabbie.

Inside, she threw the coin purse back to Doyle, who caught it with one hand while continuing his conversation on the phone. "Stay in Kingsport," he said. "I want all the details about Nova Malone's radio broadcasts." He crashed down the phone which immediately began ringing. Doyle snatched it up.

With some relief, Minnie peeled off her battered hat and coat, hanging them on the pegs nearest the radiator to dry. A small puddle immediately began to appear on the floor beneath them. Minnie grimaced. Eventually, the coat's back needed to be stitched closed, but she had pins in her desk and could probably hide the worst of the tears. Although that left the damp, the stains, and, she sniffed, the smell of the Black Cave.

Retrieving clean stockings and dry shoes from the bottom drawer of her desk, Minnie retreated to the ladies "comfort station" as Doyle uncomfortably called it, when he had to mention it at all. It had only been added to the newsroom floor after an outright rebellion by Minnie and a few other women working at the *Arkham Advertiser* over the conditions of the basement bathroom. But the publisher had, for once, agreed to spring the cash for the employees' comfort. The arrangement included one small room with a toilet and sink, and another with a dressing table, mirror, and chair where she could repair her appearance. Minnie gratefully rolled off her torn and dirty stockings, tossing them into the nearest wastebasket. She was tempted to toss her shoes as well, but the cobbler could probably clean them and repair the broken heel. She wasn't paid enough to discard a pair of shoes which could be saved.

Rolling on her clean stockings and clipping them to her garter belt, Minnie began to feel more like herself. She slipped her feet into her dry shoes, a sensible low-heeled pair that she hoped would be sturdy enough to last the day.

Using a dampened towel, Minnie managed to remove the worst of the sludge and ink from her dress. It wasn't pretty but it would have to do. She didn't have time to go home and completely change her outfit! A rummage through the dressing table turned up someone's discarded comb with a couple of broken teeth. With a slight grimace, Minnie repaired her bob. Thankfully her hair was short enough to untangle easily. The gal in the mirror still looked wan, but Minnie flashed a smile at herself all the same.

Marching back into the newsroom, she fished her smaller camera out of her desk. Like all her cameras, it was fully loaded with a fresh roll of film. The Kodak Vest Pocket wasn't the best camera in the world, but until she recovered her Speed Graphic, it would have to do. At least she could slip it into a coat pocket. But she needed a coat.

Glancing around the newsroom, Minnie noticed a trench coat hanging from the pegs by the door. She thought it belonged to Darrell, but he wasn't in the newsroom. So Minnie popped her head into her editor's office.

Doyle yelled into the phone, "No, a whole lot of dynamite isn't good enough. Find out the exact number of boxes or crates. Somebody there must know! Keep asking! We need facts, not vague descriptions. Climb on a boat and follow them. Take pictures of what happens. I don't care if they already started setting it off. Hurry. Take pictures of the aftermath." He crashed the receiver down.

"College boy! Why do I have a useless college boy covering the mayor's dynamite scheme?" he asked Minnie.

The "college boy" was the publisher's nephew, Edgar, whom Doyle had reluctantly given a job. So far Edgar had been largely confined to writing up social news, but obviously the newsroom was short of staff during this crisis of a day. A few reporters and staff had fallen to the sleeping sickness and, of course, Rex was now stuck in the hospital after being ambushed in Rivertown and dragged into the Black Cave.

"Where's Darrell?" asked Minnie, because Darrell Simmons was a far better reporter than Edgar.

"I sent Darrell to Kingsport before I knew about the City Hall's plan to dynamite down river," Doyle replied. "Darrell is working on a story about Nova Malone's efforts. Her radio station is broadcasting up-to-the-minute flood reports and weather warnings. And she's thrown open the Diamond Dog to everyone near Kingsport. Free coffee and soup for anyone who needs shelter from the storm. The woman always makes for good copy."

The notorious bootlegger, although Nova denied the bootlegging publicly, was a flashy older woman well known throughout the region for her radio station, the lively Diamond Dog dance hall, and a certain civic spirit. The Kingsport newspaper had even run a slightly hysterical editorial about the possibility of the bootlegger angling for the job of mayor during the next elections. Minnie read it and wasn't sure if Nova's probable criminal history or her being a woman made her such a threat to Kingsport's City Hall. Nova had laughed off the speculations with a quip: "I have too much to do already."

But Doyle sensed an opportunity to one up a rival, so he insisted on running articles about how generous Nova was to the people of Kingsport, much to the aggravation of his counterpart at *Kingsport Gazette*.

Minnie was a little sorry that she'd missed the assignment. Nova always gave a good quote and posed beautifully for photographs. Even the dynamite scheme sounded like a chance for a page one photograph. "How's Rex?" said Doyle. Minnie phoned her editor earlier from St Mary's as soon as Rex was conscious.

"Three broken ribs and a cracked skull," said Minnie. "The nurses hid his pants so he won't leave."

"You got out," Doyle observed.

"I only have a few bruises," Minnie explained. "And I didn't let them take my clothes away."

Doyle shook his head. "Reporters today. Not what they were." From his tone, it was obvious he didn't approve of any reporter shirking work for such a simple reason as a few broken bones or the lack of his trousers. Not on days like this.

"Rex asked for a phone set up next to his hospital bed," Minnie said. "He'll phone in reports about what's happening there." All the nurses were succumbing to Rex's charm when Minnie left earlier, so she had no doubt he'd secure some good gossip, even if he couldn't roam the hallways. Rex always found a way to get his story.

Now Minnie needed to figure out what the best move was for her contribution. If Rex managed to write more inches than her while confined to a hospital bed, she would never hear the end of it. Which reminded her of another thing that Rex requested along with the phone.

"You need to send a small typewriter to St Mary's for Rex," Minnie told Doyle. "One that can fit on his bedside table. I left him with my notebook and pencil."

"Transporting typewriters sounds like a job for Edgar when he's done with the dynamite." Doyle appeared a little less peeved now he knew Rex was still working.

"Any luck with the Miskatonic River monsters?" he asked.

"We saw something," Minnie said. She thought about telling Doyle that she lost the Speed Graphic with her only photos of Rivertown's monster. But she had hopes of recovering it if she went back there.

"Something isn't good enough," Doyle said. "We need–"

"Facts!" Minnie finished for him. "We were on it but then

we were jumped. Knocked out, tied up, and dropped in the Black Cave."

"By who?" said Doyle, always the editor ready to secure all the needed elements of an article.

"I'm not sure," said Minnie. The whole incident was still annoyingly foggy in her memory at the moment. For some reason, she kept thinking Columbia Goadby, the office's overly efficient manager, was involved. But maybe that was a nightmare. It didn't seem likely.

"But why?" Doyle said, recalling Minnie to the present.

"That's not clear either," Minnie admitted. She wished she could remember exactly how they landed in the Black Cave when they had gone to Rivertown's docks to hunt monsters. But she did have a burning certainty that if she returned there, she would find her answers.

"So how were you rescued?" Doyle said in the dogged manner that served him well during his days as a reporter and in his current position as editor.

"Oh, that was April May and friends of hers," Minnie said. The memory of April leading her out of the cave was startlingly clear compared to everything else.

Doyle blinked. "April May? The tiny gal who stands at the counter and writes down orders for classified advertisements?" When Minnie nodded, he asked in a resigned voice, "Did you at least get her picture?"

"Not yet," Minnie admitted. Then decided that she needed to confess about the Speed Graphic. "I lost my camera when we were kidnapped." And the film in it, which she thought included the creature in the river. She hung right over the end of the dock where the locals claimed some gangster named Fast Louis disappeared, scanning the water for the creature reported to haunt the river. She saw what looked like a tentacled shadow in the water. Rex kept a firm grip on her ankles and complained about her taking risks. But by the time he pulled her up, Minnie felt certain that she had captured the shadowy creature of menace on film.

"Abduction, Black Cave, brave rescue by an *Arkham Advertiser* employee." Doyle ticked the known elements off on his fingers. "I never liked the river monster stuff. But it's a good story without weird aquatic dwellers. Still, we need more…"

"More facts. Who, what, when, where, and why," agreed Minnie. As well as more on how certain monsters were popping up in Arkham, whether or not Doyle liked that angle. Because she had seen a tentacled flying fish that April fought off with a baseball bat. But, without a good photograph, nobody, certainly not the *Arkham Advertiser* or the *New York World*, would print her story featuring it. "That's why I'm heading to Rivertown. We need photos of the neighborhood now and how they are preparing for a flood. I can interview people at Schoffner's General Store about whether they'll stay or go. We'll want the people's reaction to the mayor's dynamite plan, maybe as a sidebar to Edgar's story."

Doyle sighed. "If Edgar brings back a story. But it's a start. Check in throughout the day. We're planning to print the evening edition an hour early. The mayor asked everyone to keep deliveries to a minimum after dark, when the flood crests, so we want to get the newspapers out before sunset."

Minnie nodded. She loved seeing the evening edition hitting the streets with a slap as folks went out to dinner or to see a movie at the Palace. But she supposed people would be staying home tonight and the newsstands would be closing early.

"The pressmen saw a little water in the basement, but it seems to be draining away," Doyle continued. "The more we can get done today, the better. We may need to evacuate to Kingsport to print tomorrow's newspaper." The *Arkham Advertiser* and the *Kingsport Gazette* competed with gusto for the latest news, always trying to scoop their rival, but both stood ready to print the other's newspaper in times of disaster.

"No worries, boss, I'm on it," Minnie said as she snatched Darrell's trench coat off the peg. He was a good egg, Darrell, so she knew he wouldn't mind donating it to the cause. She was on a deadline and needed to rush. That feeling was absolutely driving her now.

Besides, she could probably get Darrell's coat back to the office before he returned from Kingsport. Belted around her, his coat was a bit long but it covered her dress completely. The big pockets also held her camera, pencils, and a blank notebook.

"Got everything?" Doyle called from his office.

"I need a hat," said Minnie, marching back in. She stared at the fedora on the top of her editor's bookcase. The relic of Doyle's reporting days still sported a wilted card marked "Press" in the hatband.

"Go on, take it," said Doyle.

With a grin, Minnie grabbed the hat and shoved it on her head. Now she felt ready to chase a story. The idea that she was heading out, that she was once more on the trail of Rivertown's mysterious monster, made her feel better. This was what she was supposed to do.

"How are you getting to Rivertown?" Doyle asked. "The trams and buses were mostly shut down last night but they say the buses will be running again soon. The streetcars may be going later."

"Already thought of that," Minnie said. "I asked the taxi to wait for me. He was happy to do so after I mentioned the *Arkham Advertiser* would pay the bill."

Doyle pulled his coin purse back out of the desk and juggled it to test the weight. Then he tossed the purse to Minnie. "Take it," he said. "You might need extra. It's going to be a long day."

"It sure is," said Minnie as she stowed the coin purse in her pocket and tipped Doyle's hat to him, "but there's a heck of a story waiting out there for us."

CHAPTER FIVE

Lefty had dropped Harvey off at the student union with the other refugees from the storm.

"I should go to Flotsam Street," he said to Harvey, "and check on Mrs Garcia." Harvey knew his friend was worried about the landlady's decision to stay at her boarding house until the entire street was evacuated. The five landladies of Flotsam Street were apparently determined to stay with their houses, much like the captains of ships refusing to leave until everyone was safe.

Harvey reassured Lefty that he would be fine, despite his damp suit. "I need to do a little research," he said. "Why don't we plan to meet here in an hour and then see what type of breakfast Mrs Fox has to offer us?"

Harvey expected his housekeeper had arrived at his house at her normal early hour. It seemed unlikely a flood or storm would stop Mrs Fox from her appointed chores. He had thought about going home first, but she was perfectly capable of handling the small matter of his unexpected house guests. By the time he was done with his research and returned home with Lefty, Mrs Fox should have worked her usual magic with the coffee pot, bacon, and, if he was lucky, cornbread.

However, if Mrs Fox was peeved, his breakfast might be porridge. Harvey supposed he owed his housekeeper more than a hastily scribbled note to explain the two dogs and half-dozen people now residing at the house. Although Harvey had no doubts about Mrs Fox's ability to rise to the occasion and provide hot beverages and sustenance for all. As much as he had appreciated Schoffner's perpetual pot of coffee, Mrs Fox brewed a far finer beverage. Harvey hoped to wheedle a full cup out of her clutches with minimal apologies for the extra work.

Lefty agreed to Harvey's suggestions and rumbled away in Pequod. Harvey scanned the campus. Who would be in their offices and able to answer his questions about the umbrella? Actually, most of his old colleagues should be on campus. They spent more time at Miskatonic University than at home. But he needed very specific expertise to fully understand the green umbrella taken from Barbara Palmer.

The shaft of the umbrella resembled the ancient wands used by a cult to summon monsters out of dreams or possibly other dimensions. The Palmer sisters already demonstrated they knew how to do this. Who among Harvey's academic acquaintances would know about such deadly magic and dangerous women?

"Well, I don't know about the women but Armitage certainly knows about magic," Harvey muttered to himself as he trudged toward the library. As he walked across the campus, Harvey became more and more aware that he squelched. His tweed suit had soaked up the Miskatonic like a sponge. He dripped his way toward the library. One or two students were looking at him oddly, as students were wont to do if someone reeking of Arkham's river walked past them.

Harvey straightened his tie, also wet and starting to leave red marks on his shirt, and buttoned his suit jacket all the way up to hide as much of the mess as he could. Luckily his suit was good stout Scottish tweed and clung valiantly to its shape even after being doused in the river. Although Harvey was becoming aware of a certain sagging in a place best not contemplated too closely.

To look more like the people scurrying across campus, Harvey opened the green umbrella and raised it high to keep the drizzle off his head. His hat was floating somewhere down river. The umbrella might hold unspeakable secrets but it definitely looked like a practical item to carry on such a day. Perhaps it would lend him a little more respectability if nobody inspected the shaft's writhing tentacle carvings too closely.

People bustled through the doors of the Orne Library which had opened early on this unusual day. The place was full of academics seeking shelter from the rain or perhaps from the overstuffed student union. Harvey spent a few minutes near a radiator to dry off a little more. He steamed slightly, but so did many people shaking out their coats and stashing their umbrellas into the large umbrella stands near the door. Harvey rolled up his umbrella and stuck it under his arm. He had no intention of leaving such a cursed item in a public stand. Heaven knew what the students would do with it if they found it.

As he crossed the main lobby of the Orne, Harvey pretended the loud squeaking of his boots was coming from someone else. He did this by keeping his gaze up and focused on the distance, like a professor in a hurry to reach the research stacks. In reality, of course, he was looking for the one man who was always in the Orne somewhere.

As Harvey hunted for Dr Henry Armitage, he found his friend proved rather elusive. Several people acknowledged seeing Armitage within the last hour but couldn't say exactly where he had gone. Finally, one librarian suggested that Harvey head to the attics.

"The Orne has attics?" Harvey asked the young lady.

"Certainly," she said. "We wouldn't store any books there, of course. But we use it for old furniture and other odds and ends."

"But why is Armitage in the attic?" Harvey said, although he supposed Armitage could be classified as odd.

"He's checking for leaks. Dr Armitage doesn't trust the janitors to do it properly," the librarian replied, returning to what she obviously considered the far more important task of sorting the books on her desk and stamping them as "returned" on the correct card. Storms, floods, and a strange pandemic of sleeping sickness might be engulfing the city, but a librarian's work was never done.

Harvey found her steady stamping of library cards rather reassuring.

After a little more hunting around the edges of the Orne, Harvey discovered the stairs leading to the attics. With a heartfelt sigh, he mounted them. He climbed mountains in his youth but these days, his knees preferred to stick to level ground.

Once he ascended to the attics, Harvey found them to be actually quite spacious and airy. Even pleasantly warm, with a radiator near the door. Some tables and chairs were neatly arranged at one end, and a few boxes, probably not containing books, formed a small pyramid at the other end of the long room. In between was a large empty space with only dusty footprints marking any recent disturbance. The footprints belonged to Dr Henry Armitage, as predicted by the librarian downstairs. The man paced back and forth, his pale face turned toward the vaulted ceiling.

Here, at the very top of the Orne Library, the rain striking the multi-colored slate roof made an almost melodic and soothing sound. But Armitage was obviously agitated. Then again, when wasn't he a bundle of nerves? Armitage had to be over seventy by now, but he looked even older, with wispy white hair on top (much less than Harvey had and Harvey knew it was petty to notice, but he was glad his pink scalp wasn't gleaming through his hair). The deep grooves in Armitage's cheeks seemed even sadder than usual.

Harvey remembered some talk of retiring Armitage or, at least, making him head librarian emeritus as befitting his long service to Miskatonic University. Nobody thought they could actually remove Armitage from the Orne completely. The man had keys. But some of the younger faculty and librarians thought it might be nice to have a leader more accepting of the Dewey Decimal System. After all, most college libraries had switched to it.

Armitage's only response to this request was "Dewey never classified what I've seen."

So the Orne's book classifications remained untouched with every volume organized by the principles laid down by the founding librarians and passed on to each subsequent generation. Except Armitage proved reluctant to train his possible successors among the younger librarians. Harvey never believed Armitage was hiding tomes within the complicated classification system, neatly documented on cards housed in splendid cabinets made of golden oak.

However, Harvey also never doubted the man didn't like certain books examined even under his watchful eye.

He didn't know what Armitage's exact position was these days. Harvey joyfully lost track of university politics as soon as he retired. Armitage might still be an employee or he might be pacing the attics like Mrs Rochester as a volunteer.

Whatever Armitage's current position and worries, they had managed to work together in the past. So Harvey hoped Armitage would answer his questions now. If he could distract the man from his ceiling gazing.

"Any leaks?" Harvey asked.

"No, no, I don't think so." Armitage remained staring at the ceiling. "Except maybe there?" He pointed at a shadowy corner. "Does that look damp to you?"

"Not particularly," Harvey replied. "But I have an umbrella that I'd like you to examine."

At this, Armitage blinked and lowered his gaze to peer at Harvey and his umbrella. "Walters!" he exclaimed. "Did you carry a wet umbrella through the stacks? Don't you know what water does to books?"

"I kept the umbrella far away from the stacks," Harvey promised him. He hoped Armitage wouldn't notice how damp the rest of him was.

"There are umbrella stands at every entrance point," Armitage snapped. "Large ones."

"I doubt it would be wise to leave this umbrella in a public receptacle," Harvey said. He opened the umbrella in the center of the attic. A few drops of water did drip upon the floor.

Armitage moaned. "Walters! What are you doing?"

"Imploring you to look at this umbrella's shaft. What can you tell me about it?" Harvey said. Seeing Armitage stooping to dry up the drops on the floor with his handkerchief,

Harvey shook his head. "Such a small amount of water is not going to leak through several floors and damage the books."

"But what if we flood?" Armitage said. "We might have to bring the books up here."

The thought of trying to shift the library's vast collection to the attic boggled Harvey's mind. No wonder Armitage appeared ready to collapse. Harvey would have suffered nervous prostration too if he had to relocate all the Orne's books. Moving his own books from his office and his apartment into his house had been horrifying enough.

"It is not going to flood," Harvey said in as soothing a tone as possible. "The newspaper said Miskatonic University was too far from the river to suffer any damage. That's why City Hall is sending people to shelter at the student union. Although making them eat any of the food there seems unkind."

"The basements smell damp!" Armitage practically shouted, obviously not mollified at all.

"Armitage, the basements have smelled damp since the 1880s," Harvey said. "Possibly even longer. But there is no water coming in."

"Are you absolutely sure?" Armitage asked, finally collapsing into one of the wooden chairs that Harvey had noticed when he first entered the room. The chairs were lined up next to the tables as if waiting for a meeting of some secret society. Actually, given this was Miskatonic University, Harvey wouldn't be surprised if some society did meet in the attic.

"You think the basements are safe from flooding?" Armitage said.

"Certainly," Harvey lied because he had more pressing problems. Actually, he had no idea if the basements would remain dry, but he needed Armitage to concentrate on other things. Harvey flipped the open umbrella upside down, so it resembled a boat that an owl and a pussy-cat might sail away in. Harvey thought those famed sailors would have been on a very strange voyage given the sinister eye carved into the shaft. He passed the umbrella to Armitage. "What do you think the meaning of these carvings are?"

Armitage cautiously twirled the umbrella, examining the shaft and its peculiar carvings from all sides. He shuddered and passed the umbrella back to Harvey.

"Close it up," Armitage said. After Harvey complied, he continued, "I think, no, I know, that is a very evil thing that you're carrying, Walters. What arcane research are you conducting now?"

"I'm not the original owner." Harvey defended himself from the accusatory stare being leveled by Armitage. "The umbrella was taken from a woman named Barbara. Or rather, she handed it to my friend, Carolyn, and never retrieved it. Carolyn gave the umbrella to me. I'm not sure exactly what the Palmer sisters intended to do with it, but I have my suspicions. I was hoping you could clarify how this might be used."

"Better you should burn it," said Armitage with a disgusted expression like he had encountered a bookworm in his library. Not the usual student bookworm but the actual insect. "Wait. Did you say Barbara? And the Palmers? Are you talking about Barbara Palmer, one of the Palmer triplets?"

"Yes," said Harvey, now surprised that Armitage could trot out those names so easily. He had never heard of the Palmers until this week. "How do you know about them?"

"There's a pamphlet about the seance that they performed in the 1870s," Armitage said with a worried frown. "They were children at the time. The seance left one man in a permanent coma. The others involved all suffered from a variety of headaches and nightmares for years. Very similar to this sleeping sickness being reported in the newspapers, although it only claimed the one victim. A man named Cartwright."

"I always said you had an amazing memory," Harvey said. "Can I take a look at this pamphlet?"

Armitage shook his head. "It's out on loan. I don't like letting pieces go out of the library but the pamphlet wasn't on any of my restricted lists. And she made considerable donations over the years to the archeology fund. So the university board granted her privileges such as the ability to check out materials."

Armitage seemed ready to plunge into a speech about the folly of allowing outsiders access to Orne, so Harvey said quickly, "Who took this pamphlet?"

"Valeska Stange," said Armitage.

Harvey immediately knew why Armitage sounded so worried. In the occult circles of Arkham, there were meddlers. Harvey might have even been one on occasion. Simply for academic research and the advancement of knowledge, of course. But then there were troublemakers. Harvey couldn't think of a bigger troublemaker than Valeska. Not that anyone actually caught her at it. But everyone knew that Valeska took incalculable risks. If she was interested in the Palmer triplets, it might be very bad news indeed.

Or, Harvey considered, it might be a way to find the answers that he sought. Even more than Armitage, Valeska understood arcane magic and dangerous women. Possibly because she practiced the first and was definitely the second.

"When did Valeska take the pamphlet?" Harvey asked. Last he had heard, Valeska had been in Budapest, searching for a fragment of a book best left unnamed.

"Just yesterday," said Armitage. "I saw her checking it

out along with a copy of Lucius Galloway's latest book of poetry. I tried to tell the librarian how risky it was to allow such a pamphlet to be read, let alone leave the Orne. This younger generation has been so opposed to my sensible lists of restrictions. They seem to think libraries are for sharing knowledge, not archiving volumes for safer times. Actually, Galloway's poetry is a bit disturbing too. Have you read it?"

"Yes," Harvey said, who had been worried enough by the poet's descriptions of a sunken city to seek Galloway out in New York. He enjoyed the party but he feared the poet had dismissed his gentle hints about danger as the nervous twitterings of an old man. He said as much to Armitage.

"How many times have we tried to warn students away from pursuing such knowledge?" Armitage said. "Some books are not meant to be opened."

"Ah," said Harvey, who had been opening every book that he came across in the Orne since his undergraduate days.

"Look what happened with Willoughby," Armitage said, flapping his arms about like an agitated old crow.

Harvey winced. Willoughby had been his student, and a very promising student too. Armitage had warned him that Willoughby was making some unusual forays into certain stacks in the library. At the time, Harvey had thought it showed initiative.

Armitage must have caught the wince. "Sorry," he said. "Pay no attention to me. Old memories. Not worth discussing."

"It's fine," Harvey said. "I think about Willoughby too, sometimes. Especially on days like this."

"Doesn't matter," Armitage sighed. "This new crop of librarians think they have all the answers. But they don't know the questions. We do. Why don't they listen to us?"

"They're young," said Harvey, giving the easiest explanation. "And we're old. We didn't listen nearly enough to our elders either."

Armitage appeared even more depressed by this answer. "When did we become elderly, Walters?"

"I'm not sure," said Harvey. "Some time last Wednesday? But we're not dead yet, Armitage."

It was clear that Armitage could be of no further help, but Harvey decided that visiting Valeska might be well worth the risk. But he needed to go home and change into a dry suit. Valeska wouldn't be swayed by someone dripping in her parlor. Harvey would have to be impressively turned out to learn anything useful. Besides, he did not want Valeska to compare him unfavorably to any of her five husbands. She always married elegant men who happened to suffer ignoble deaths within a year of their wedding. Once, some wag at the *Arkham Advertiser* commended her fashion sense and ability to turn a wedding veil into a widow's weeds. As Harvey recalled, the reporter fled town with a most unusual rash.

"Buck up, Armitage. We possess more experience combined than most of the faculty in this building. That must count in our favor. I still have things I can do to protect Arkham," Harvey said as he prepared to tackle the stairs. At least he would be going down this time.

Armitage nodded. "So do I. At least to protect the Orne." Despite his fragile look, Armitage stood up smoothly. His knees seemed to be working much better than Harvey's, even if he had less hair. A little color pinked Armitage's cheeks. The master librarian now seemed determined, if possibly subject to being blown over in a stiff breeze.

Harvey clapped Armitage on the shoulder. "Good for

you." He closed the umbrella and rolled it tight so no water would drip upon the floor.

"Where are you going next?" Armitage asked as they descended back to the main hall of the library.

"Breakfast," said Harvey. "A man can't plan on an empty stomach. Then I'll visit Valeska." Also, he was beginning to think longingly of dry clothing for other reasons. He didn't remember being wet as chafing quite so much during his younger adventures. Was he growing more feeble with age? Or just more concerned about his comforts? Perish the thought, Harvey told himself sternly.

"Be careful," said Armitage, cutting into Harvey's ruminations. "Dealing with Valeska Stange can be very risky."

"She may be inclined to help me. Even Valeska should want to avoid a city in ruins."

"So you do think the flood is going to be serious?" asked Armitage.

"Maybe," said Harvey, who actually thought "catastrophic" would be a better description of what was coming next. But he did not want to upset Armitage too much. Keeping his allies calm was going to be crucial to their success, just as keeping himself calm had helped him weather some truly atrocious arcane encounters. Then again Armitage should be informed that water hitting the books might be the least of his worries. "But I suspect an entity even more monstrous than this flood is on the horizon. Do what you can to protect the Orne, Armitage. Every bit helps."

CHAPTER SIX

Lefty liked his landlady Mrs Garcia. He had great respect for her forthright manner and how she took care of her houseful of boarders. But at the moment, he was considering picking up the sturdy lady and dumping her in the cab of his truck. As gently as possible, of course.

"You cannot stay on Flotsam Street," said Lefty. "The river is rising. One of the docks washed away this morning. They say all of Rivertown will go under." The rain beat relentlessly on his sou'wester while he stood and argued about her leaving the neighborhood. Actually, he was the one arguing. Mrs Garcia simply stared silently at him from the portico of her house.

"Then it is good we are nearly on French Hill," Mrs Garcia said when Lefty ran out of words. The landladies of Flotsam Street often said "almost on French Hill" to calm any potential boarders nervous about renting in Rivertown.

French Hill, being one of the richest neighborhoods in Arkham and full of mansions with large gardens, looked nothing like the narrow Flotsam Street with its old family homes converted into five boarding houses, all run by widows. Even the street itself was a short and now largely bypassed way between two more important roads. But once these houses had been the better homes of Rivertown, occupied by those aspiring to move up to French Hill. In some ways, it was still a street full of people hoping for better lives or, in the case of the landladies, trying to hang on to what little they had left of more comfortable times.

Lefty hadn't cared where he lived in Arkham. He only wanted a cheap room and good meals once he secured a job at the garbage company. His sole aspiration was moving out of the flop house where too many mistakes to list had landed him. Mrs Garcia provided both the room and the meals. Even though the garbage company was located in Northside, he never considered one of the many apartment buildings there, not after he tasted the chicken enchilada casserole served regularly at Mrs Garcia's table. Over the years, he had made Mrs Garcia's basement a comfortable space for himself, furnished with salvage from his garbage runs and stocked with his many books and magazines collected from his customers.

Now Lefty's home was probably going to be underwater by evening. Or maybe sooner, if the mayor's dynamite scheme didn't alleviate the water backing up through Arkham's sewers. To say nothing of the rumored cave system stretching from the Black Cave into multiple neighborhoods. Flotsam Street might stand a little higher than its neighbors, but it was unlikely to be spared by the flood.

"Please," he said to Mrs Garcia, playing the one card that he had to persuade his stubborn landlady. After that, he wasn't sure what he should do. Except he would not abandon her. "You promised April that you would come with me as soon as you closed up the house. She is worried about you."

Mrs Garcia gave him a disapproving look for invoking the name of her injured boarder. It was a dirty trick, but Lefty was not above using Mrs Garcia's tactics against her. She had promised to follow them to Professor Walters' house. And Mrs Garcia was fond of little April May.

"That was before I talked to Mrs Alba," Mrs Garcia said. "Now it is better for me to stay here on Flotsam Street. At least for a few more hours. April will understand."

April might but Lefty definitely didn't.

"Sol and his gang have sandbagged all the lower doors," he said. "Your house is as protected as it can be."

"Which is why I am going to Mrs Chiebek's house," said Mrs Garcia, snapping open a sturdy black umbrella. She picked up her suitcase in her other hand and descended her front stairs. "Mrs Chiebek's house is the closest to French Hill. It is the highest point on Flotsam Street. We will wait there."

"Wait for what?" Lefty huffed a bit. Mrs Garcia made a beeline for the high ground that she had picked out. His landlady could move at a very brisk pace.

"Mrs Alba. What she attempts is very difficult," Mrs Garcia said.

Lefty did not understand what Mrs Alba was trying to do. Last time he had heard anything about her, she was one of the victims of the sleeping sickness gripping most of Arkham. However, Mrs Alba had woken up earlier in the evening. He did remember Ollie, a nurse who lived at their boarding house, mentioning this as a hopeful turn in the unusual illness gripping far too many in Arkham.

"Can't Mrs Alba do this elsewhere?" he asked as he followed Mrs Garcia down the street. "I can take you all to the professor's house. If you need to make a phone call or…"

He could not think what else the landladies were planning. Besides, Mrs Alba was the one with a phone installed in her house. He could not remember if Mrs Chiebek had one. Of course, sometimes the ladies gathered for baking parties around the holidays. But they couldn't be organizing one during a flood? Could they?

"Is this about cookies?" Lefty realized how ridiculous this sounded. Then he had a thought. "Are you making meals for Father Iwanaki?" He knew the priest was staying at Christchurch as long as possible, holding it open as a refuge for those who needed help. Arranging for meals did sound like the landladies of Flotsam Street.

He assumed the other four landladies were already at Mrs Chiebek's house from Mrs Garcia's remarks. They tended to socialize together and also organize as a group, such as when petitioning the garbage company for one extra pick-up a week. The garbage company had agreed when Lefty figured out how to squeeze the extra service into his schedule. His supervisor also knew arguing with the landladies of Flotsam Street was a useless endeavor.

But even if the landladies were a formidable force when working together, they were not indestructible. At least he didn't think they were. Maybe they were. But he still wasn't going to leave them on Flotsam Street when the city was about to suffer from the worst flood ever, according to the newspaper.

Lefty knew he was useless at the weird stuff which cropped up in Arkham. Except when it came to whacking it with a baseball bat. He had to do that occasionally when things crawled out of the river to rummage through the garbage cans. But he wasn't a brain, not like the professor or some of his favorite heroes in the pulps. He wasn't able to come up with dozens of plans to thwart some otherworldly threats.

But he did remember some advice about persuading people. It involved flies and honey, or carrots, being better than baseball bats when it came to getting folks to go where you wanted them to go.

"The professor's house has a big kitchen," Lefty said, although he had never actually been inside the kitchen. "I am sure Mrs Fox will let you use it for any meals you need to make."

He was not certain about the latter statement. But he had admired Mrs Fox over the backyard fence and from comments dropped by the professor, he thought Harvey's housekeeper was the type of woman to help provide food for those in need.

"We have already sent meals to Father Iwanaki. Mrs Alba has other tasks. But with Mrs Chiebek and Mrs Iskander to help her, we will be fine," Mrs Garcia replied as she marched up Mrs Chiebek's stairs and stopped. With one hand clutching the suitcase and the other holding her umbrella, his landlady finally needed assistance.

"Allow me," said Lefty with manners which would have surprised his ex-wives. But he had learned a thing or two living with Mrs Garcia. Like wiping his feet and opening doors when a landlady looked at him in a certain way. He reached around her to unlatch the door. Mrs Garcia handed him her umbrella to close and stepped inside. Lefty shook the umbrella out, relieved to see this one had a very plain shaft. Nothing mystical about it. Then he rolled the umbrella tightly and deposited it in the hall's umbrella stand. The less said about the taxidermied elephant's foot, the better, but he understood that Mrs Chiebek's husband had traveled to shoot big game, much like Teddy Roosevelt. The widow probably kept the elephant's foot for sentimental reasons.

Lefty disliked taxidermied anything. For one thing, he was fond of animals. His only foray into deer hunting with the fellows from his baseball team left him vomiting in the bushes.

For another, whenever the last generation's craze for stuffed monkeys playing cards or hunting trophies hit the garbage pile, the objects were disgusting. Dead, of course, and usually leaking sawdust. Moths would rise in clouds from such items as well. Discarded polar bear rugs always had moths. Lefty wasn't very fond of bugs, although he encountered insects daily in his work. At least moths just fluttered, and didn't bite or sting.

The elephant's foot in Mrs Chiebek's hallway appeared well cared for and unlikely to end up in the garbage heap any time soon. Which was a relief as Lefty collected on Flotsam Street, the rest of Rivertown, and French Hill. Most of the stuffed animals came from French Hill. As well as some very nice furniture, because the rich always replaced perfectly useful items with new pieces. The garbage from Rivertown tended to be simply garbage. By the time a wooden chair made it to a Rivertown burn pit or was discarded on the street, it was already kindling.

"Rosario," said Mrs Chiebek, advancing into the hallway, "I am so glad that you are here."

After a moment's stupefaction, Lefty realized that Rosario was Mrs Garcia. He didn't remember ever hearing her addressed by her first name.

"Of course I am here, Violette," said Mrs Garcia. "Are the others ready?"

"Oh yes," said Mrs Chiebek, apparently named Violette, which was an interesting moniker for the tall broad woman who nearly topped Lefty in height.

"Good," said Mrs Garcia as she stripped off her hat and gloves. Then she turned to Lefty and said, "You will want to help Professor Walters."

"Yes, you should leave now," chorused Mrs Chiebek.

It was a clear dismissal. Lefty wasn't used to arguing with ladies who were twenty years his senior, but he had to give it one more try.

"This street is going to flood. It's dangerous to stay here," he said as firmly as he could. He definitely felt that they were listening to him out of politeness. Lefty knew those blank stares that older ladies gave to people who were wasting their time. He'd encountered such looks at numerous back doors when explaining why the garbage company wanted cans placed closer to the fence. After he finished talking, the ladies simply said, "The can stays by the kitchen door. It's more useful there."

He never won those arguments either. He always carried the cans to the truck, tipped them in, and then brought them back to their original spot by the kitchen door. Never mind what the fancy efficiency expert decided in his office after only spending a day riding around Arkham with one of the garbage trucks.

But this time, he had to try one last plea.

"If we leave now, I can take all of you wherever you want to go," Lefty said. "The Palace Movie Theater is taking people in."

The ladies left Flotsam Street for an evening at the cinema nearly every week. Mrs Garcia had been looking forward to seeing Lon Chaney's *London After Midnight*. "It's supposed to be much safer there at the Palace," Lefty said even as he thought these women were not impressed with this argument.

"How nice," Mrs Garcia said. "Perhaps they will play a Charlie Chaplin film to make us laugh while Arkham burns."

Lefty stopped talking. He couldn't think how to answer her last remark. Mrs Garcia was like that. She had a way of making pronouncements which, on the face of it, sounded fairly benign – until a man started to consider what she actually said.

"Floods first," said Mrs Chiebek, "then fire. Mrs Alba is certain now that fire will be seen in the sky."

Mrs Garcia nodded. Turning to Lefty, she lost a little of her briskness. "Please, Herman," she said. "Do not hesitate. Go now. Take this with you." She handed Lefty a sealed envelope. "Give it to Mrs Fox when you see her. We will need her aunt to help."

Nobody but Mrs Garcia ever called him Herman, even though it was his real name. She usually said "Lefty" in casual conversation like everyone else. If Mrs Garcia was asking Herman for a favor, then Herman Googe needed to do the favor.

Besides, he could never win an argument with a dame, Lefty told himself as he walked back to his truck. He would find Harvey at Miskatonic University, take him home, and give the letter to Harvey's housekeeper, Mrs Fox. Just as Mrs Garcia asked. As Lefty climbed into Pequod's cab, he gave one more look around the street. So far, it appeared to be safe. Mrs Garcia had not asked him to stay away forever. Just deliver a note. He could return for the landladies later in the morning, after he had helped Harvey.

Feeling a little better now he had a plan, Lefty turned Pequod around and headed back to Miskatonic University.

But he was still worried about the women left behind on Flotsam Street. Most of all, Lefty wondered why they mentioned fire on a day when all the waters in the world seemed to be pouring down on Arkham.

CHAPTER SEVEN

The first thing Harvey noticed during the ride back to his house was how quiet his driver was. Lefty wasn't the most talkative of men, which, of course, was one of the reasons that Harvey enjoyed chatting with his garbageman on pick up days. Anyone who could listen in silence to Harvey's excessive explanations of his favorite desserts, his puzzling roses, and the general state of Arkham was sure to win Harvey's approval.

You could take the man out of Miskatonic University, but you couldn't take the professor's propensity to lecture out of the man, Harvey acknowledged. Lefty kindly tolerated Harvey's bad habit of talking too much. The big man even seemed interested in what Harvey had to say.

But during this drive, as Harvey shared Armitage's remarks about the umbrella and younger librarians, he had the distinct feeling that every word leaving his mouth was dropping like the rain into the gutters and running uselessly away.

"What is bothering you?" Harvey asked. His wet clothing continued to aggravate him, but Harvey knew a dry shirt was on his horizon, a fact which considerably gladdened his heart. Also, Harvey now had a fairly good idea of where to go next for some answers about the strange green umbrella. Valeska Stange might be a dangerous woman, but she definitely possessed knowledge of the more deadly manifestations of the arcane.

Lefty grunted in reply to Harvey's question. His eyes remained glued on the road, an indistinct blur as the rain sluiced down the windshield. Lefty cranked on the lever that wiped the water off the windshield but it was a battle of man against elements, with man definitely on the losing side this morning.

"They should automate those wipers," Harvey mused out loud. If Lefty wouldn't answer a direct question, perhaps he could prompt his friend to start talking about his beloved truck. Harvey never was inclined to the natural sciences or mechanical devices, as archeology and the occult occupied all of his academic years. But the world was changing, and Harvey sometimes considered changing with it. Maybe. He had a telephone installed in his home and recently bought a radio. Both fascinating contraptions although best left to other people to use.

However, Harvey had tried a ride or two in an airplane. Perhaps he should consider purchasing himself a car. At least for driving on sunny days.

"Crank works," Lefty said, giving it another turn. "Pequod's not the newest truck in the company, but it runs sweet. Easy to repair."

Harvey nodded. "Sometimes older appliances are worth more than we perceive. Mrs Fox swears by our stove-top percolator. I purchased an electric percolator but she says the Westinghouse fails to make coffee as good as the stove-top."

Lefty grunted again, but it was a more relaxed grunt. "People throw away working stuff just because it is old. Never understood why."

"Human beings are naturally wasteful creatures. Which is a blessing for archeologists," Harvey said. "What would we know about Troy or Rome if there were no garbage dumps to dig up a few thousand years later?"

"So you're saying that you're a garbage collector too?" The thought seemed to amuse Lefty.

"Very much so," Harvey replied, relieved to see his friend looking a bit more cheerful. What was coming would be dire. Harvey knew it in his bones. But dwelling on disaster before it arrived could be fatal, as it had proved for his poor student, Willoughby. If only Willoughby had not believed so completely in his own doom, he might be teaching at Miskatonic in Harvey's place.

As Harvey had come to learn during his own sinister encounters, it was better to meet the challenge with a hopeful heart. But how could he inspire an entire city to hope when so many calamities were literally raining down on them?

As he pondered the question, Harvey kept up a light stream of chatter about trucks and new cars with Lefty.

"A Ford is always reliable," said Lefty as Harvey speculated about the type of car which would suit his needs.

"But so dull," Harvey said. "There are Fords everywhere. I was considering a more sporty car, just to shock the neighbors."

"Chrysler," Lefty said with conviction. "You can get up to seventy miles per hour on a good road."

"Perhaps not that fast," Harvey said, trying to imagine what it would be like to be in control of a ton of metal hurtling down the road at seventy miles per hour. Far more terrifying than facing murderous cultists or dismantling deranged spells, he was certain. But, then again, he had never shied away from new experiences.

Arrival at his house meant Harvey could drip his way into the vestibule and inquire about his guests. Mrs Fox handed him a towel with a shake of her head and a stern admonition to remove his boots before walking through the house.

"There's been enough mud and water tracked inside," she said. "And there were animals in my kitchen when I arrived."

"Only two dogs," said Harvey, toweling his hair dry, "and one is a very small poodle."

"And the other is the neighbor's German shepherd," Mrs Fox replied. "How did Fritzie end up in my kitchen?"

"It's a long story," Harvey said. "But Fritzie was trapped in the basement." Along with Ira, Harvey's terrible assistant, who intended to practice animal sacrifice to further his sisters' occult plans. Harvey managed to save the dog and send Ira to the hospital, but he didn't want to discuss the details while water dripped off him onto the tiled floor.

"They are both very well behaved dogs," said Mrs Fox. "I'll take Fritzie back to his owners before lunch. For now, I have them settled in the parlor with a couple of ham bones. It's a much better place for dogs than my kitchen."

While Harvey owned the house, Mrs Fox had laid claim to the kitchen on the day that she came to work for him. In return for her deft hand with baking cakes, Harvey had happily ceded the kitchen to be her domain. The study, which held the more pertinent part of his book collection, was definitely his territory. The remainder of the rooms housed the rest of his books wherever a bookcase could be placed and such utilitarian items as beds, tables, and chairs were normally found.

After receiving a small inheritance, Harvey had been talked into purchasing a house for his "golden years." Harvey hadn't exactly planned to retire but somehow it happened. Being a homeowner and man of leisure still felt shockingly new for Harvey. He hadn't come to terms with what this phase of life meant yet. Actually, he had never expected to grow old at all, when so many of his colleagues had been lost in Antarctica or felled by the more mundane disasters encountered in a life filled with occult mysteries and undergraduates.

"How's April?" Lefty asked as he hung up his rain gear on the coatrack. Harvey knew his friend wanted to send April to St Mary's Hospital with the two reporters rescued from the Black Cave. But April preferred to stay with them. Harvey had reassured Lefty that she would receive equal if not better care at his house. St Mary's was nearly full already, due to a mysterious plague of sleeping sickness, although his friend Dr Carolyn Fern had managed to revive some patients. The storm probably created additional emergency visits following the usual accidents and injuries such weather caused. All in all, it was better to leave the beds in St Mary's for those who had no one else to care for them.

"Poor child, fast asleep," Mrs Fox replied to Lefty. "The nurse who came with you strapped up April's arm and gave her a sleeping draught from the professor's medicine cabinet."

"Not the laudanum?" Harvey asked. The stuff, a staple of his youth, was becoming harder to find. Although he shouldn't begrudge an injured young lady a healing sleep. April witnessed terrors in the Black Cave but rallied marvelously against the Palmers in his opinion.

Mrs Fox shook her head at Harvey's question about the laudanum. "No, we gave her the powder the doctor prescribed the last time you complained of insomnia. The nurse said the drug was very mild."

"Probably why it didn't work for me," said Harvey, who preferred whiskey or laudanum or both combined, depending on what monstrous memory was plaguing his sleep. Which was why he was going to keep purchasing both as long as he could, even if that made him a scofflaw.

Mrs Fox ignored his interjection, as she often did. "We put April to bed in the big front guest room. Her friend Nella is sitting with her, although I'm sure she's asleep too by now. I fed everyone and sent them off to various bedrooms with all the clean linen that we had. Next time, professor, you might give me a little warning. I barely had enough in the pantry for a decent breakfast."

Harvey mumbled some type of assent. He didn't expect another catastrophic flood to wash a half dozen visitors up on his doorstep, but he understood it did put a strain on the household supplies.

Mrs Fox continued, "After we settled April, the nurse…"

"Ollie," Lefty supplied the name of another boarder from the Flotsam Street house.

Mrs Fox nodded. "Ollie left for St Mary's just before you arrived. I called her a taxi, professor, and paid for it out of the emergency tin." Harvey kept an old tobacco tin filled with small bills and change in his study. It used to sit in his office at Miskatonic University for the days when he wanted to make a quick escape from Arkham. He also gave the money to students short of funds by the end of term. Since retiring and moving into the house, Harvey's tin had grown a little dusty. He was glad Mrs Fox found a use for it and told her so.

"You are very wet." Mrs Fox observed the growing puddle

around Harvey's feet as he tried to wring out the tails of his suit jacket without her noticing. "Is it raining so hard?"

"He fell into the river," Lefty said.

"When did that happen?" Mrs Fox exclaimed, momentarily distracted from the pool of water forming around Harvey.

"Before we went to Miskatonic University," Lefty said, ignoring the desperate waggling of Harvey's eyebrows. Although Harvey liked to talk, he knew there were times when a man should remain silent for his own protection.

Mrs Fox drew herself up another inch and leveled an awful look at Harvey. "You dunked your good suit in the river and are now wringing it out like it is an old dish towel?"

"I dunked me in the river. The suit was an unintended casualty," Harvey said. Mrs Fox oversaw the care of his clothing as well as his house. He knew she wouldn't be happy about the bedraggled suit, but he hoped to tuck it into the back of his closet before she took a closer look at it.

"No wonder the jacket is sagging. Stop pulling at it, you will make it worse," Mrs Fox said with a terrible frown. "I hate to think about the state of your trousers. Never mind, go and change. Do not hang your suit back in the closet. I will take everything to the tailors. I only hope they can clean and block it into shape."

Then, because she was Mrs Fox and in many ways a treasure beyond price, she handed Harvey a mug of hot coffee. "Take this upstairs with you. I'll make more breakfast. I saved some eggs and bacon for you. And made fresh cornbread while I was waiting." She glanced at Lefty, who had stayed reasonably dry under his sou'wester. "We might have a shirt which would fit you, if you need it."

Lefty shook his head, looking a bit bashful. "I'm fine," he

said. "I dropped off a bag with my things when I brought the others earlier. I wouldn't mind a shave."

"Come along," said Mrs Fox. "Unclaimed bags are in the kitchen. It's the warmest and driest room without anyone sleeping in it. You can use the washroom off the pantry."

Harvey escaped to his bedroom, glad to see it remained free of visitors both human and canine. While he was happy to throw his house open to refugees from the storm, a man liked a little privacy for shedding his clothes and changing into dry underwear.

With that satisfactory chore done, Harvey took up the brushes from his bureau and gave his hair a few vigorous swipes. The silver mane, as he liked to think of his hair as leonine, was mostly dry. It settled into its usual shaggy nimbus around his head. Harvey took a bit longer with his mustache and beard, and then picked up the tiny silver comb for his eyebrows. A quick stroke on each eyebrow and the face staring back at him in the mirror looked like Professor Harvey Walters rather than a soggy tramp.

A crisp white shirt, one of his many red silk ties (he ordered them by the dozen from a shop in San Francisco), and his second best suit (which was made with the exact same cloth and cut as his best suit) completed the transformation.

Because Valeska would notice such items, Harvey rummaged through the top drawer of his bureau for his gold cufflinks and tie pin. These fastened into place, he decided it was time to retrieve other items from his safe.

Harvey spun the dial of the tall Mosler safe taking up half of his bedroom closet. His special combination, a numerical sequence derived from "abracadabra," clicked open the lock. He swung open the heavy metal door and surveyed the shelves.

From inside the safe, Harvey pulled out the locked box containing the smallest of his handguns. The key from his watch chain opened the box and he retrieved the pearl-handled derringer. Others might dismiss it as a lady's pistol at first glance, but the Remington Double Derringer had been recommended to him by a Secret Service agent many years ago. After snapping the gun open and loading it, Harvey tucked the derringer into the specially made inside pocket of his suit jacket.

Then he exchanged his river-soaked pocket watch for a drier and still ticking model with an interesting occult history. As usual, Harvey became distracted by the symbols engraved on the watch's platinum case, but he put the watch on his chain after a few moments of contemplation of the symbols that contradicted the meaning of time. Next, Harvey extracted a dry billfold stuffed with enough money to carry him through the day and even a little bribery. Not that Valeska could be so persuaded, but he might need to question others as well.

He pondered the two money belts also stored in the safe. Should he take one? The money belts were essential for travel in foreign places, but he expected to return home at the end of the day. Or, if he did not return, Harvey doubted he would need any more cash in the afterlife. Just a coin for the ferryman, if the classics were to be believed.

Harvey weighed the larger belt in his hand, heavy with foreign gold coins collected in his travels. Very heavy, Harvey decided, but rather than returning it to the safe, he tucked the gold-filled money belt into the top drawer of his bureau. Should he not return, the house and all its contents would go to Mrs Fox. His will contained a request that his books find their way back to Miskatonic University, as his work there inspired so many purchases. However, Miskatonic had enough benefactors that the rest of his estate should go to the woman who washed his socks and spared him the chore. As houses were needy things, in Harvey's experience, some ready cash could help Mrs Fox surmount any troubles until the settling of his estate.

He scribbled a small note telling Mrs Fox to look in the top drawer and stuck it into the corner of the bureau's mirror. Then he crossed the room to close up the safe.

Before he shut the heavy metal door, Harvey pulled out the second money belt. It was only a small pouch strung on a strong leather cord. This bag felt insubstantial next to his other money belt, as three dozen fine diamonds weighed very little. Harvey tipped one of the glittering gems into his hand simply to see it sparkle in the watery light coming through his bedroom window.

With a shrug, Harvey tipped the diamond back into the pouch and hung the cord around his neck. With a small adjustment of his collar and his necktie, the diamonds were safely hidden under his clothes. It never hurt to be prepared for the unexpected, he decided, and even Charon might row a little faster for a diamond.

Harvey swung the safe door closed with a click that echoed behind him as he went in search of breakfast.

CHAPTER EIGHT

There was much to be said for being clean, dry, and fed. Lefty appreciated all three. Especially the breakfast being served to him by the lovely Mrs Fox. She was a tall woman with waves of dark hair pinned up in the style favored by the girls of his youth. Lefty judged her to be about his age. He gathered from Harvey that Mrs Fox was a widow, having lost her husband during the last war. Several times, when seeing her over the fence as he picked up the garbage cans, Lefty tried to think of something to say to her. But then he'd remembered that he was dirty, sweaty, and holding a garbage can on his shoulder. So he'd stayed silent.

But now he was freshly shaved and wearing a clean shirt from his bag, he probably looked as good as he ever would. However, Lefty remained at a loss for words.

"More cornbread?" said Mrs Fox, picking up the serving dish and handing it to him. "Take what you want before the professor comes down. He'll clear the plate."

"Thank you," mumbled Lefty as he took another piece, searching for witty words or even mildly interesting ones to add to the conversation. Then he remembered the commission given to him by Mrs Garcia. "I have a note for you," he blurted, wriggling on his seat like a schoolboy, trying to extract the envelope from the pocket of his overalls. It was a little crumpled when he pulled it out.

"Here," he said, handing the envelope to Mrs Fox. "It's from Mrs Garcia," he added to make it clear that he wasn't the author of the note that he was handing her. Then he pushed another piece of cornbread in his mouth to prevent speaking any more of his jumbled thoughts.

She took the envelope from him with a nod of thanks. After ripping it open and scanning the contents of the single sheet of paper, Mrs Fox said, "She wants my auntie to help her." Folding the letter away, Mrs Fox tapped the corner of the envelope against her lush lips.

Lefty swallowed his cornbread in one gulp. The crumbs made him cough. Mrs Fox immediately thrust a glass of water toward him. She also whacked him smartly on the shoulder blades.

"How are you?" she said.

"Fine, fine." An embarrassed Lefty waved her away. "Swallowed too fast, that's all."

She lingered for a moment, apparently to be sure that he was breathing. Then Mrs Fox turned back to the stove, briskly breaking eggs into a frying pan.

"I smell cornbread! Mrs Fox, have I ever told you that you are one of the wonders of Arkham," said a jovial voice from the doorway. "Ah, the wilderness is paradise now."

The professor once again resembled a gentleman of learning in a well-cut tweed suit, natty red tie, and crisp white shirt.

"Yes," replied Mrs Fox to Harvey. "You generally misquote the *Rubaiyat* when you want extra cornbread."

"I feel that misquote is harsh judgment," Harvey said as he pulled out a chair and settled himself at the table. "Fitzgerald's translation is riddled with inaccuracies although pretty in parts."

Mrs Fox merely raised one eyebrow as she flipped the eggs expertly onto a blue-and-white china plate. Some still sizzling bacon went next to the eggs. She finished with a pile of cornbread. Upon setting the plate in front of Harvey, Mrs Fox said, "Honey and butter are already on the table."

"Thank you," said Harvey, reaching for both, which he applied lavishly to his cornbread. After a couple of large bites, he sighed and said, "Perfection. But, please, could I have some more coffee?"

Mrs Fox had the cup on the table before the professor finished speaking.

Their interaction amused Lefty, although he hid his smile in another sip of his own coffee. It felt like the boarding house chatter over meals. A warmth pervaded the kitchen which charmed him as much as Mrs Fox. Thunder rumbled outside to remind Lefty that everything he valued might soon wash away.

"I better go now," Lefty said, setting his cup back in its saucer.

"Go where?" Harvey polished off his eggs and cast a beseeching look at Mrs Fox. She sighed as she cracked another egg into her frying pan. She flipped it twice as the men watched.

"Back to Flotsam Street," Lefty said. "I need to convince the ladies to leave."

"There's no rush," Mrs Fox said as she ladled the additional egg onto Harvey's plate. "The flood won't reach its high point until nightfall."

"Is that what they're predicting?" Harvey asked. "Did you see it in the newspaper?"

Mrs Fox shook her head. "Auntie said so. I wouldn't have left her alone this morning otherwise."

"Your aunt is a meteorological expert?" Harvey said, in a tone closer to wonderment than scorn. Which surprised Lefty, who thought a university professor would have very little regard for the predictions of old ladies.

"Auntie can see the future," Mrs Fox said. "Surely I told you?"

Lefty caught a slight note in her voice which indicated, based on his experience with past wives, that the casual dropping of this information into the conversation was not so accidental. Which made him both curious about her aunt and what exactly Mrs Garcia had said in her note to Mrs Fox.

"No," said Harvey, now putting down his coffee cup and turning his full attention to Mrs Fox. "Never once have you mentioned that your aunt can predict the future." Then in a slightly more peevish tone, he added, "And you know I've been writing about the sibyls of Delphi and their possible descendants for the American Society for Psychical Research's journal."

"Have you? How should I know what you're researching, when you have so many projects?" said Mrs Fox. "I have my own work. The floors won't clean themselves. Nor will your breakfast appear without my labor."

"Your work is multitude. I agree. But so is mine. I have ambitious plans for more than eighty articles over the next few years," Harvey said.

Lefty calculated Harvey's plans might last him a decade, or maybe longer. Based on earlier discussions over the backyard fence, Harvey liked research and always had new things that he wanted to learn and then write about. Ambitious plans seemed the best description for Harvey's work. Admirable, too, as Lefty considered Harvey's age. Rather than slowing down, the professor seemed to be speeding up in his supposed retirement.

"Exactly!" Mrs Fox said. "Every time you tell me about your work, it's completely different. Last week was stone circles and this week was wands. How am I to remember what else you've discussed?"

"But I am sure I told you recently about my examination of ancient accounts of sibylline prophecies," Harvey said. "How I was researching similarities over the ages, especially among the Grecian sibyls."

"Our family came from Naples, Italy, not Greece," Mrs Fox said.

Lefty nodded and absently took another piece of cornbread from the plate in the center of the table. This seemed a good opportunity to learn more about Mrs Fox and how her family came to Arkham.

"Naples!" Harvey exclaimed. "But the area was famed for harboring the Cumaean Sibyl!"

Mrs Fox finally stopped working at the stove and sat herself down at the table with a cup of coffee. She took her own slice of cornbread gracefully from the dwindling pile on the china plate and spent several moments buttering the cornbread, leaving Lefty with the distinct impression that she was carefully considering her next words.

"All the women in our family have some talent for palmistry or reading tea leaves," Mrs Fox said and then held up a hand for silence when Harvey started to sputter. "We don't talk about this talent much as it causes trouble. It's one of the reasons that my family left Naples. But my aunt doesn't need tea leaves or palms or anything at all to make predictions. They simply happen. She was the youngest of my grandmother's sisters. She's actually my great-aunt, but only a few years older than my mother. The prophecies are hard on her, and the family has done what they can to keep her safe."

"So why are you telling me about this now?" Harvey asked.

"Because a disaster is coming to Arkham, something greater than a flood," Mrs Fox said. "Auntie says so."

"Flood and then fire in the sky," Lefty said, remembering the odd conversation in Mrs Chiebek's front hall. Was that what Mrs Garcia had written in her note to Mrs Fox?

"Mrs Alba had a vision," Mrs Fox said with a nod. Before Harvey could shoot a question at her, she added, "Her family came from Turkey, near Hisarlik."

"The Trojan sibyls," Harvey muttered. "Are there any other descendants from the sibyls in Arkham?"

"Mrs Iskander's family came from Libya originally," Mrs Fox said. "And we don't know if Gloria Goldberg is a sibyl or not. She keeps to herself."

"Gloria Goldberg?" Lefty asked. "Isn't she a writer?" He had read some of her stories, good stories too, in his beloved pulps. What Mrs Fox was saying was a bit peculiar, but not actually unusual for Arkham. As a man who regularly read the advice columns in *Tales from Nevermore*, Lefty knew there were folks with odd talents in the city. Actually, he could have deduced that from the contents of many garbage cans.

"But none descended from the Delphi priestesses?" Harvey asked, his hands patting his pockets as if he was searching for something. He pulled out a small notebook and a mechanical pencil to scribble down notes.

"The Palmers might be," Mrs Fox said.

Harvey gave a surprised exclamation echoed by Lefty. He hadn't met the Palmers, but Lefty heard a lot about the triplets last night at Schoffner's. April hadn't said much about her encounters with them, but she'd asked Lefty to look after Harvey when he dropped everyone off at the professor's house. Then there was the wicked umbrella that Harvey had, the one he said belonged to a Palmer sister. Altogether, Lefty gathered the Palmers posed a threat to Arkham, one which truly worried his friends.

"Augusta Palmer certainly is a sibyl," Mrs Fox continued. "Powerful enough to worry Mrs Alba, who has known Augusta since she was a child."

"I can't believe you know the Palmers and didn't tell me," Harvey said. "We had Ira right here in the house."

"I didn't realize Ira was one of those Palmers," Mrs Fox said, looking very troubled. "And I never met the sisters, only heard gossip about them. They left Arkham before I was born. Auntie also told me stories about the Palmer triplets. She never mentioned someone named Ira."

"He's a half-brother," explained Harvey about his former assistant. Lefty had met Ira at Harvey's house and thought him a regular chap, a bit fussy but that wasn't unusual for a university man. "Much younger and from a later marriage of their father."

"Obviously. Ira wasn't even thirty," Mrs Fox said, "but the sisters would be in their early sixties by now. Auntie remembers the headlines in the newspaper about Babies A, B, and C born in Rivertown."

"So your great-aunt and Mrs Alba both told you that Augusta Palmer is a sibyl?" Harvey asked.

Mrs Fox nodded. "Augusta is the only one of the triplets

who can foresee the future. But her sisters worked to enhance Augusta's skills, which was a terrible thing to do. There was a seance that went very wrong."

"I heard about the seance today," Harvey said. "But what has that to do with Augusta's abilities?"

"It gave the triplets a taste for magic," Mrs Fox said. "At least, that's what my aunt told me. It was around then that Augusta realized she could see the future. But like most with the talent, just bits and pieces, not enough to truly help her. So the triplets started asking questions, dangerous questions, about how to change the future."

"Why?" asked Lefty, who wouldn't have minded seeing how parts of his life would turn out before he made mistakes. Most of all, he wished someone had predicted a spitball would kill a man. If they had, he wouldn't have advised his friend to crowd the plate and avoided what happened afterward. Ray's death rattled him horribly, leading to more drinking and bad choices.

"The more you can see of the future, the more likely it becomes exactly what you saw," said Mrs Fox. "Augusta Palmer always wanted it both ways. To see the future and to change it. You can't have both."

"The old conundrum of destiny and free will," Harvey muttered. "How can you be granted one without destroying the other?"

Mrs Fox nodded and then shook her head. "It's never so simple. But talented seers like my aunt know the less possibilities, the greater chance for disaster. Judging from Mrs Alba and my aunt's predictions, there may be as few as three possible outcomes for Arkham over the next day or so. All end in destruction very soon. By tomorrow morning at the latest."

"What should we do?" Lefty asked. There had to be a way to protect his friends, even if it meant driving them away from Arkham. But Pequod could only hold so many people and where would he take them?

"Nobody knows," Mrs Fox replied. For the first time she sounded truly agitated. "That's the whole point. None of us should know exactly what to do over the course of the next day. If we try to create a set pattern of events, we might very well cause the worst possible outcome."

"But can we do anything to improve matters?" Harvey asked the question before Lefty could voice it.

"I hope so," Mrs Fox said. "Mrs Alba and the others are trying to find a way to use their powers to help without forcing a particular outcome on Arkham."

"A tricky dance," Harvey said as Lefty puzzled over how such a scheme would work. It would be like a baseball game, he decided. His team always played to win, knowing the other side was doing the same. He could never predict exactly how they would win, but knew if he played hard enough and was lucky, the outcome could be good. Enough to save a house on Flotsam Street if not the whole city.

When Lefty asked if they could protect one small part of Arkham, such as Flotsam Street, Harvey looked troubled. "Is it right to save just ourselves? If others suffer?" the professor said.

"But should we let Flotsam Street flood because everywhere else is flooding?" Lefty asked. "If we can save even one house, isn't that better than saving none?" He wasn't a thinking man, not like Harvey, but Lefty felt the moral high ground shouldn't mean saving no one. Even if it was just helping one or two people, that was better than nothing. He had made a number of boneheaded decisions in his life. Now he couldn't stand sitting on the sidelines. Waiting outside the Black Cave had been a mistake. He hated how he'd felt when he saw his battered friends emerging from the cave yesterday.

So he asked Mrs Fox what she thought. The question left his mouth so easily, it took a moment for Lefty's brain to catch up and realize that he was holding a conversation with Mrs Fox without worrying about how he sounded. With an inward smile, Lefty acknowledged disaster was good for something.

As for Mrs Fox, she looked as troubled as Harvey. "That's what they are discussing at Mrs Chiebek's house," she said slowly. "And why they want to hear what my aunt thinks. Ways we can use our knowledge of the future to aid as many as possible without hastening the destruction of Arkham."

"What will Augusta Palmer be doing with her ability?" Harvey asked.

"Augusta Palmer will try the opposite, with the help of her sisters," Mrs Fox said. "That's the warning from Mrs Alba, and what they wanted me to tell you, professor. Mrs Garcia sent me a note. Augusta wants to force an outcome favorable to her, even if it leads to Arkham's complete destruction."

Harvey nodded, finishing up his breakfast. "But Mrs Alba doesn't want to predict what I will do with this information?"

"She really can't," Mrs Fox assured him. "We need to find a way that doesn't destroy Arkham in the process. It will take all of us, but we can't start telling people exactly what to do. Or forcing them into a certain action, like Augusta."

"Ah, well, I may have a place to start," Harvey said, getting up from the table. He turned to Lefty. "Can you continue to act as my chauffeur for a few hours more?"

"Are they safe on Flotsam Street?" Lefty asked Mrs Fox. He still didn't understand why knowing what would happen was such a bad thing. But he trusted the landladies of Flotsam to know what they were doing. He'd never known them to fail. It boiled down to what one of his coaches once told him, "Don't worry about the whole game, that's my job. You focus on the next pitch and hit the ball. That's your job."

"I think they are safe on Flotsam Street. Mrs Alba does too," Mrs Fox answered him. "At least until sunset."

Lefty nodded. "Thank you for breakfast," he said as he followed Harvey out the door. They grabbed their coats and hats, including a new one for Harvey to replace the hat lost in the river. Harvey retrieved the green umbrella. Outside they found the rain had diminished to a fine mist. The air even smelled pleasant, almost fresh. Only a very faint boom echoed in the distance and then it stopped too.

"Where are we going?" Lefty asked as they climbed back into Pequod.

"To see a dangerous woman," Harvey replied. "One who might have answers about what comes next."

"Is she a sibyl too?" Lefty asked as he mulled what he had learned. Arkham held some strange characters, and women who could predict the future didn't seem too odd for the city. He wondered if Mrs Fox also could see bits and pieces of what would come. And if he was in any of her visions. He hoped it was so, a nice dream to distract him from the problems of the day.

For now, Lefty decided he would focus on doing his job as well as he could, whether it was driving Harvey around or helping the ladies of Flotsam Street. They could make the big plans. He would be there to step up to the plate and swing for the fences when they needed him.

Harvey shrugged and grimaced when Lefty asked about if Valeska was a sibyl. "I would not put prophecy past her. Valeska Stange is many things, and not all of them good."

CHAPTER NINE

Minnie stood on the path leading to the Black Cave and considered her options. The rain was easing up, turning into swirling vapor that resembled a low-hanging cloud. Her borrowed hat and coat kept her relatively dry. But once inside the cave, who knew what she would encounter? Still, the Black Cave was the only place in Rivertown that she hadn't searched for her camera. She wasn't ready to give up on finding the Speed Graphic, the best press camera that she ever had.

Besides, Minnie felt a certain urgency to search the Black Cave for the tentacled fish that April had smashed with a baseball bat. She had promised Doyle a story, and she had enough to write about the flood's potential impact on Rivertown. But she still wanted the other story, the one that sent her and Rex to Rivertown in the first place. The story where monsters swam below the surface of the water and stole grown men from the docks of Rivertown. If she could find her Speed Graphic, she might have the photos to prove the tall tales true. If she found April's strange monster, that would work too.

"Hey, you can't go in there," called a young man jogging down the hill. "The Black Cave is flooded."

"The path is clear," Minnie said. True, the river was lapping along the edge of the path leading to the Black Cave. But the entrance was still visible in the morning light. It looked dry, or as dry as anything could be given the recent rain.

"Once you're inside, the floor slopes down," the guy said as he caught up to Minnie. "Water is already running into the Black Cave. You could be trapped inside or drown. Wait a minute, don't I know you?"

Minnie turned from her contemplation of the cave entrance to look at him. A slender young man wearing simple clothes, he looked like any of the men who worked on the docks around Rivertown. His cloth cap didn't fully cover a riot of brown curls swirling over his forehead and around his large ears. He seemed familiar, although Minnie had talked to so many Rivertown residents in the last hour that she couldn't say for sure.

But he suddenly grinned and stuck out his hand. "I'm Sol, April's friend. Well, Nella and April are really pals of my girlfriend, Genevieve. How's April doing?"

This all came out in a rapid patter as Sol shook her hand.

"I don't know," Minnie admitted. "I think she's fine. Her friends took her home."

She remembered a group of young men with April. They rescued her and Rex from the Black Cave. Along with a lot of dogs, as Minnie recalled. Annoyingly, she still couldn't remember exactly how they became trapped in the Black Cave or everything that happened there, although some details of their rescue were becoming clearer in her head. But she recognized Sol. She remembered him outside of the cave, dancing around and issuing orders like someone much older after they all escaped. The other men, all about his age, obeyed him without question. Just scattered to wherever he pointed them.

"And you went to the hospital!" Sol exclaimed. "I sent you off with Ervin. Don't tell me the goof brought you back here."

"No," said Minnie. "He took us to the hospital. Your friend Ervin drives very fast."

Minnie turned around again, staring into the Black Cave. She had a vague memory of the bag banging against her hip when she was trapped inside. So this seemed like the most likely place to recover the camera, and more importantly, the film inside it. "Ervin is a fast driver," Sol said, breaking into her thoughts. "That's because he usually drives the getaway–" He broke off with a grimace.

"Drives a getaway car, does he? Bank robbers or bootleggers?" Minnie said, suddenly back in a world that she understood. A world where criminals and reporters rubbed shoulders, traded tips, and best of all, created stories. Other women might be afraid of being caught on a damp path with a criminal, but Minnie always had been a good judge of character, even crooked characters like Sol and his friends. She didn't think he was a threat. He had just tried to warn her about the dangers of the Black Cave.

Sol shrugged, a noncommittal answer.

"Doesn't matter what Ervin drives or who he drives for," Minnie assured him. "I'm glad Ervin took us to St Mary's. Rex was hurt pretty badly."

"He your boyfriend?" Sol asked, obviously happy to switch topics.

"Rex is my colleague," Minnie said, because a reporter was allowed a private life and she never discussed hers with near strangers. "We both work for the *Arkham Advertiser*."

Sol nodded. "So what were you doing in the Black Cave yesterday?"

"I wish I knew," Minnie said. The last thing she remembered clearly was arriving in Rivertown and finding Rex. He was following up on a call about monsters seen in the river, big things with tentacles. Which tied into a story that he had been working on, all about why the O'Bannions and the Sheldons were fighting across Arkham. There was a story going around about a gang member being tossed into the river and drowned. Which one bootlegger blamed on a river monster, but Doyle had cut that part out. So Rex wanted to learn more and, possibly, secure some photographic evidence.

Then they got a call at the newspaper that this monster had been spotted near the pier yesterday. Which was another reason to go snooping around the Rivertown waterfront.

They'd spent some time interviewing people along the waterfront. A number had heard about the drowning of Fast Louis. Some agreed that the creature or creatures had been spotted in the river recently, but nobody knew exactly who first made the call to the *Arkham Advertiser*. It felt like one of those frustrating "well, my cousin knew this guy who talked to this gal" stories that sprang up so often in Arkham. Except Rex said a man called and said in as few words as possible that there was a monster in the river and it killed people. And, Rex added, he didn't sound like the kind of guy who made up stories.

Every reporter, whether they admitted it or not, knew the unexplainable lurked at the ends of Arkham's alleys. Even Doyle, old skeptic editor Doyle, occasionally mentioned "seeing things" but then he'd harumph and say, "But you can't write stories about shadows in the mist. You need facts.

Facts which can be verified. And photographs, real pictures of identifiable objects, not just vague shapes!"

Finally, Rex suggested they go straight to the source. Take a boat out on the river and see if they could spot an actual monster in the water. Which nobody in Rivertown thought was a good idea. Captain Tavares, a tough one-armed woman met on the docks, told them the river had turned too dangerous for amateurs to be out on it. She pointed out how fast and how high the water was running under the pier. She said all the fishing fleet was moving their boats so they could ride out the coming flood.

But Rex and Minnie searched along the pier, trying to find someone to take them out. Then she saw the shadow under the water, as big as a man, maybe even bigger, with fins, tentacles, and legs. Minnie was certain about the legs. It swam right under the pier, so she threw herself flat and hung half off the dock trying to snap a picture. She definitely remembered nearly toppling into the water, along with Rex clutching her ankles and dragging her back from the edge.

Minnie also recalled the smell. Decay, like rotting seaweed, and salt, like the ocean, even though the Miskatonic River was fresh water. She blamed the smell on the fishing boats bobbing nearby, decks piled high with nets.

Once Minnie scrambled to her feet, she stuffed the camera safely away in its waterproof bag. She slung the strap over her shoulder, turned around to tell Rex to stop fussing as she hadn't dunked herself in the river.

The next thing she remembered clearly was waking up in the Black Cave with April bent over her, trying to unknot the ropes tied around her. "We were jumped, probably by one of the bootlegging gangs, and then trapped in the Black Cave," Minnie told Sol, because she thought that was the most logical explanation. Except it didn't feel right. She kept remembering gold watch fobs and green umbrellas, but she couldn't think why.

"Nah, it wasn't bootleggers," said Sol with conviction. "We were all too busy moving the hooch the last couple of days. This whole part of the city is supposed to flood. Even if the mayor's trick with the dynamite works, the sewers and caves probably will go under water. So we shifted the stuff out of the Black Cave. If someone grabbed a couple of reporters, nobody would have put you in there."

"But that's where you found us," Minnie said, still trying to reconcile the memories in her head. Now she was starting to feel a little queasy. Because it seemed somebody had rummaged around in her mind, her bright inquiring reporter's brain, and stolen her memories. No wonder her head still ached.

"I remember the cave," she said. "It was damp. And full of dogs, lots of dogs barking and whining. It stank too. Seaweed and worse."

"That was probably the dogs," Sol said. "We found so many dogs in the cave last night."

"No," Minnie said. "This smelled like terror."

"Terror has a smell?" Sol asked, looking as confused as Minnie felt confronting her memories of the Black Cave.

Terror smelled sickly sweet, like a graveyard full of rotting flowers, Minnie almost said. But as soon as she thought it, the wind shifted and a well-remembered whiff of fear emitted from the mouth of the Black Cave. Sol backed up a step as Minnie leaned forward. She remembered this scent. This was the stink of the ocean, but it wasn't the edges, the gentle lapping tide along the beach.

In her heart, she knew this emitted from the creature

glimpsed below the dock in Rivertown. A creature born out of the unfathomable depths, which most definitely should not be in Arkham. But if it was here, then she was going to capture a photo of it.

"I need to go in there," she said, starting forward on the path.

"Wait!" called Sol. "It's truly not safe. The water gets deeper the farther in you go. Some of the passages will be flooded by now."

"There has to be a way," Minnie said. She remembered being on a shelf of stone, a good way above the floor. At that point, Minnie felt the lump of her camera under her. Later she'd rolled and wriggled, trying to free herself or wake the unconscious Rex. It took hours, almost a full day, for April to find them. By then Minnie was half delirious and she had forgotten the camera.

"Did you find a camera?" she asked Sol. "Or a leather bag about this big?" She gestured with her hands, sketching out the well-remembered proportions of her camera bag.

Sol shook his head. "It was confusing," he admitted. "We had all these dogs, and the two of you to carry. Luckily the dogs followed April out of the cave after she ran off those two weird women."

Normally Minnie would have jumped on the topic of two weird women, but somehow the questions slid out of her head. Instead, she asked, "Was there a green umbrella?"

Sol nodded. "April broke it up," he said. "Don't you remember? She practically smashed it right next to you."

Minnie shrugged, not even sure why she wanted to know about the green umbrella. The camera was what was important. If Sol had not found it, it had to be in the cave.

"I must return to where you found me. I need to find my

camera," she said to Sol. "If the water is too deep, I'll turn around. I promise."

Sol heaved a great sigh. "I can't let you go alone," he said. "April will hear about it if I do. She'll tell Genevieve and Genny would take my head off."

"You have an interesting code of ethics for a bootlegger," Minnie said. Although several of the bootleggers that she had met, including the infamous Nova Malone, were surprisingly normal. Involved in the community and concerned about their neighbors, they didn't seem like crooks. Over her time as a reporter, Minnie had come to believe nobody was simply one thing or another. Everyone had many stories to tell and multiple sides to their personalities.

"We're not all bad guys," Sol said, echoing her thoughts. "Some of us are just enterprising in how we make a living. Wait here, I'll grab my canoe."

"Your what?" Minnie said but Sol had already charged up the hill. A rustling of bushes marked his activities at the top of the small rise. Then he came trotting back down the hill, holding a small canoe over his head.

"Let's go," he said. "You follow me. Step where I do. That's the best route."

With a shrug, Minnie followed him.

With the canoe held over his head, Sol picked his way down the path and into the cave. Then he stopped.

"What now?" Minnie asked.

"We need the lamp," Sol replied, holding the canoe a little higher so she could see him gesturing with his chin. "It's behind the rock there."

She found a pair of small camp lamps stashed behind the rock. "Where's the matches?" she said.

"They're self-lighting," Sol replied, setting down the canoe and showing her how to light the lamps. He hooked one on his belt and handed the other to Minnie.

"Clever," she said, securing her lamp to the belt of the raincoat.

"Yeah, I ordered them from a magazine," Sol said. "They'll last about three hours, but we shouldn't be in the cave that long." He shouldered the canoe and continued down the path that Minnie remembered vaguely. The sound of running water echoed through the cave. When Minnie brushed against a wall, she came away with a soaked sleeve. Practically a small waterfall ran down the stone.

"See, it's filled up during the night," said Sol. He pointed to the passageway stretching away into the dark. Minnie unhooked her lamp and held it high. The light reflected on rippling water.

"How deep is it?" she asked.

"Deep enough," Sol said, flipping the canoe in the water. When he pulled it close to the edge of the path, she saw a single paddle stashed inside.

"That's too small for two people," Minnie said.

"No, it will be fine," Sol said, holding out his hand. "You go first and then me."

"But there's only one bench," Minnie said, pointing at the single seat toward the back of the canoe.

"You kneel in front," Sol instructed her. "You'll fit. I've stashed a couple of kegs of beer there. I paddle. We go in and out as quickly as we can."

With some misgivings and a lot of help from Sol, Minnie managed to kneel in the front of the canoe. The thing dipped and bobbed under her. Minnie breathed a short prayer that the tiny boat would stay afloat.

Sol settled easily onto the bench at the back of the canoe,

shifting his weight a bit and then dipping the paddle into the water. They shot forward. Minnie gripped the sides of the canoe as tight as she could.

"That won't help anything," Sol said when he spotted her white-knuckled grip. "If we go over, it is better to be loose. I'll right the canoe. It's easier if you're not hanging on to it."

"I'd rather we didn't flip over," Minnie muttered but she lifted one hand off the edge of the canoe to adjust her lamp. She wanted to give Sol as much light as possible. They slid forward into the passage, the water making an eerie hiss beneath them.

"We could turn back," Sol said again. "Is your camera that important?"

"Yes," Minnie replied, absolutely convinced this was what she should be doing, although she couldn't be more articulate than that. But her natural curiosity prompted her to say, "But why are you helping me? You don't have to be here."

"Told you," Sol said as he dipped the paddle into the brackish water. "If anything happens to you, April would probably tell Genevieve. Gen would definitely tell Mrs Alba. And trust me, you don't want Mrs Alba to be mad at you."

"Who is Mrs Alba? One of the weird women from the cave?" Minnie asked.

"Nah. She's one of the landladies on Flotsam Street," Sol said. "They are not weird. They are fierce. And know far too many ways to make a young man very, very sorry for his actions."

Minnie made a mental note to ask April about the landladies. It sounded like their story could become an interesting article.

Sol rowed them past a wall painted with a green circle

with a dot inside it. Minnie fumbled in her pocket to pull her little Kodak free. The light was poor, but she might be able to get a shot of it, just to mark where she was going rather than anything usable for the *Arkham Advertiser*.

"Don't," Sol said. "That's a bad luck sign."

"What is it?" Minnie asked. "A warning to other bootleggers to stay away from your stash?"

"No," Sol said. "It's older than Prohibition. Maybe older than Arkham. My grandfather said it was a warning not to go any farther into the Black Cave."

"Warning or not, I need my camera back," Minnie declared. "So onward, please."

"Hope this will be worth it," Sol said as they glided deeper into the Black Cave.

"So do I," Minnie said as the smell of brine and death grew stronger.

CHAPTER TEN

Harvey wasn't surprised to see people hurrying out of Valeska Stange's house. On a day like today, he expected people to be consulting Valeska about what was going on. Her understanding of forbidden lore, ancient rituals, and cosmic entities was second only to himself in his opinion. Valeska's opinion of who was more knowledgeable differed. What did surprise Harvey was the identity of the three women who descended the steps and hurried down the street. He knew two of them very well, Columbia and Barbara. Which meant the third woman with similar features had to be Augusta Palmer.

"There they are, Babies A, B, and C," Harvey said, pointing them out to Lefty. "The Palmer triplets." Whatever they had learned at Valeska's house did not seem to make them happy. Valeska rarely gave information without exacting a steep price, which might account for the sour looks. Also, Valeska never sugarcoated the arcane world. If she expected death, doom, or destruction, she would say so. She also would tell the listener that it was all their fault as well, in Harvey's experience. Not that he thought the whole fiasco of 1912 was entirely due to his actions.

Harvey wondered what exactly the sisters sought from Valeska. The Palmers certainly suffered some setbacks yesterday, both in the Dreamlands and in Arkham. Were they after a new route to the power that they failed to appropriate from the Ancient One's dreams? Or were they seeking Barbara's umbrella?

"You want to follow them?" Lefty asked as the Palmer sisters continued walking away from them.

"In a garbage truck?" Harvey said. "They might notice."

"No," Lefty explained. "Nobody notices garbagemen. I can go slow. Even hop out and rattle some cans. They'll think I'm working."

Harvey was torn. He wanted to talk to Valeska, but he hated to lose sight of the Palmer triplets. He would love to know what they were planning, especially after his recent discussion with Mrs Fox. Also, he wondered about their family ancestry and whether it contained sibyls or witches (he suspected both were in the Palmer family tree). However, he also needed to understand exactly what powers the umbrella might unleash before he possibly traded it for information. Or perhaps destroyed it.

Of course, if he destroyed the umbrella, he would have to figure out a diplomatic way to mention its loss to the triplets. Or he could just lie and say he dropped it in the river. It was that kind of day.

"Why don't you talk to your friend and I'll follow the Palmers?" Lefty said, interrupting Harvey's internal debate before the Palmers disappeared around the street corner. "I'm no good for the academic occult stuff, but I can keep an eye on the three dames for you."

"Be careful," said Harvey, who truly didn't trust the Palmers. As much as he wanted to know more about how they fit into Arkham's arcane past and uncertain future, he hadn't forgotten their recent attempts to capitalize on the sleeping sickness infecting so many in the city. "Do you have a watch?"

Lefty turned his arm to show off his battered wristwatch.

"Good," said Harvey, retrieving his pocket watch out of his vest. "Give me half an hour. Perhaps forty-five minutes if Valeska has the information I need. No more than an hour."

Lefty nodded. "I'll follow them as long as I can and then come back. Look for me there." He pointed to where an alley ran between two houses. A garbage truck could park in such a spot without anyone noticing.

"Oh, and she is not really a friend," said Harvey, feeling he should clarify this to Lefty. Not that he'd ever been able to define his relationship with Valeska in his own mind. Harvey retrieved the green umbrella from under the seat.

Lefty just grunted. It was a far more satisfactory answer than most, especially when it came to Valeska Stange.

Harvey hopped out of the truck's cab, giving a little wave to Lefty. "I will try to be quick," he added.

Lefty started Pequod, following slowly behind the Palmer sisters. Harvey watched for a minute and then crossed the street. He rang Valeska's doorbell.

To his surprise, Valeska answered the door. Generally, she was surrounded by people. Some might call them acolytes. Harvey always thought of Valeska's assistants as minions. Whoever or whatever they were, they took care of menial tasks for her, like answering the door.

"Walters," Valeska said, without any warmth in her voice. "What is it? I am going out."

Unlike Henry Armitage and Harvey, Valeska lacked white hair, but only because hers had been dyed the palest blonde.

Her locks were also artfully trimmed into an asymmetrical bob. She still looked as lovely as the day that she appropriated the best seat in the class about the history of the Sumerian dynasties. In those days, her hair had been a rich auburn chignon with a flirtatious cluster of curls arranged against her pale nape. Young Harvey had been fascinated by those curls, sitting exactly three rows ahead of him at Miskatonic University. Old Harvey was surprised how vivid the memory was. He remembered the other students as well, almost all men, and all now sporting bald spots, thinning beards, or wildly uncontrolled eyebrows.

"So many old men," Harvey muttered as he considered the alumni who still remained in Arkham.

"Walters, what are you mumbling about?" Valeska said. She generally refused to call any of the Miskatonic academics by their first names. According to Valeska, all the Harveys, Henrys, and Howards were just too confusing. "I don't have time for your philosophizing today.

She wore a severely tailored overcoat of soft charcoal gray wool with a merino wool scarf in a muted plaid wound around her neck. Her purple hat, while a touch old-fashioned, was obviously from one of the better haberdasheries of Boston. She carried a pair of blue leather gloves in one hand. As usual, Harvey noticed Valeska sported a serpent bracelet on her left wrist.

"I have an object which might interest you," Harvey began, because the best way to deal with Valeska was to appeal to her greed. She collected arcane artifacts in the same way that Harvey accumulated books, which meant Valeska might be willing to pause her activity if it meant adding to her collection.

"Ah," said Valeska. She carefully lifted off her hat and set it on the side table, dropping her gloves beside it. "I have been looking for an artifact. But I thought Tillinghast had it."

"Tillinghast," Harvey snorted. "The man's a junk dealer or possibly a fence."

"Tillinghast is definitely a fence," Valeska agreed. "But he does acquire some very interesting objects from his sources. What do you have?" Valeska opened a door and gestured to Harvey to follow her into a small study. Unlike Harvey's study, the room was almost unnaturally clean. The bookshelves were bare of books but full of artifacts. Harvey barely glanced at the Roman, Grecian, and Egyptian antiquities. A nice collection but nothing too unusual. Behind Valeska's desk was another bookcase with glass doors. Barely visible on those shelves were stranger objects, ones that seemed to slither out of sight when examined too closely. Harvey dismissed an urge to circle around her desk and investigate the bookcase more closely. After all, he reminded himself, curiosity killed the cat. Besides, Valeska would surely object.

"I can give you fifteen minutes," Valeska said, settling into the leather chair behind the desk. Harvey took the chair opposite her, placing the umbrella across his lap.

She flicked a glance at the green umbrella and frowned. "If the artifact that you want to discuss is that umbrella, make that five minutes," Valeska said. "I've already endured a rather tedious conversation about it."

"The Palmer triplets?" Harvey said. "I noticed them leaving your house."

"Obviously they didn't notice you," she said.

Harvey shook his head. "I was in a garbage truck across the street."

"Why were you…?" Valeska began and then frowned.

"I neither care nor want to know more. I have no interest in adding another umbrella to my collection. I am busy, Walters. Far too much of my morning has been taken up with rank amateurs finding signs and portents in the coming storm."

"So you consider the Palmers amateurs?" Harvey said. Such a dismissive assessment didn't align with his experiences.

"No, of course not," she snapped. "Powerful practitioners, if misguided in their attempts to plumb the unknown regions. If they only allowed themselves to be advised by older and wiser heads, much tragedy could have been averted."

"You mean if they had let the men tell them what to do?" Harvey couldn't resist the jab, which might cause Valeska to lose her temper and drop a few hints about the Palmers.

Valeska made a disapproving sound, a little "tetch" click of tongue against teeth, at Harvey's admittedly impolite question. "Or more experienced women," she replied. "But they always thought they should be leaders."

"I'm surprised that you find that offensive," Harvey said. Valeska had never been a woman to hide her talents.

Valeska sneered, but in a very elegant fashion. "I never fought to prove myself. The Palmers exhausted themselves running after Elizabeth Cady Stanton, Susan B. Anthony, and those other women in white. Actually, Columbia and Barbara did. Augusta never bothered with anyone outside of her family. And then the sisters were furious that the world didn't change overnight when the vote was finally won."

"We all expected more than Prohibition," Harvey said. "But it has become somewhat better, you must admit."

"Still defending the suffragettes, Harvey? They won the vote. Then what did they do? Elect more men," Valeska said with a bitter edge to her voice. For a woman who had gone her own way throughout her life, Valeska was very dismissive of those who fought for the rights of women. Harvey once heard her say that the only interesting suffragist was Victoria Woodhull and she had been run out of the country when they were both youths.

Harvey almost listed off a few women who were making strides in national government, but he knew Lefty would be returning for him soon. Debating politics with Valeska was a useless endeavor. They would always disagree on the way the world should be. However, her comments revealed a greater knowledge of the Palmers than Harvey expected.

"How long have you known the Palmers?" he asked.

Valeska shrugged. "A number of years. Most of my dealings were with Columbia and Barbara, of course, as Augusta has been locked up in various asylums for the last three decades."

"I understood that they left Arkham as children," Harvey said, recalling the stories told at Schoffner's General Store.

"They did. But I am not anchored to this city. I do travel," Valeska said. "There's also the US Mail. Even telephones. I have ways of communicating with others."

"If you knew them already, why check out a pamphlet about their childhood seance?" Harvey asked, genuinely intrigued. Valeska's research was almost always directed toward her own profit, but she seemed uninterested in the umbrella and dismissive of the Palmers. So why spend any time at all on reading about them?

"I need to know my potential allies and enemies," Valeska admitted. "Tillinghast's greed unleashed a horror, as you already know. But the Palmers are useless for my purposes. They are far too focused on their own needs. Selfish, really." She sounded genuinely astonished that somebody other than herself would want to triumph in the upcoming cataclysm.

"What did the Palmers want from you?" Harvey asked and immediately knew that was too direct a question for Valeska.

She proved that he was right by her evasive answer. "What most people want. What do you want with me? To hash over old news and even less important business dealings?"

"Not at all," Harvey said, reluctantly abandoning his curiosity about the Palmers' dealings with Valeska. "I need your opinion on why the Palmers want this umbrella so badly."

The only place where they sometimes met in agreement was on the value of careful experimentation in pursuit of better occult understanding. Although Harvey often suspected that Valeska's definition of careful experimentation was slightly different than his own. However, Harvey could not fault the woman's intelligence or knowledge of arcane objects – just how she used them.

Harvey unfurled the umbrella, revealing the carved shaft. "Armitage says it is dangerous. What can you tell me?" Harvey lifted the umbrella higher so Valeska could see the strange carvings of tentacles and the single eye made of mother-of-pearl at the base of the shaft.

"Henry Armitage is an overeducated librarian with the soul of a mouse," Valeska said, reaching across the desk for the umbrella. Harvey drew back a little. Valeska clicked her fingers at him like he was a tardy waiter. "I have already told you that I don't want or need another conjuring stick, even one hidden in an umbrella. Hand it to me so I can examine it. Or take yourself off. It doesn't matter to me what you decide. I have a great many things to do today."

Harvey handed Valeska the umbrella.

"Definitely a wand," Valeska said, rotating the shaft slowly. "The carvings are possibly based on the staffs carried by the priestesses of Mu."

"Really? I thought it might have been created by descendants of the Ignoti," Harvey said.

The sound that Valeska made could have been called a snort if she wasn't a refined lady. As it was, she sniffed more emphatically than most ladies did. "Like Armitage, you are too much wedded to your books. Knowledge should never be confined to accounts written after the invention of the printing press."

"Are you insulting my books?" Harvey drawled. "Be careful, Valeska, because them's fighting words."

"Ring Lardner ruined the English language," Valeska said as she continued rotating the umbrella. "A man with as many degrees as you have should not be quoting him."

"I enjoyed *Gullible's Travels*," Harvey said. "When was the last time you read anything humorous?"

"Oh, please," Valeska said, "as if the *Arkham Advertiser*'s articles on strange occurrences aren't laughable enough." She passed the umbrella back to Harvey. "It is a wand, which you already knew, and one which is most often used to cloud the minds of followers."

"Manipulate their memories?" Harvey asked, thinking of the problems encountered by his friend, Carolyn Fern, recently.

"Certainly," Valeska said. "A priestess could create false memories of miracles and apparitions. Which is useful if you're trying to control a cult. I can see why you thought of the Ignoti."

"But why did you immediately name the wand as belonging to a priestess of Mu?" Harvey said.

"Various sources claimed the high priestess to be a virtuoso of shadows woven from the dreams of the gods. Able to alter reality itself. The sheer power of these shadows could save a city or drown it. Indeed, it's one of the reasons given for the destruction of Mu," she said. "There's also some who claim the sibyls of Greece descended from the high priestess of Mu."

"Except Mu is a myth," said Harvey. "A case of mistranslation by Le Plongeon."

"Next you'll be saying that Atlantis is a fairy tale and R'lyeh only a fable," Valeska said and, for the first time during this conversation, almost smiled. At least her painted lips curled slightly upward. "When did you grow so old and staid, Walters?"

"I've been asking myself that very question all week long," Harvey admitted. He tightly rolled the umbrella's green material to hide the wand and the staring eye at its base.

"What else can the wand do?" Harvey asked.

"A more interesting question than any that you've asked so far." Valeska straightened back in her chair, steepling her fingers. Harvey noticed her manicure was immaculate, each fingernail polished a deep scarlet.

Harvey decided to lean back in his chair. He often used this gesture before lecturing a wayward student. Such a maneuver said, "I'm in charge of all knowledge here." Harvey leaned back as far as possible and gave Valeska a skeptical look. Two could play at being the most knowledgeable in the room.

Valeska's lips might have twitched, and she dropped her pose. "I may dislike Augusta Palmer and her sisters but they have done more with their wands than hypnotize people or cast shadows on the wall. It's possible they can use the wands like keys, to open doors best left locked."

"What kind of doors?"

"Passages to other places, even other dimensions." Valeska tapped one polished fingernail on her desk. "So drawing power out of those places to fuel their spells. In fact, I would say such power would be essential for Augusta to sustain her spells. The sisters are strong but they are not inexhaustibly so."

"Are the Palmers causing the problems today?" Harvey asked. He had thought they had been attracted to the magical upheavals, very much like flies to honey, but perhaps he had underestimated them.

Valeska shook her head. "I am most emphatically saying that the Palmers did not cause our recent troubles. I blame Tillinghast for the unusual weather and a few other things. But the Palmers definitely want to take advantage of the situation. I told you that they were selfish women."

Harvey restrained himself from muttering about pots calling kettles names.

"It's been suggested to me that Augusta Palmer wants to change the future," Harvey said instead.

"There's no denying she is a powerful sibyl." Valeska nodded. "If Augusta hadn't been confined to an asylum for the last thirty years, she might have become a rival."

"To you?" Harvey asked, a little surprised Valeska would rate Augusta's powers so highly. Valeska rarely admitted to equals or even the possibility of equals.

"There was a time when the Golden Leaf was interested in the Palmer triplets," Valeska said, neatly sidestepping the question. "But those three broke the men who sought to use their power. Deliberately or unintentionally? It's hard to say. But three little girls did open a window into the dreams of a dead god."

"I've never heard of the Golden Leaf." He had heard of a dead god dreaming but he had been careless with the name before. He promised friends to be more careful.

"A very minor organization of the last century," Valeska continued. "The Golden Leaf disbanded soon after their seance with the Palmer triplets. Over the years, I've met a few of the surviving members and acquired one or two trifles from them."

"Mementos of the Ancient One?" Harvey dared to use one of the dead god's many pseudonyms. That wasn't breaking his promise not to name the dead god.

"Possibly hints of its continued existence. Mentions of R'lyeh." Valeska shrugged. "My guess is the Palmers did the same research, although Augusta's access to such knowledge would naturally be more limited over the last few decades. Barbara and Columbia seem to have continued her work where they could, once they shed themselves of inconvenient husbands." She waved one hand. "And, before you ask, I neither know nor care how those two became widows." She leaned back again and waggled her fingers at Harvey. "But you should."

Harvey blinked. "Why should I care about their late husbands?"

"Because they are rather peeved at you, Harvey Walters," Valeska said with a smile broad enough to be clearly recognized as an almost Cheshire Cat grin and using his full name for the first time in the conversation. "They want their umbrella back."

"But why? To open a door? Or a more nefarious action?" Harvey said. He wasn't truly worried about the Palmer triplets. A number of people had tried to curse or kill him over the years. So far, nobody had succeeded, not even

Valeska. Among all the mounting dangers of the coming day, he counted the Palmers as a lesser threat.

"That's your problem," Valeska said. She turned a silver carriage clock on her desk. Three upward arrows were engraved on the case. A gift from Carl Sanford, Harvey grumbled to himself, having seen the symbol before. Valeska had always favored the pompous Sanford, whose views on exploiting occult knowledge were very similar to her own. Or perhaps Valeska had looted the clock from the scorched remains of the Silver Twilight Lodge. That thought made him feel a little better.

Valeska tetched again at the clock. "Time's up, Walters. I have places to go today before there is no place left standing."

"So you do think the Ancient One will manifest in Arkham?" Harvey knew the question was blunt, but he, too, sensed time was ticking away for them all.

"If we are lucky, the Ancient One will only brush past us on its way to somewhere else. Certainly, that is an outcome that we should all encourage," Valeska said as they left the room. She collected her hat and gloves as she ushered Harvey outside. She thrust the gloves in a coat pocket and paused before a hall mirror to adjust her hat on her head.

Harvey descended to the street as Valeska locked the door and pocketed the key.

"Walters," Valeska said quietly and with an odd look of concern crossing her face, "try not to get yourself killed too quickly."

"Why, Valeska, does our friendship mean so much to you?" Harvey said with a smile. He made the joke as he supposed she was poking at his dignity. Valeska did like having the last word.

To his surprise, Valeska did not immediately respond with a devastating riposte. Instead, she stared steadily at Harvey. "Arkham may need you before the day is done. As much as you academics annoy me, your knowledge may be our only weapon of worth. And if that is true, then we best hope for a minor miracle or two."

Valeska pulled on her blue gloves and strode away.

CHAPTER ELEVEN

As promised, Harvey found Lefty and Pequod parked in the alley. "Learn anything useful?" Lefty asked as Harvey climbed back into the cab.

"Other than Valeska Stange never gives the answer that you expect?" Harvey grumbled. Exchanging barbs with Valeska had been part of his life for decades. But Valeska almost turned sentimental on him during the last exchange, which Harvey found unsettling. Still, it confirmed his own judgment that what was coming outweighed the petty rivalries of Arkham's occult scholars.

"Maybe I did learn a little," Harvey confessed to Lefty. "Where did the Palmers go?"

"To a little café around the corner."

"Are they still there?"

"No. They borrowed the phone and called a cab. It picked them up a few minutes ago." Lefty started up Pequod during his recounting.

"So we've lost them." Harvey sighed. "Maybe that's just as well." Perhaps he should spend the rest of the day gathering what forces he could find to assist those who would fight for Arkham's future. Nothing in his recent conversations with Armitage and Valeska changed his original diagnosis of cosmic terror being far too close for comfort. He needed to learn more about the sibyls' predictions, including a chat with the often mentioned Mrs Alba.

Harvey considered Augusta's plans and her willingness to change the future. Perhaps it was a bad idea for Augusta to do this. But might he not borrow a little from the Palmers' techniques to help Arkham in a very dire time? After all, he had the umbrella. If it was the key to unlocking a better outcome for the Palmers, shouldn't he use it to help his friends? Of course, somebody was sure to quote the old adage about the path to hell being paved with good intentions if he tried to explain this idea to Mrs Fox.

"Oh, I know where the ladies are going," Lefty said as he backed onto the street and turned Pequod around.

"Really, how?" Harvey inquired.

"Asked the waitress if she'd overheard the call." Lefty rolled down the window and hand signaled a left turn. Traffic wasn't heavy but brisker than it had been earlier in the morning. With the easing of the rain, Arkham seemed to be coming back to life. Harvey saw more people wandering down the street as well. It seemed the early morning fears of flood and devastation had abated as the day continued without any serious damage to the town. Even the booms of the dynamite project were gone.

"So where are we going?" Harvey asked.

"They wanted a cab to St Mary's," Lefty said.

"But why would they go to the hospital?" Harvey answered his own question next. "Ira! They intend to retrieve their baby brother."

At least he assumed the sisters wanted Ira. It was hard to imagine anyone wanting Ira, but families were odd.

When they pulled up at St Mary's, the place also appeared a little quieter than the last time they visited. The lull that Harvey noticed in the rain seemed to extend to the hospital. At least there were no ambulances with bells jangling as they sped to the entrance. Even the pair of orderlies sneaking a smoke just outside the main doors looked reassuringly relaxed.

Before leaving Pequod, Harvey slid the green umbrella under the seat. He might want to interrogate the Palmers, particularly Augusta, but he didn't want to wave the umbrella in front of them. Not yet. Better he should claim knowledge of its whereabouts and see what he could secure in trade.

"So how do we find the Palmers?" Lefty asked as they entered the main hall.

"Ask where Ira is," Harvey said, bustling over to a desk. The nurse seated there directed them to another desk, and its occupant told them to try the East Ward.

At the East Ward, yet another nurse flipped through a stack of cards which reminded Harvey of the Orne Library. Apparently "checked in" meant similar things for books and patients.

"He broke an arm?" the nurse inquired. "And unconscious when he was brought in?"

"Yes, most unfortunate," Harvey said. "A small accident in my basement." Involving a pipe wrench wielded by himself, but Harvey didn't think that was necessary to mention. "I hoped to see my assistant and reassure myself of his well-being."

The nurse nodded and flipped a few more cards. "Here he is. Room 304," she said. "The elevator is around the corner or you can take the stairs at the end of the hall. When you arrive on the floor, they will let you know if he can receive visitors."

"Thank you so much," Harvey said. He gestured to Lefty and the garbageman followed Harvey to the elevator. Harvey had had enough of trotting up and down stairs after the Orne.

"Which floor?" asked the elevator operator.

"Third," Harvey said.

The operator nodded and clanged the door shut. The elevator car rose with minimal creaks and settled almost smoothly into place on the third floor.

"Here you are," the operator said, "just go straight down the hall to the nurses' station."

Harvey and Lefty got off the elevator. Signs of the hospital's storm preparations were evident. Old-fashioned oil lamps stood ready on tables up and down the hall in case the lights went out. Buckets of sand were filled and positioned beneath more modern fire extinguishers, perhaps an extra precaution warranted by the oil lamps.

At the desk, Harvey repeated his story of concern over his assistant. They were waved toward Room 304 by an obviously tired nurse, who did not even bother to check if Ira was conscious and able to receive visitors. Nobody mentioned Ira's sisters, but Lefty grabbed Harvey's arm and pulled him aside.

"The Palmers would have gotten here before us," he said to Harvey. "Don't you think we should be careful? Maybe not charge into the room?"

Harvey shook his head. "Nobody mentioned seeing the three sisters or that Ira has had visitors. Maybe they went somewhere else or the cab was delayed."

"The ladies left a good fifteen or twenty minutes before we did," Lefty said. "It would be a pretty poor taxi driver if he couldn't beat us to St Mary's."

"Nothing ventured, nothing gained," Harvey said, quoting his favorite motto. He strode down the corridor and flung open the door to Room 304.

The room was empty.

"Well, that's a disappointment," Harvey said, who had fully expected to confront all three Palmer women as well as his assistant. He looked around the room, hoping for a clue on where Ira could have gone. The small closet and bedside table were both empty. A discarded hospital gown lay under the bed as if kicked there by someone. Ira had obviously left his room fully dressed since nobody had mentioned an unclothed man wandering the halls. Even on a day like today, such a sight would have set the nurses buzzing.

Harvey wondered if Ira had simply pulled on his clothes and left the room to meet his sisters elsewhere. Harvey opened the door and glanced down the hallway. He could see the back of the nurse's head. She appeared to be slumped in her seat, fighting to stay awake. Obviously, the long night had taken its toll on the staff. The door to the staircase was directly opposite the room's door. "Ira could have easily slipped out without anybody noticing," Harvey said.

Lefty put his hand on the still rumpled bed. "It's warm," he said. "He must have left just minutes ago."

"Down the stairs is better than climbing up the stairs," Harvey said as he crossed the hall and opened the staircase door. He leaned over the banister to peer down the well. Nobody could be seen on the levels below, but Harvey thought he heard the faint thud of a closing door. He hurried down the stairs with Lefty close on his heels.

The antiseptic green walls were interrupted with long narrow windows at each landing. Glancing outside, Harvey estimated that the stairs must end in a side door. Catching a glimpse of old boxes and garbage cans, he thought this was one of the alleys running along the back of the hospital. He couldn't see the main road from the landing.

Once they reached the bottom, they found a latched door that opened easily from the inside. "If we go out, it may lock behind us," Lefty observed.

"Ira must have come this way," Harvey said. "Otherwise, the nurse would have seen him."

They hurried down the alley but caught no glimpse of the elusive Ira.

"It appears to be a dead end," Harvey declared as the alley led them back to a courtyard of St Mary's. "Ira has vanished so we have no way to find the Palmers now." He sighed. "Well, there are other things we can do."

They turned another corner, heading to where Lefty parked his truck. Harvey was lost in his thoughts, trying to decide where to go next. Perhaps he should return to Miskatonic University and find his colleagues. Surely someone was already working on a plan to protect Arkham, or, at the very least, their beloved campus.

"Ah, professor, we have company," Lefty said.

Startled, Harvey looked up and saw a trio of angry looking ladies blocking the alley in front of them. Standing slightly behind the women was Ira, a white bandage covering his head. Harvey's former assistant appeared both wan and irate.

Well, at least one of his deductions had proven correct. The sisters had come to fetch their baby brother. Now he had to gauge their mood and possibly prevent them from killing him before he could discuss the green umbrella.

"Ladies," Harvey said, raising his hat politely. "This is a fortuitous meeting."

CHAPTER TWELVE

Minnie peered into the gloom. The lamps barely illuminated the water rippling underneath the canoe. The walls and ceilings were lost in darkness. A musty odor, like dirty laundry moldering in a basement, rose around them. Other than the quiet swish of Sol's paddle, the only sound was a steady trickle of water coming into the Black Cave.

"Why is so much water coming down the walls?" Minnie asked Sol. "The river is behind us."

"This water is coming from the city, not the Miskatonic," Sol replied. "With all the rain, the sewers and storm drains are overflowing. It all leads to the river eventually but there's so much water that it has to go somewhere. These caves will fill long before the river goes over its bank."

The thought of overflowing sewers made Minnie shudder in disgust. It also explained the rank and uninviting atmosphere. At least the wind and the rain outside smelled clean. But she wanted her camera back, so she urged Sol to keep going. They entered the larger cavern where April had rescued them.

Feeling more confident of her position in the canoe, Minnie stopped clutching the sides and used her free hand to raise her lantern. She let the beam play across the dripping walls and stagnant water.

"There!" Minnie said, pointing to the long platform of stone which ran along the edge of the chamber. She recognized the rock, remembered lying upon it, and being wedged between Rex and her camera case. The rest of the event might be fuzzy in her brain, but the hard square of her camera case was now so clear in her memory that she almost felt it at her hip. Sol paddled forward until the canoe bumped up against the rock. He stretched out one arm to pull the canoe tight against the platform. "See anything?"

Minnie straightened a little more from her crouch in the front of the canoe. Again, she swept the beam of the lantern across the wet stone. Tight against the wall was her brown leather camera case. Although water trickled around it, the platform had kept it from being submerged. She hoped the camera bag manufacturer's promises to keep her equipment dry in all conditions would prove true. Minnie leaned out of the canoe and reached across the platform. She snared the camera case's leather strap in her groping hand with a cry of triumph.

"Careful!" Sol said as Minnie's actions caused the canoe to bob in the water like an agitated duck.

Minnie shifted her weight fully back into the canoe, cradling the camera bag against her chest. Even in the lantern's dim light, she could see it was still shut tight. With luck, the waterproof bag not only protected the camera, but also kept the flash lamp dry enough to work.

Thinking to capture a picture of the Black Cave filling with water, Minnie opened the bag, practically assembling her equipment by feel in the poor light. Sol continued to clutch the platform to give her some stability.

"Maybe I should crawl out on the rock and take my picture," Minnie told him.

"I don't know if that's a good idea," he said. "Do you think you could get back into the canoe without overturning us?"

"Perhaps not," Minnie acknowledged. She pulled the camera free of its case along with the flash. She hooked her lantern in her coat's belt to make it easier to manipulate her camera equipment. It would be tricky getting the shot in the rocking canoe, but she had captured photographs in worse conditions.

Something moved outside of the small circle of illumination cast by Sol's lamps. It sloshed – no other word would do – at the far end of the cave. Minnie immediately swung to face the noise, her camera momentarily forgotten. Sol shifted in his seat, directing the beam of his lantern toward the noise.

At the very edge of the light, a vaguely humanoid silhouette emerged from the water. The creature's flesh gleamed like an oil slick upon the sea. It twisted toward them, expanding and contracting in an unsettling flux of features. Sol shifted his lantern so it shone directly upon a mass of writhing tentacles which formed a shape approximating a human head. Large bat-like wings unfurled from its back, scraping against the damp walls of the cave.

But it was the taloned hands which caused Minnie to gasp and Sol to swear. Each ended in a cluster of obsidian claws. The creature slithered forward, its immense mass appearing to stretch and then compress, as it waded through the shallow water. As it drew nearer, it also grew impossibly larger, continuing to spread upward toward the ceiling. The smell of decay and destruction intensified. A gust of icy wind swept through the cave, rocking the canoe.

The tentacled head was maddeningly indistinct. As the lanterns bobbed in their unsteady hands, its features wavered in a manner reminiscent of shadows creeping up the bedroom wall. Minnie remembered nights huddled in the bed as the moon shone through cracks in the curtain, creating nightmare figures shifting toward the void which was the closet. On those nights, she had pinched her sister awake, certain monsters lurked behind the closet door or under the bed. She almost reached back and pinched Sol, simply to make sure he also saw what was oozing toward them.

The monstrous entity seemed to be her bedroom shadows given form, stirring into impossible life in the depths of the Black Cave.

Minnie blinked, feeling as if she stood on the edge of a bridge or tall tower, looking down instead of up at the creature's visage. Her disorientation grew and she dropped her eyes to the camera cradled in her lap. The camera's solid shape anchored her to the world confined in the Black Cave. This creature might be fantastical in the most horrific sense, but it was there and she could take a picture, a photograph that could fill the entire front page of the *Arkham Advertiser*.

Sol let go of the rock platform, his lantern dropping a bit so they could only see the edge of the creature swimming toward them. He clipped his lantern to his belt, pushing off from the rock, and then paddling them back toward the cavern's entrance.

"What is it?" Minnie hissed as she struggled to aim her camera, grasp her flash, and keep her eyes trained on the advancing monster. As always, even as the immediate terror chilled her skin and raised goosebumps, she lamented that her distant ancestors had lost their tails when they descended from the trees. She truly wanted three hands at this moment.

"How should I know?" Sol whispered as he continued to paddle away from the creature as quickly and quietly as possible. "But it's too big to follow us into the passage."

Both kept their voices as low as possible, instinctively trying to avoid the creature's attention. The swaying of its head, and the absence of visible eyes, made Minnie think it might be blind. As such, they might be able to slip away from its notice.

A faint, low thrumming vibrated from its face tentacles, as if it sought them through sound as much as sight. Or was responding to Sol's assertion about it being unable to follow them, an even more disquieting thought.

"Keep your eyes on it," Sol said. "I need to watch the walls here so I don't scrape the canoe." Sol aimed them for the narrow opening leading back to the Miskatonic River, shooting the canoe expertly between the rocky walls.

Behind them, the monster gave out a hideous wail or perhaps it was the foul wind that it pulled in its wake, shrieking through the caverns. Minnie would later swear the cave walls seemed to buckle in and out, fluctuating with the terrible cry. She lifted the camera from her lap, pointed the equipment at the creature pursuing them, and set off the flash. The bright burst of light revealed a still undefinable body with webbed appendages now filling the chamber behind them. The same burst of light also seemed to startle the creature, causing its face tentacles to retract. Like smoke in the wind, the taloned hands reaching toward them quavered and then dissolved in the short burst of light. The creature sank itself beneath the surface, another unexplainable action as Minnie knew the water was only a few feet deep in this cavern. But the creature was gone, not even a ripple to mark where it had been.

"Let's go before it comes back," Sol said as he maneuvered the canoe through the passage leading them out of the Black Cave. His face was pale in the lantern light. Sweat dotted his brow, but he kept a steady rhythm with his paddle, carrying them swiftly away.

"Probably a good idea," Minnie said, but she shifted around so she could peer back over Sol's shoulder, wondering if the creature would emerge from the water again. As hard as her heart was pounding, she almost longed for it to emerge so she could take another picture. With the immediate terror past, she now feared that her first hasty shot failed to capture the enormity of the creature. Still, her body wanted to put as much distance as possible between the Black Cave's otherworldly shadows and herself.

As they left the passage into a broader chamber, Sol swore again.

"What is it?" Minnie looked around, expecting to see the horror pursuing them here. Could it have passed through solid walls to cut them off at the entrance of the Black Cave? It seemed physically impossible but nothing about the creature seemed to be ruled by any laws that Einstein would recognize.

"The eye!" Sol said, pointing to the circle with a dot painted on one wall. "It wasn't glowing when we passed it the first time."

The circle shone in the light of their lanterns. A sickly glowing green that they would have noticed when Minnie took a picture of it the first time.

"Maybe it is luminescent paint," said Minnie. "Like the radium used on watch faces. It only needed to absorb more light." But where would the light have come from? Their lanterns provided the only illumination. They had shone the lanterns on the circle for a few brief minutes when they passed it the first time. Would that have been enough to cause it to glow?

Sol shook his head. "Whoever painted it used ordinary green house paint. I showed it to April and her professor friend when I brought them in here. Someone repainted the old warning symbol a few days ago. But it didn't glow then!"

With a glance at the passageway that they had recently exited, which might contain a monster on the other side, Minnie considered her options. Flee as quickly as possible or stay and risk another attack as she sought answers to the mysteries encountered. As always, she only considered one option. Get the picture, follow the story.

"Can you take me a little closer? I want to photograph it again," she said.

Sol gave the same uneasy look around the cave, obviously calculating the odds that they were being followed. But they heard nothing and even the oppressive smell of decay seemed diminished so close to the entrance.

"Please," Minnie added. "I need this photo." Then she grinned. "I'll tell April what a great guy you are, a regular hero. She'll tell Genevieve and maybe Genevieve will tell Mrs Alba…"

Sol pursed his lips but apparently the opportunity to appear a hero won out over other considerations.

"Be quick," Sol said, paddling them a little closer to the glowing circle.

Minnie pulled out her camera and took several shots of the circle. How well it would appear in a black-and-white photograph weighed on her mind. But it was part of a larger story, she was certain, and she needed this evidence for Doyle and other doubters.

"Tell me again what it means," she said to Sol.

"We all grew up knowing about the Eye," Sol said. "It's supposed to be a warning, to stay out of this section of the cavern past this point."

"Why do you call it the Eye?" Minnie asked. "Why not the Circle? Or the Dot?"

"Don't know," Sol said as he resumed paddling. "That's what my grandfather used to say. Don't go past the Eye. There's trouble deep in the Black Cave."

"But you store booze in here," Minnie pointed out. "So you don't seem too worried about the legends."

"After the last two days, I'm not sure I'll be putting any hooch here again," Sol said. "Hey, are you taking notes on this? I don't need to appear in the newspaper!"

Minnie tucked her notebook back into her pocket. Suddenly it struck her that he was a criminal, and they were alone in a dark cave, moving through a deep puddle of sewer water. Rex would say she was taking unnecessary risks. But Doyle would tell her to pursue the story. And Sol didn't look threatening, simply a little concerned.

"I won't quote you by name," she promised. "Or mention the bootlegging. But if the Eye is a warning, what exactly is the warning about?"

"Keep out of the cavern when it floods because there's things with tentacles back there?" Sol said. "I don't know. My grandfather never talked about a man-shaped octopus coming out of this cave."

"Do you think it was an octopus? Washed into the cavern by the rain?" Minnie couldn't believe that was what they saw. But she knew what Doyle would say when he reviewed her copy. She hoped the picture turned out clear enough to refute such theories.

"An octopus with talons, legs, and wings?" Sol said, sounding skeptical. "I don't think so. But I do believe the Eye is a good warning if it's telling us to get out of here before the creature comes back."

"If it returns, I could get another picture," Minnie mused as she put her camera back in its bag but left the flap unfastened. That way she could pull the camera out again in a hurry.

But they reached the entrance of the Black Cave with no further incident. Minnie wanted to return to the *Arkham Advertiser* as quickly as possible to develop the picture. Had she captured the photo of the century? Would she be known as the reporter who caught the monster of the Black Cave on film?

But as she scrambled out of the canoe, Minnie felt a certain relief. The weird compulsion driving her all morning seemed to be mollified by the recovery of her Speed Graphic. She had enough material to go back to the office and work on her story. But she also wondered where the creature had gone. More importantly, where would it appear next?

CHAPTER THIRTEEN

Harvey nodded to the quartet confronting him in the courtyard as he replaced his hat on his head. "Ira, you appear a bit better," he said to his former assistant. Ira stared back with a disdainful look.

"Professor Walters, I presume," said the woman in the center of the group.

"That's him, Augusta," said Barbara, who Harvey had recently confronted at the Black Cave along with her sister, Columbia.

"He's a troublemaker," Columbia confirmed. "And a friend of that interfering doctor."

"If you are referring to my friend, Carolyn," Harvey said, "from my perspective, you were the ones meddling with her life." The sisters turned Carolyn's own skills at hypnosis against her in their attempt to manipulate the dreamers of Arkham. Without the intervention of April, they might have succeeded in stealing a great deal of power from the Dreamlands awash in turmoil caused by the awakening of a certain not to be named entity.

Augusta stepped forward. "You have our umbrella," she said. "You will give it back to us before you die."

The other two women moved one step forward in unison. Ira stayed where he was.

Harvey once faced down a cosmic entity with eyes like swirling clouds of ice. The creature's indifferent observation was cozy compared to the cold gaze of Augusta Palmer. Her matter-of-fact certainty concerning his future irked him too. While he never doubted he might meet his death someday making a heroic final stand against the forces invading Arkham, Harvey disliked Augusta's assumption that he would return her umbrella so easily. So he began to lecture the collected Palmers as if they were a group of tardy freshmen.

"I would need far more information about an invasive extra dimensional entity before I could even contemplate the transfer of a dangerous artifact into the hands of those who have proven to be inexperienced practitioners of arcane rituals," Harvey said without having to take even one breath. Practice over the years had perfected his technique of droning out a great many big words while contemplating several things at once.

At the moment, he was wondering if the Palmers constituted an immediate physical threat. None of them appeared to be armed. He did have a derringer in his pocket. Of course, firing on a group of unarmed women and one annoying former assistant was not what a gentleman would do. But they did not know Harvey was a gentleman. So perhaps he could wave it about and exit stage left as Shakespeare would advise.

"Careful, professor," breathed Lefty behind him as the trio of Palmer sisters advanced one more deliberate step toward them.

Harvey added Lefty's probable aptitude for physical

combat to his calculations. He doubted his friend would engage in fisticuffs with any of the women, but he might be willing to punch Ira. No, Ira was injured and that would probably cause Lefty to hesitate. So it was up to Harvey to talk themselves away from the glowering Palmers while extracting as much information as possible.

"Madam, if my calculations are correct, we will soon face a nightmarish amalgamation of cephalopodic, draconian, and anthropomorphic components embodied in a gigantic being. The implications of its reawakening portend the very bending of the conventional three-dimensional space which we occupy. It would behoove you to aid us without resorting to petty threats. I cannot be menaced. I can, however, be persuaded to return your lost umbrella if you will aid us in saving Arkham," Harvey said.

Augusta did not blink, for which Harvey gave her full credit. Most of his students would have blinked and even retreated by now, concerned they faced a gibbering occult fanatic at the podium. He folded his arms and glared. Harvey also stayed silent, a more difficult task, as the Palmers glowered back at him.

"Why would we care about the fate of Arkham?" Augusta finally said. "What has this city or its citizens ever done to earn our assistance? They publicly mocked us as babies A, B, and C in our youth. Now that we are old women, we are invisible to them. Hags to ignore."

Barbara nodded her head and Columbia nodded in time with her. "Walk into a store and be overlooked by the clerk," Barbara said.

"Have everyone tell you how little your experience matters. If they acknowledge that you have any experience at all," Columbia added.

"When you voice an opinion, be called a scold and reminded old women are only good for minding grandchildren," Barbara continued.

"Lock us away when we make them uncomfortable," Augusta concluded.

While Harvey held some sympathy for their complaints, he knew Augusta Palmer had been locked away for hacking her stepmother apart in an occult experiment which turned even his stomach. So he felt that the "uncomfortable" was a misnomer. "Terrified" would be a better description of people's reactions to Augusta according to the tales that he had heard at Schoffner's. As a child, her crimes extended from arson to kitten snatching. She was certainly more disturbing as an adult. Perhaps it was a trick of the light, but she cast a long shadow which seemed to writhe and spread like a pool of oil upon water.

Lefty hissed at him, "Look behind them."

Augusta's shadow climbed the blank back wall of St Mary's Hospital. The inky shape shifted slowly, forming a shape almost humanoid in appearance. Certainly, it had a pair of legs and a pair of arms. But this materialization also had wings, wide bat-like wings, which stretched impossibly large across the building and up into the sky.

Harvey tried to calculate the scale of the creature but it defied normal reality. It spread across the hospital's wall but was also immense on a cosmic scale. The biggest part appeared to be the head, even though its shape was a biological impossibility. Still, his eyes insisted on seeing the tangled mass of writhing tentacles at the top of the body as a head. Even though heads didn't normally come with feelers which entangled themselves like living whiskers.

"It is not at all like the head of an octopus," Harvey

said, remembering one of his ancient tomes describing an infamous manifestation as "containing the head of a monstrous octopus." Cephalopods, whether octopus or squid, may be "head-footed" but they weren't tentacle-headed. This shadow thing matched nothing found on Earth.

He also remembered a time when Valeska said to him, "Harvey Walters, stop analyzing the monster in front of you and fight back!" But she was often hasty when it came to destroying possessed artifacts, despite her love of such objects.

"What is it?" Lefty asked. To give the garbageman his full due, he asked it in a calm voice as if Harvey would have a comforting answer. Harvey had known students to run screaming from a mere drawing of a similar entity on a chalkboard. Except for poor Willoughby, who had unfortunately been transfixed and later obsessed beyond the point of reason.

"A grotesque impossibility," Harvey said because that was the fascinating truth if not the most reassuring answer. Then turning his eyes away from the enormous and still growing shadow creature, he said to Augusta, "And it is not completely corporeal, is it?"

She smiled slightly. "The legacy of my encounters with the Ancient One's dreams. Isn't it amazing? You will find it can interact with physical objects. More so, once you return our umbrella."

"It's dangerous. You play with shadows and you may well attract the true Ancient One to you." So Valeska was right, the Palmers needed the umbrella to help power this shadow. Which was a good argument for keeping the wand away from Augusta.

"But the Ancient One is what I want in Arkham," Augusta

said and Harvey did not doubt her. This was the most terrifying thing to happen so far in this encounter.

"Nobody wants to meet Cthulhu," Harvey retorted, then cursed himself for speaking the name out loud. He most definitely did not want to bring the actual Ancient One to Arkham any more quickly. "Oh, we all know the cultists in the basement think they want to encounter their god." He glared at Ira, who had an unfortunate history in Harvey's own basement. "They believe their devotion will result in unfathomable rewards, but their god does not exist to grant wishes like a genie from a fairy tale."

"Are you so sure?" Barbara asked, turning glowing eyes on her sister. "Look how only its dreams have transformed our sister."

"And are you not one of those academics willing to sacrifice everything for a scrap of forbidden insight granted by such an encounter?" Columbia asked Harvey.

"Not my sanity, not my soul," Harvey said sternly. "Not even my magnificent eyebrows." Then he gave the sisters the same lecture that he once used when trying to persuade Willoughby to abandon his quest. "Consider what we know, which is minuscule and fragmentary. Yet it is clear that every significant interaction with entities of such magnitude leads to the destruction of the mind and malformation of the body. Should you survive an actual encounter, it is most likely you will spend the rest of your lives imprisoned in an asylum."

Of course, this argument had failed to save Willoughby. The Palmers looked equally unimpressed.

"I have wasted half my life in confinement," Augusta retorted. "I will have my freedom and the ability to change the world into what I want, not what petty moralists claim we should desire."

As she spoke, the shadow began to seep into the walls of St Mary's. The tentacled head ducked into the roof, reminiscent of a child peering into a cookie jar. Screams could be clearly heard through open windows. From the third floor, there was a pop and flash, and smoke began to pour from the window. A shout of "Fire!" and a clanging of alarms followed.

"Just a taste of the future," Augusta said. "Soon this hospital could be engulfed in flames."

"Stop!" Harvey shouted, throwing his empty hands high into the air in a gesture of surrender. Behind him, Lefty remained absolutely still, an admirable response to a dangerous predator like Augusta. "We don't have the umbrella with us. You can see that for yourselves. But we will bring it to you."

Augusta narrowed her eyes. Harvey felt as if she was looking past him or possibly through him. He resisted the urge to turn his head and look over his shoulder.

"You will bring the umbrella to us," she said, sounding almost surprised. "On the Thomas Ward Bridge."

Behind her, the shadow stretched, abruptly withdrawing from the walls of the hospital and melting upward into the leaden sky where it spread like a miasma, rising like smoke from a wildfire, and drifted toward the Miskatonic River. If it moved with any intelligence or purpose, Harvey could not detect its rationale. Nor did he assume Augusta was controlling its movements. She half turned to watch it disappear with an expression of dissatisfaction which gave Harvey a small jolt of hope.

If the shadow came and went as it pleased, with monumental indifference to the people watching its trajectory, perhaps it could be pushed away from Arkham with the gentlest of occult nudges. A small charm to send the shadow in a different direction, preferably as far from people as possible, a charm so minuscule that it would not attract the attention of the Ancient One who cast the shadow in the first case.

Or perhaps the Ancient One would follow its shadow? Creating the "brushing past" desired by Valeska and himself. Harvey felt the frustration of not having a clear plan. There were almost too many choices to be made despite the sibyls' prophecy of limited options, according to Mrs Fox. He really needed to question the women about this. He wanted to shake more information out of Augusta Palmer, but the woman was still staring at the sky, apparently now oblivious to her sisters and brother, all watching her in a disturbingly intense way.

A nurse on the third floor threw up the sash and shook a smoldering pillow out of the window. Charred feathers, like flakes of shadow, fell down into the courtyard. The alarms fell silent.

"Do you need help?" Lefty called up to her, stepping a little out of Harvey's own shadow. The courtyard's brick walls gave his voice such amplification that Harvey wondered if they could hear him at Miskatonic University. Certainly, the nurse seemed to understand him clearly.

"No," she yelled back. "Everyone is fine. It was mostly smoke." Then the nurse leaned a little farther out the window and took a good look at their group. "Mr Palmer!" she yelled. "What are you doing down there? We have been searching for you everywhere! You should not be out of your room!" She popped her head back inside.

"Time to go," Augusta said to her family, turning her longing gaze away from the vanishing shadow. "Before we have to explain Ira's recovery." She flicked a hand at Harvey.

"We will meet you at Thomas Ward Bridge at sunset."

"Why there?" asked Harvey, because it seemed an odd choice to pick the middle of a bridge. Surely a coffee shop like Velma's would be more comfortable. Also, he had anticipated Augusta to demand the immediate return of her umbrella. However, sunset would give him almost eight hours before he had to deliver the wand to the terrifying woman. Eight crucial hours if he wanted to create a workable plan to overcome the predicted terrors of the night. So he wasn't going to object to her choices of time and place.

"Because the bridge is where this event will happen," said Augusta as if he was a simple minded child who demanded "why?" from an adult too busy to explain. She shook her head as if amazed by her own words. "It is very clear. Almost an unchangeable event, and those are very rare. We will meet on the Thomas Ward Bridge, and you will have my umbrella with you."

"My umbrella, dear," Barbara said with awful emphasis.

"Our umbrella," Columbia said with equal weight. "As it is the only one that we have left."

Ira was the only Palmer who made no claim on the umbrella, but then the man didn't seem to speak when his sisters were talking. In fact, he hadn't said a word during this entire meeting. Harvey noted his former assistant's glassy stare and wondered if Ira was even aware of the events which had just transpired. The expression that Harvey had taken for ire might simply be Ira's normal impassivity in the company of his sisters.

Augusta listened to Barbara and Columbia, but Harvey noticed that she neither agreed nor disagreed with her sisters. After sunset, he was willing to wager that if anyone wielded the wand hidden in the umbrella, it would be Augusta.

"If we try to change the time or place where we receive the umbrella, we may lose our connection to the shadow," she pronounced. "We need the shadow's power amplified, not diminished, to achieve our goals. The professor will bring the umbrella to us on the bridge." Then she added in a slightly more questioning tone, "And he will be riding in a garbage truck?"

"You bet he will," Lefty spoke up. "You're not going to meet with" – here Lefty paused and obviously reconsidered his words – "these women alone."

"Until sunset, Professor Walters," Augusta said.

The three women stalked away from St Mary's. Ira trailed behind them, lurching slightly as he stumbled down the alley. Just before he turned the corner, he looked back at Harvey. Ira mouthed, "Save me."

Harvey almost called out to Ira, but Columbia reached out one hand and jerked Ira closer to her.

"Don't dawdle, baby brother," she said.

Augusta ignored her siblings, moving swiftly to wherever she wanted to go next. The group turned the corner and were gone.

"Women keep walking away from me," Harvey observed. "And I'm wearing my second best suit."

"Can't say that I'm sorry that they are gone." Lefty shook himself like a big dog coming out of a puddle. "If you hadn't been so calm, I think I would have run screaming out of the alley."

Harvey chuckled. "I doubt that. You are a brave man, my friend."

Lefty shook his head. "I'm just an ordinary joe."

"Thank goodness for ordinary people," Harvey said and sincerely meant it. "There are far too many occult obsessed individuals in this town. Sometimes I think Arkham would be a much better place without us."

"Don't even think it," Lefty said. "We need you to see us through the weird stuff today. Mrs Fox would say the same thing."

Touched by Lefty's sincerity, Harvey looked up to the sky. Were the ominous clouds simply puffs of water vapor or were they wisps of tentacles stretching over the entire city? And how could he solve the weird stuff before it overwhelmed them all?

Chapter Fourteen

Lefty asked the professor where they should go next. He didn't understand what he had just seen. He simply felt an immense relief that the shadow was gone, but a lingering memory of his initial terror shamed him as well. He had frozen in place. Only Harvey's droning voice had kept him anchored in the alley when his first natural inclination was to run away. That and his conviction that the professor needed him as much as he needed Harvey, even though Harvey appeared calm throughout their encounter with the Palmers. But Lefty hoped he would forget the sight of the shadow soon. Was it really a shadow, a trick of the light, which crawled up the hospital wall? Or was it a manifestation of the nightmares plaguing so many of his friends in Arkham?

He stopped dreaming a long time ago. At first it bothered him, to wake up every morning with no memories of dreams. As a kid, Lefty dreamed all the time. The typical weird dreams of boys sent him chasing monsters through the town or flying above a sleeping city. He still remembered his early dreams in a hazy way. Later, his dreams were all about girls or baseball, and some dreams almost came true.

But disastrous bad luck killed those dreams and the booze created new nightmares, ones he finally conquered when he left the bottle behind.

Now Lefty slept without nightmares or any dreams at all. Instead, he filled his idle hours with the dreams of others, the pulp stories that he loved so much. The writers packed their stories with strange creatures, but nothing like the shadow which crawled up St Mary's and into the glowering sky.

"What do you think we should do, professor?" Lefty asked. He wanted Harvey to have answers to more than a simple question of where to go next. He needed Harvey to voice a plan, a clever way to avoid the disaster that the landladies of Flotsam Street expected. And a way to avoid future encounters with whatever they had just seen.

"That's an excellent question, Lefty," Harvey said. He looked down the alley for a few minutes more and then shook his head. "Let us return to my house. Mrs Fox will have lunch prepared shortly. A man needs a full stomach to make a plan. At least I do."

As much as he wanted to see Mrs Fox again, Lefty confessed, "I'm worried about the ladies still on Flotsam Street." If flooding didn't overrun the streets of Arkham, it appeared other things might go slithering through the city.

Harvey pulled his watch out of his vest pocket, checking the time and then clicking it decisively closed.

"Still an hour until Mrs Fox will be ready to serve. I suspect today will be a pot roast as we have a house full of guests. And she's already made the cornbread." Harvey nodded his head. "We can give Mrs Fox time to prepare while we visit Flotsam Street."

"Thanks, professor," Lefty said, starting up Pequod. "The streets look dry so far, but I'll feel better checking the situation there." Doing something, doing anything, was the only real answer to beating the shakes, as Lefty learned some time ago. That was one of the reasons he liked his garbage route. It was hard work, lifting cans and dumping out the contents, but it kept him moving and not listening to the unhappy thoughts when they started buzzing in his head.

"A visit to Flotsam Street is an excellent suggestion. We apparently need their advice. They seem to know more about Augusta Palmer and the power of sibyls than anyone else," Harvey said.

Lefty shrugged. "They know a lot about Arkham, at least the part in Rivertown. They all grew up in the neighborhood and married local men, as I understand it."

"No husbands left?" Harvey asked. His tone was cheerfully curious.

That was one of the things that Lefty liked about Harvey. When he asked, "How are you?" over his roses, he listened to the answer. Harvey actually cared about people. And, as free with words as he was, he never tried to tell anyone how to act. Harvey once quoted Voltaire, a phrase which stuck with Lefty as sensible advice about thinking for yourself and letting others do the same.

So Lefty shared what he knew about the landladies of Flotsam Street with Harvey, knowing he wouldn't judge them like their neighbors on French Hill. "None of them are rich," he said, "but they own their houses. Like I said, they grew up in Rivertown. Most are around your age. Mrs Bernard is the youngest and she's closer to my age, I think."

"A spring chicken," Harvey chuckled.

"My pitching arm says differently," Lefty replied. "But they are all widows. A couple lost husbands during the influenza pandemic. Mrs Garcia's husband died young of a heart attack while working on the docks. Mrs Chiebek's husband was killed while big game hunting in the Rockies. Mrs Bernard's husband volunteered early in the war and didn't come home."

"Sad histories but not unusual," Harvey commented. "Many women outlive their husbands, especially if there are no children. Were there any children?"

Lefty considered. "Mrs Chiebek may have a daughter, but she was grown and gone by the time I moved onto Flotsam Street. Mrs Garcia has some nieces and nephews, but they are all in Boston or New York, I think. I don't know the others well enough to say." Although the more he thought about it, the more he had a vague memory of Mrs Alba having a relative or two in Rivertown. Maybe a connection to Sol? Or was Mrs Alba's connection with Sol's girlfriend, Genevieve?

"But when did they become landladies?" Harvey asked.

"Mrs Garcia was the first," Lefty said. "She told me once. When the others were left with big houses and little money, she encouraged them to take in boarders. Seems to have worked well for them. They run nice houses, and there's usually a waiting list for rooms."

Harvey nodded. "An enterprising and resourceful group, it seems."

"Yeah, they're good women, all of them. But stubborn too. I wish they'd leave their houses and go somewhere safe. Sol and his gang will keep an eye on the street. We've sandbagged where we can and cleaned the drains. It might not be as bad as the early predictions, but I hate the ladies taking the risk."

"Let us see if we can lure our responsible landladies away with a request for aid with our own problems. We can take them to lunch at my house. Then we can all have a conference of war, as it were, over dessert," Harvey proposed.

"Won't Mrs Fox want to know you are bringing five more people to the house?" Lefty asked as he turned Pequod toward Rivertown.

"A good point!" said Harvey, who was groping under the seat for the umbrella that he had stashed there. With a grunt, he pulled it out and straightened himself. "We will call Mrs Fox from Flotsam Street to inform her about the extra guests."

"If you say so," Lefty said, glad it was Harvey and not himself who would be informing Mrs Fox about five extra guests to feed. However, he had no doubts that she could rise to the occasion. Mrs Fox seemed capable of handling anything, including Harvey's sudden invitations. Also, he considered Harvey's idea a good way to lure the landladies away from Flotsam Street. They might go if they thought they were helping to save others.

After a night when flooding seemed imminent, the streets now looked almost normal as they rolled past the Witch House on their way to Flotsam Street. The standing water seemed to have drained away, although Lefty drove carefully through the larger puddles. He even spotted one of his company's garbage trucks making the usual rounds. Which reminded him he should be making a phone call or two as well. He had never reported in, and somebody might be wondering where Lefty and Pequod had gone.

On the other hand, last night's evacuation of the garbage company's main yard had been chaotic. The crew boss had shouted directions about where the men were to take the trucks and when they were to return. But the boss had been vague about how long to wait to see if the city flooded.

Lefty figured he could probably show up tomorrow and write today off as having helped with the emergency. The company owners weren't the most understanding of men but Lefty was good at his job. Luckily, men willing to haul garbage from one end of the city to the other were not easy to find. Which meant the Arkham Sanitation Company tended to put up with some real characters.

For the rest of the drive, Harvey seemed to be running through a list of ideas in his head, arguing with himself about possible outcomes. Finally, he muttered, "Agatha?" and, "Maybe. She certainly knows more than most."

"Anything I can do to help?" Lefty asked as they reached his part of Rivertown.

Harvey shook his head. "Right now, providing me with a way to traverse the city is the best aid. I wish I knew a way to gather the people we need in one place."

"Offer free beer?" Lefty joked.

"Even in these dry times, I doubt the ones that I want would come," Harvey said. "Other preoccupations will be consuming their attention."

Parsing through the large words, Lefty observed, "You mean they are all distracted by what is happening now?"

"Precisely! The distraction will only grow greater as the day progresses. By nightfall, I expect all of Arkham to be experiencing hallucinations, paranoia, catatonia, or violent outbursts."

It was a disturbing statement, but it also felt a little unreal. Lefty couldn't imagine how such a prediction would play out. Would people be running around, screaming at the top of their lungs, or would the doors and windows slam shut as they tried to barricade themselves away from the horrors? Lefty suspected he might be frightened when it happened, but for now, a lack of imagination and inability to dream seemed like a good thing. He said as much to Harvey.

To Lefty's surprise, Harvey agreed. "There are metaphysicians and theorists who argue a life lived in the present moment is the best armor against eldritch terrors. Be grateful that you have achieved this state of mind. But how do we turn everyone's thoughts away from overwhelming despair? Free beer, as attractive as that sounds, might not be the answer that we need."

"I admit the booze didn't treat me well when it came to sorrow. Seems the more I drank, the sadder I became," Lefty said. While once he might have hesitated to propose any idea to an educated gent like Harvey, he now felt confident enough to confide in him. "Funny thing, even after I left baseball, there was nothing that made me happier than seeing my team win. I used to sneak back into the stadium, way up in the stands where nobody expected me, and watch them play. You know they talk about Casey striking out leading to despair. But, oh, there is nothing like a crowd shouting when the hitter drives home the winning run."

Even as he spoke, Lefty remembered the crack of the bat and the roar of the fans. The smell of beer and hot dogs permeating the air. The wind snapping through the flags as the organ played its cheerful tunes. There was nothing, absolutely nothing, as grand as a Saturday afternoon at the game, as he tried to explain to Harvey.

Harvey blinked. "Why, Lefty," he said, "you are truly a philosopher for our times. Arkham needs to see the hitter hit a winning run. Or the equivalent."

"You are going to stage a baseball game?" Lefty asked in astonishment.

"Not at all," Harvey said. "But perhaps a slight modification of your idea could shift the future a little more in our favor. Let us see what the ladies think. If I understood Mrs Fox correctly, we can still have some free will even during the course of predestination. We must create a desired resolution with balance and finesse, rather than using brute force like Augusta Palmer and her shadow. We need to find a solution which does not create a worse problem."

Remembering the puzzling conversation over breakfast, Lefty decided such conundrums were for Harvey to solve. At least he had made a contribution. They pulled up before the house on Flotsam Street. Mrs Garcia was waiting for them on the front porch.

"You seem to be expecting us," Harvey observed as he climbed out of the truck.

"Mrs Alba said you were coming," Mrs Garcia answered. She glared at the green umbrella that Harvey clutched in one hand. "You still have it."

"I do."

Mrs Garcia nodded. "Come in," she said. "Mrs Alba wants to discuss the umbrella with you."

"We came to issue you an invitation to lunch," Harvey said. "Even on a day like today, perhaps especially on a day like today, we should take time to fortify ourselves against what will happen in the coming hours. I believe Mrs Fox was planning a pot roast as we already have a number of guests. A few more would be most welcome, I am sure." Then Harvey hesitated. "Well, Mrs Fox will find a way as soon as I inform her that we will need to seat five more for lunch. I am sure we have enough chairs in the dining room."

Mrs Garcia did not actually roll her eyes, but Lefty had to hide a smile at her expression.

"Come in!" she said again, even more forcefully. "I will

phone Mrs Fox and see what food we should bring as well as warn her that we are coming."

"Thank you," said Harvey, obviously relieved at not having to make the call himself.

"You," she said, pointing at Harvey, "will speak with Mrs Alba before we leave here. It is urgent. She is anxious to tell you what she has seen."

"How can I help?" Lefty asked as they went into the house. He was relieved and a little surprised that Mrs Garcia capitulated so quickly to Harvey's invitation. Perhaps it was the mention of pot roast.

"I am glad you are here," Mrs Garcia said to Lefty, which surprised him after her earlier objections. "It is time to go now and we need your help."

"Whatever you need me to do," Lefty said out loud, although he knew Mrs Garcia understood he would always be there for her.

"You will help me pack the food for Mrs Fox," Mrs Garcia said. Then more softly as Harvey walked into the sitting room ahead of them, she added, "Later, stay with him. Mrs Alba believes his fate is entwined with all of Arkham. And the outcome she sees is not good."

CHAPTER FIFTEEN

Harvey found himself in a pleasant parlor with walls displaying a few too many dead heads of animals. However, the watercolor paintings and the mirrors interspersed amid the elk, deer, and gazelle softened the hunting lodge atmosphere.

Four women sat on pink chintz-covered chairs facing the door. A round low table between them bore the remnants of a mid-morning snack. Tea and cookies, with possibly a cake reduced to a few crumbs on a gilt-edged plate.

Harvey judged three of the women to be near his own age, just as Lefty described. The fourth was a slender woman of approximately the same age as Mrs Fox. Mrs Garcia stepped into the room with Lefty. She introduced the other ladies to Harvey, going from left to right around the circle. "Mrs Chiebek, this is her house. Mrs Alba, Mrs Iskander, and Mrs Bernard." The last was the younger woman with a sorrowful air.

Harvey gave a nod to all and asked for permission to sit. Mrs Garcia tapped Lefty's arm and led him from the room. Mrs Bernard followed them out. Mrs Chiebek waved him to an overstuffed chair near Mrs Alba.

"You are a sibyl," Harvey said to the impressively large Mrs Alba. She reminded him of a time when women were rounder than the slender flappers of the college campus and the practical females like his friend, Carolyn, or Mrs Fox. A hefty woman with no need of petticoats and bustles to fill out her shape, Mrs Alba however sported a modern crop of short gray hair curling just above her broad lace collar. The old-fashioned plum colored dress plunged all the way to her ankles and her feet were covered with very practical heavy shoes. But when she shifted in her seat, Harvey caught a glimpse of embroidered stockings covering her plump ankles. Mrs Alba was a woman of contradictions, Harvey decided.

Mrs Alba gave a soft chuckle. "Sibyl is not a word commonly used these days," she wheezed. An ebony cane leaned against her chair. She caught Harvey's look of concern and waved off any comment he might make. "I suffered from the great flu," she said, "but I survived. More recently, I was caught in the dream blanketing all of Arkham. I woke from the nightmare cast upon us. Sadly, I may outlive you, Professor Walters, and that was not a message that I wanted to give."

"Ah," said Harvey. Perhaps he should have been startled by her message but he had a feeling himself that today marked a great change in his circumstances. While the mere thought of Cthulhu no longer had the power to cast him into despair, he also was realistic enough to know a visitation of the Ancient One generally did not bode well for those who knew what they were seeing. "You have had a vision concerning myself?"

Mrs Alba nodded. "You will face Augusta Palmer on the Thomas Ward Bridge." She cocked her head at him.

"Carrying a green umbrella." She raised one hand to point at the umbrella that Harvey held, now resting against one knee. The palsy in her fingers was visible but her voice never wavered. "This umbrella, as I think you know."

"I met Augusta Palmer a little while ago. She told me our meeting on the bridge was a certainty."

Mrs Alba nodded, but then shook her head. "This entire day and coming night is a flux of possibilities. You must understand nothing is ever certain. But sometimes a moment has to happen to make all else even feasible."

Mrs Alba went on. "But as predestined as your meeting with Augusta seems, the second vision concerning you worries me more. I have seen your memorial at Miskatonic University. It is clear you die in Arkham."

Harvey caught the troubled looks from the other two women, both far more concerned with him than their friend. He waited for a reaction from himself as Mrs Alba's words tumbled through his head. Oddly, he felt no fear or even sorrow. His pursuit of the occult always carried a strong element of risk. His death never seemed too far away, although he had cheated a few times to stave off the Grim Reaper. Eventually all debts must be paid.

And how nice that they would put up a memorial to him at the university!

"Do they erect a statue in my memory?" he asked Mrs Alba. Harvey knew of one or two artists teaching on campus who would do an admirable job of casting his likeness in bronze. Not on a horse, of course, because such statues were reserved for the military types. But something nicely academic, clutching a book and looking over the heads of the students with a wise gaze. Would they be able to replicate his eyebrows? Should he mail them a photograph or two of himself when he went home for lunch? Perhaps he could simply leave the photographs on his desk with instructions to Mrs Fox to give them to whoever was planning his memorial. That might seem less presumptuous.

Mrs Alba interrupted his musings. "A small plaque. On a wall in the library."

"Ah," Harvey said again, now knowing a slight twinge of disappointment. "I know the area. There's a number of plaques there for past professors." Willoughby deserved a plaque, Harvey always thought, but Willoughby had only been a student when he perished.

"I would prefer a statue," Harvey admitted. "Are you sure the two events are connected? A meeting on the Thomas Ward Bridge, followed by a plaque on the wall?" Prophecies often tricked both sibyl and audience in the ancient classics. One seemingly leading directly to the other, conveniently leaving out a few major opportunities for change in the time between events. Although the more grim the prediction, the more certain it seemed. Look at poor Oedipus, whose mother failed to ask some crucial questions about how she became a widow and exactly who the new man in town was.

Mrs Alba smiled. "You are clever. No, it is not certain at all. Simply probable. A strong possibility."

"If I destroy the umbrella now, will the act change anything in the future?" Harvey asked. It seemed the most sensible question to ask at the moment, although he was still curious about the memorial plaque. What would they inscribe on it? Perhaps a few notes left for Mrs Fox to distribute would not be inappropriate after all.

"If you can destroy the umbrella," Mrs Chiebek said, "we don't think it will make any difference." Like Mrs Alba, she was a sizable woman, although she appeared more solid than rounded. Harvey thought she might be the taller of the two when they stood up. "You will still meet Augusta Palmer on the Thomas Ward Bridge with something like the umbrella."

"A piece of it," Mrs Alba expanded on Mrs Chiebek's statement. "Or a wand unexpectedly found somewhere else." She leaned forward to grasp one of the teacups, which Mrs Chiebek obligingly filled for her. "We have asked ourselves the same questions. Unfortunately, the answers are not as varied as we would like."

"Well, that's certainly annoying," Harvey said. He glanced around the room. He did not see anything in the parlor which would lend itself to umbrella destruction. No fire in the fireplace. No handy axe leaning against the wall.

"Forecasting events often is annoying," observed Mrs Iskander, the quietest of the trio and the smallest. One of those neat little ladies who worked unceasingly on beautification projects throughout the city, seeming indispensable on all volunteer committees, especially those concerning gardening. "Seeing the future baffles even the most experienced, because you can never see all of it. We peer through pinholes at single moments, missing so much happening even in the moment glimpsed."

Mrs Alba finished her tea. She placed the cup back on the table and fiddled for a moment with her lace collar. "None of us like accepting an unchanging future," she finally said. "But some moments in time do seem fixed. There's an unnatural disturbance on the horizon, an event so immense that it carries a flood before it. Its shadow alone can wreak havoc. Arkham can be destroyed because nothing is indestructible. However, we are not women who patiently accept a predicted fate. If we were, we would have never started our own businesses and changed the course of our lives."

"Yes, dear," Mrs Chiebek interrupted in the manner of an old friend who has heard a certain argument numerous times. "But accepting Mrs Garcia's advice and changing the fate of Arkham are two very different things. The latter simply kept Flotsam Street afloat, as it were, and didn't truly impact the future of the city."

Mrs Iskander twisted her wedding ring around her finger. "But we did more than that by not accepting what appeared to be our fate," she said. "We all saw Flotsam Street as a place of abandoned tenements but that has not happened."

"So you can change the future using the knowledge of what you have seen?" Harvey asked, considering how this might impact his planning.

Mrs Alba held up one hand, two fingers only a whisper apart as if she was taking a pinch of the air in front of her. "A little bit can be done," she admitted. "But you cannot shove the shadow of the Ancient One on a city and have it create the future that you want. Such an action… it is like a bully in a schoolyard. The bully can push all the children down and be king for a moment, but such actions end with many children in tears, including the bully, as the world goes back to the way it wants to be."

"I have seen Augusta Palmer's shadow," Harvey said, catching the analogy with ease.

"A disaster piled upon even bigger disasters." Mrs Alba frowned. "Augusta has stolen power as if she grabbed the last cookie on the plate or pulled another girl's pigtails to make herself feel more important. Augusta was an awful child. I fear her sisters only encouraged her."

"But can Augusta Palmer accurately predict the future?" asked Harvey.

"Certainly better than most," Mrs Alba said. "It took all

three of us, piecing together individual visions, to describe one thing specific to you. You will meet Augusta on the Thomas Ward Bridge. But what will happen there, we cannot see clearly."

"Yet Augusta saw the meeting on the bridge including what transportation I would use," Harvey told them.

"Yes," said Mrs Alba. "She's always been very strong, while neither Columbia nor Barbara seem to have any predictive abilities at all."

"Augusta probably stole their power in the cradle," muttered Mrs Chiebek.

"I wouldn't put it past her, although I have no idea how she would accomplish it," Mrs Alba concurred. "You must understand Augusta is the most ruthless of the three. Also, she has been pursuing a way to change their future for years. To the detriment of all around her."

"What future is she trying to escape?" Harvey asked. If he could understand Augusta's fears, he might be able to use the knowledge to strike a better bargain with her.

"She saw all three of them dying impoverished and far from Arkham," Mrs Chiebek said. "Barbara told me once, when we were at school together. Barbara was always the easiest going Palmer and actually liked to play games with other children. The other two kept to themselves or did what they could to rule the playground."

"And nothing so far has changed Augusta's vision of their future?" Harvey asked, feeling this was key to the ladies' unease about the Palmers.

"We think not," said Mrs Iskander, who left off her nervous twisting of her wedding ring to recount the Palmers' history. "Augusta did try to inherit their father's money by murdering her stepmother, which only imprisoned her in an asylum. Columbia and Barbara both married money but lost everything when Columbia's husband died and Barbara's husband disappeared."

"So it seems Augusta can't avoid her fate, or, at least, her actions haven't done much to improve their future," Harvey pointed out. "Then why worry about her now? Even if she gains the umbrella, what can she do?"

"Too much," Mrs Alba said. "I saw her while I was dreaming. She's stolen terrific power from the cast off dream of an undead god. She will wield it like a sword with the wand you have there." She pointed at the green umbrella. "At some point, she will force the shadow upon all of Arkham."

"But if Augusta is only protecting herself and, possibly, her family from an unwanted fate, can her actions truly make everything worse? Would it not be the small action that you said was possible?" Once again Harvey wondered how Augusta's actions could be wrong but his own efforts to save Arkham could be right. Weren't they both meddling in the predestined fate of the city? Gads, if he did survive (which was looking increasingly unlikely), he would take up teaching in the philosophy department and give the graduate students fits with the moral and ethical questions raised. Or better yet, perhaps he could write a series of monographs on the topic.

"Unfortunately, we think everyone will suffer more if Augusta triumphs," Mrs Alba said. "This day will end in the appearance of the Ancient One. We cannot stop it from coming to Arkham. But we hope you can separate Augusta from its shadow. We believe if she raises it on the bridge, the shadow will multiply and amplify the damage to every person living in Arkham."

"It will kill the heart within them," Mrs Chiebek added. "Their courage, do you understand?"

"The Ancient One is destruction in its most awful form," Mrs Iskander said. "But not every single building should fall to the flood and fire that it brings. Not every person must succumb to despair. If we can alter even a little, then those who love this city can find a way to restore it."

"So Arkham could be rebuilt," Harvey concluded. "It might survive what is coming."

"Not if all hope is lost," Mrs Alba said. "We think Augusta is trying to escape her fate by imposing it on all who live here, forcing everyone to die alone and far from an Arkham which vanishes forever."

Chapter Sixteen

Minnie pinned the last dripping photograph on the line to dry. She stared at her pictures taken with the Speed Graphic. A disappointing lot. The photograph taken of the shape swimming through the Miskatonic River could be simply a submerged tree. The one that she just added to the line looked like rocks and shadows in the Black Cave. Yes, a hint of a tentacled head or a massive wing might be seen, but the photograph was frustratingly blurry. Nothing was as clear as the terror which had gripped her and Sol. Even her picture of the glowing circle painted on the cave wall appeared nothing more than a vague shape.

A hammering on the door startled her. "Klein! Are you in there?" Doyle shouted.

"Yes, boss, almost done," Minnie yelled back.

"Get out here! We've got a lead."

"Five more minutes," Minnie said as she cleaned up the trays and secured the chemicals. The last thing the *Arkham Advertiser* needed was an accidental fire started in the dark room. Making sure everything was secure, she unlatched the door. Doyle was already gone, back to his office to bark on the phone.

When she appeared in front of his desk, Doyle crashed down his phone. "Would you believe the college boy actually uncovered a story?" he said to her.

"Edgar? Wasn't he following the dynamite down river?"

"He did. Says he even took a few photos of the blast site," Doyle said. "Oh, and boats make him seasick."

"Poor Edgar," Minnie said with a laugh. "But what's the story?"

"There's a boat of dynamite gone missing!"

"What do you mean?" Minnie asked. "Did it blow up?" She calculated how quickly she could get back to Rivertown and find a boat to take her down river. An explosion always made the front page of the newspaper. She tried not to feel too smug about getting first crack at this story. Darrell and Rex would have other front page opportunities, and Edgar would not know a front page story if he stumbled over it. Which it sounded like he had.

"I mean missing as in stolen right out from under the mayor's nose," Doyle said with his eyes shining. He loved stories of crime, especially when he could partner them with jabs at City Hall. "Edgar counted the number of boats loaded with dynamite. Who knew the kid would actually listen to all my lectures? Fourteen boats were loaded with thirty crates of dynamite in Rivertown. But when Edgar arrived at the blast site, he only counted thirteen boats there. The dynamite exploded, and then everyone headed back to Arkham. They pulled into the docks in Rivertown less than an hour ago. That's when Edgar decided to count again, just to confirm his numbers. Counted three times, he said, but only thirteen empty boats docked in Rivertown."

"So what happened to the fourteenth boat?" Minnie asked. Already she could feel the excitement stirring inside her. This could be a front page story.

"Good question! We need an answer," Doyle said, rapping his big fist on his desk. "Edgar asked around. Apparently only thirteen boats were contracted to take the dynamite. They made their run and returned home. Nobody seems to know who was captaining the fourteenth boat or even noticed it in the confusion of boats pulling in and out of the dock."

"Clever," said Minnie, pulling her notebook out of her pocket and jotting down the facts as Doyle had related them. "With all the confusion of the loading and setting off, somebody nipped in and helped themselves to some dynamite."

"Probably two or three crates," Doyle said. "They might have slipped a bribe to the guys doing the loading."

Minnie nodded and licked the tip of her pencil. She wrote the number down as well as a name that occurred to her. "Or the dockworkers knew them already. Or the thieves were the guys loading the boats. Sounds like a gang in Rivertown decided to help themselves."

"What is it?" Doyle asked. "You've got a look."

"I met someone at the Black Cave who might have a very good idea of where dynamite might go," Minnie said. Sol had considerable knowledge of hiding places in the Black Cave. Wouldn't he be equally knowledgeable about smuggling items other than booze up and down the river? If she found him again, Minnie was certain Sol could lead her to the dynamite. He had been hiding something in the bushes above the Black Cave. She had thought it was just his canoe, but what if it had been crates of dynamite?

"Who can help you?" demanded Doyle.

"Now, boss, you know I can't name my sources," Minnie said. "I need to go to Rivertown to find him." The photos retrieved from the Speed Graphic had not proven as good as she had hoped. Also, the absolute burning desire that had driven her all morning to search for monsters seemed to have finally snuffed out. Not that she would reject a decent photograph of a tentacled horror, if she could capture one, but a story about stolen dynamite seemed a better bet to make the front page of the evening edition.

Now all she had to do was find someone who knew more about the dynamite. Which, as she had told Doyle, should not be hard in Rivertown.

After they left the Black Cave, Sol walked back to the road with Minnie and waited with her at the bus stop until a bus arrived. She gathered from remarks that he made, Sol intended to head back to Schoffner's General Store. Minnie knew a small crowd had collected there to wait out the day and see what happened with the flooding. If Sol wasn't there, somebody would probably know how to find him.

"How about the photos?" Doyle asked. "Anything good?"

Minnie handed him a stack that she'd taken with the Kodak before she found the Speed Graphic. While those pictures had been drying, she had typed up her notes. It was not monsters, but it was the news that she had promised Doyle. She had gotten some decent shots of the destruction done last night by the rising waters, including a broken dock. But Minnie preferred the pictures of people walking away from their homes this morning, defeat slumping their shoulders as they carried suitcases full of their worldly belongings. More than the destruction of the dock, those photographs showed the impact that the floods might have on all of Arkham. A loss of home and community loomed over them all.

Doyle hummed as he sorted the photographs on his desk. "You have an eye," Doyle said, which was his highest compliment. He tapped a photograph of the broken dock, the wreckage of a fishing boat swirling in the churning water. "We'll use this. And the one of the little boy sitting on his suitcase." The latter showed a child left for a few minutes as his mother ran back inside their apartment house to fetch more belongings. The boy looked bewildered by the other people passing on the street with their luggage.

"It's good," Minnie agreed. She flipped back through her notebook and pulled out a page. "Here's his name and age." She handed it over to Doyle. "I typed up the particulars about Rivertown's evacuation efforts. The article is in your tray."

Doyle nodded, pulling the pages out of his inbox. He grabbed a pen to mark the copy. "Anything else?" he asked.

"Not yet," Minnie said, thinking of the disappointing pictures drying in the dark room. She needed to understand the creature glimpsed in the Black Cave if she wanted to write a convincing article. A blurry photograph was not enough to persuade Doyle of the merit of her story nor intrigue her readers. Strange shadows in the Black Cave? It was not a place most people went. But what if she could show the monster clearly and its impact on real people, like the photo of the boy sitting on the suitcase? Then she would have a story.

If she returned to Rivertown, she might find more information while she hunted for the dynamite. "I'm off then," Minnie told Doyle. In some ways, this was what she loved best about the news business. Never a dull moment because there were always new things popping up.

"Bring me back a story!" Doyle said with a wave of his

hand, his head already bent and his attention riveted on the commas or lack thereof in her copy.

"Sure," said Minnie, grabbing Doyle's hat off her desk and clapping it on her head. She checked the coin purse in her pocket and decided speed was essential. She would call a cab.

With both her cameras loaded with fresh film, Minnie set out to find the dynamite and, possibly, a monster made of shadows.

CHAPTER SEVENTEEN

Harvey looked at the people filling his dining room. The sibyls of Flotsam Street, as he had come to regard Mrs Alba, Mrs Chiebek, and Mrs Iskander, sat in a row down the left side of the table. Mrs Bernard, like Mrs Garcia, seemed to be a practical soul who accepted her friends' talents but didn't have any particular skill at prognostication. Mrs Bernard and Mrs Garcia flanked Mrs Fox at the far end of the table. Mrs Garcia's boarders, Sally, Lefty, and an elderly married pair who didn't speak much, sat in a row down the right side. Harvey's dining room no longer felt impossibly large. In fact, it was a good thing that April was still in bed and her friend had taken lunch up to her. There simply wouldn't have been enough chairs to seat them all.

"So how do we change the fate of Arkham?" he asked the crowd as soon as he had finished dessert, a rather nice apple pie which sadly was all gone. No seconds left with such a group all taking a slice.

His question was met with silence, possibly due to the fact a number of people were still eating. Which was perfectly fine with him, as Harvey was used to answering his own questions. It was a rhetorical device he employed often in his university days.

"We need to inspire people," Harvey continued. "I believe this will be crucial for our success. Stop them from falling into despair and abandoning the city to destruction. Encourage them to make every effort possible to save Arkham."

"City Hall has been doing that," Lefty pointed out. "Distributing sandbags yesterday. Using dynamite this morning."

"The *Arkham Advertiser* published special editions," Sally, a schoolteacher who lived in Mrs Garcia's house, added. "Telling people where to go and what to do."

The married couple whispered to each other and then the man spoke up. "Nova Malone's radio station has been broadcasting reports too. Along with some very nice music." His wife nodded vigorously. "We listened to the radio in your parlor," he added.

"All very helpful," Harvey said, "but apparently not enough to save Arkham from complete annihilation according to Mrs Alba's visions."

All eyes turned to Mrs Alba. Harvey had been rather surprised that nobody in the room had disputed Mrs Alba's dire predictions when she had first recounted the possibility of Arkham's abandonment by its citizens during the serving of the pot roast.

Mrs Alba stuck largely to flood, fire, and Augusta Palmer's enormous shadow, the last being corroborated by the eyewitness accounts of Lefty and Harvey. Mrs Iskander added information about the foreseen meeting on the Thomas Ward Bridge. Mrs Chiebek nodded along but had left out the part about the memorial plaque.

Harvey had made a quiet request to all three sibyls when

escorting them to the dining room to avoid discussion of his impending doom. Not only would the ensuing discussion have given him indigestion, he didn't want to distress Mrs Fox.

Harvey slipped into his office for a few moments before lunch and wrote a necessary letter for his housekeeper. Along with the note stuck on his mirror in the bedroom, Harvey felt his possibly last missive would be enough. If he managed to survive the meeting on the Thomas Ward Bridge, he could always consign those documents to the fire. If not, Mrs Fox would know what to do.

As for himself, he had not given up all hope. Things were dire but he had managed to survive dire several times. But it gave him some comfort to know that his affairs were in order.

Mrs Alba looked around at her neighbors. "I have never been one to push my advice on others," she began.

Mrs Chiebek made a small choking noise and grabbed for her glass of water. Mrs Bernard, Mrs Iskander, and Mrs Garcia exchanged looks that Harvey thought indicated Mrs Alba was a champion dispenser of advice. He had seen a few such looks directed at himself for the same offense.

"Please go on," he said to Mrs Alba, who was obviously ignoring her friends.

"If we rely on someone else, whether it is City Hall or the *Arkham Advertiser* or Nova Malone," Mrs Alba said, "I fear it will not be enough. At the same time, I am not sure we can do anything that impacts the entire city. Then we fall into Augusta Palmer's folly of trying to change everything all at once."

"So what do we do?" Lefty asked the question before Harvey could.

But Harvey had an answer. "Small actions. You said those were possible, Mrs Alba, to bend but not break the course of the future."

Mrs Alba nodded ponderously. "On Flotsam Street, we made small changes, over a long period of time, to prevent a fall into decay and despair. How to do this in a single day, in even less time, is the problem."

Everyone looked down at their plates, then looked up at the ceiling, and then looked at Harvey, who wished he had a good answer to give them. He was about to make a reassuring but basically meaningless pronouncement, much as he would bolster freshmen before their first exam, when Mrs Garcia spoke.

"Perhaps I was wrong," she said. Nobody spoke but her boarders looked slightly shocked by this pronouncement. "Perhaps we should play Charlie Chaplin movies while Arkham floods. At least it will lift the hearts of those sheltering at the Palace."

Harvey nodded. "Distract them from their miseries somewhere they are safe. Yes, that might work."

"Games!" Sally exclaimed. "Some days, when the children are very restless, we organize games to keep them occupied. It's better than letting them fret about a storm."

"The student union certainly has badminton equipment. It can be played indoors. The dean frowns on it, but in these circumstances, a tournament might be warranted," Harvey said. "It will distract those sheltering there from the food as well as the flood."

"We keep cleaning," Lefty said. "Take anyone who wants to help. We clean the streets of any debris that might be blown about in a storm. Make sure the drains are clear. Pick up the garbage. Nobody has to clean the whole city, but they can do a patch wherever they are. There's a warehouse full of burlap sacks and brooms down in Rivertown. We could load Pequod and pass out the brooms throughout the neighborhoods."

"Wouldn't the owner of the brooms object?" Harvey said. The mention of brooms gave him pause, but he tried not to show his unease. He did not want to explain Willoughby's fate to this group, who were all starting to whisper new ideas among themselves.

"Nah," Lefty said, responding to Harvey's question. "The place has changed hands a few times. The new owners want the brooms and bags out. They called the company about clearing it, but all the trucks were busy these past few days. So we put it off until after the storm. Everyone would be glad to see the stuff go. I'll tell my supervisor that I've taken care of it, which will make him happy."

"All excellent ideas," Harvey said, stuffing all thoughts of Willoughby as far back in his head as he could. Willoughby had tried to fight a cosmic monstrosity, a small Star Spawn, with a broom. It had not gone well for him and the tale was a cautionary one told to select students at the university. But the order of the day was hope and not despair, so he concentrated on bolstering the confidence of the people around the table. "Small actions happening throughout the city. But how do we let others know? Better yet, even add their own suggestions to ours? We don't have a newspaper or a radio station."

"But we do have a phone," said Mrs Fox. "And we all know people."

Harvey nodded. He did not like talking on the phone himself, still preferring letters for correspondence with academic friends. But he paid the bills. So they might as well use the thing.

"Yes," said Sally. "I can call the other teachers from my school. Everyone was sent home yesterday when they thought flooding would happen immediately. I am sure the teachers would be glad to visit their neighbors and talk to the families that they know. We should make a list. That's what Ollie says. You can survive anything with a good list."

The married couple poked each other in the ribs. Then the gentleman drew out a small notepad with a King of Hearts printed on the cover. A gold pencil was attached to it by a red ribbon. He handed the notepad to Sally.

"Oh, thank you, Mr Sullivan, I'll take good care of this," she promised. When she flipped the pages, Harvey glimpsed neatly totaled bridge scores. On the first blank page, Sally carefully wrote "A List of Things to Do Today" across the top.

"I do feel a little better already," she said.

Mrs Alba collected her cane and pushed away from the table. Harvey stood up from his own seat and made his way around to her, helping pull out her chair. She rose slowly and leaned heavily on his arm until she got her balance with the cane.

"I hope you will take a short rest in my parlor," Harvey said as he led her from the dining room. "Just while we organize a few things."

"They told you that I would fall asleep after lunch and not insist on being driven back to Flotsam Street," she observed as they paced slowly into the other room. "Especially if you placed me in a comfortable chair."

She sank into Harvey's widest and most comfortable reading chair, positioned near the window for the best light.

"I am afraid you know your friends too well," Harvey said as he snagged a light blanket from the back of the sofa and swung it over her knees.

"I know their pasts, I see their futures," Mrs Alba said. "It's not a difficult prediction to make." She sighed. "It is not a bad plan to make small actions across the city. It will give them all something to do. But I do not think it is enough to dispel the shadow that Augusta will raise. Nor turn aside the Ancient One."

"No," Harvey said, staring out the window at the darkening clouds. The rain may have stopped for the moment, but it would return soon. Thoughts of Willoughby and his broom crowded his head with unexpected and unwelcome gloom. He needed to do more if he wanted to vanquish Augusta Palmer and yet, so unusually for him, Harvey hesitated.

He wanted to turn the coming meeting on the Thomas Ward Bridge to his advantage, but he needed to keep the shadow away from his friends. Last time, the thing had been supremely indifferent to the wishes of Augusta Palmer, abandoning her in the alley outside the hospital. However, with the wand concealed in the umbrella it might be another story. The encounter could be dangerous for others as well as himself. Although he never minded gambling with his own safety, Harvey did not want to expose his friends to the mind-bending presence of the Ancient One or even its shadow. Not after what happened to Willoughby.

"You are still worried," Mrs Alba said and Harvey turned away from the window.

"You are psychic as well as a sibyl," he guessed.

She chuckled. "I am a landlady. I know worried when I see it. Can you not pay your rent?"

"I had a student…" Harvey began and stopped. He hated this story. So why was he telling it now? But Mrs Alba made an encouraging noise. "His name was Thomas Willoughby."

Harvey stopped again to clear his throat. Mrs Fox must

have failed to dust this room. Or perhaps it was the rain. But he was Harvey Walters and the one thing that he always tried to do was face the truth about himself.

"I encouraged Willoughby to pursue knowledge. To seek to understand what we cannot, what we should not, perceive. That which dwells behind our dreams in the darkest corners of the cosmos. Eventually, as happens with far too many unfortunate souls, he found actual proof of amphibious entities spawned beyond the stars. And it destroyed him. Literally. Although he did try to whack it with a broom before he died."

Mrs Alba reached out and patted his arm. "I suspect the courage to attack such a creature came from his professor."

"That is my great regret and shame," Harvey admitted. "That I was foolish enough to give Willoughby hope that he would survive such an encounter when I could not persuade him to turn aside from his studies."

"Hope is a good beginning to a better future. I am a sibyl. I know," Mrs Alba said with reassuring confidence. "You have given the people in this house a little hope." She sighed and pulled the blanket more tightly around herself as if feeling a draft. "Do not let anyone stop you from trying to do more."

"My dear Mrs Alba," said Harvey, who did indeed feel a little better for this discussion, "you have been enormously helpful."

Harvey retreated quietly from the parlor, certain Mrs Alba was asleep before he even closed the door. Standing in the hallway, he debated whether or not to return to the dining room and the conversation which sounded as if it had become even more lively.

He resisted the urge to retire to his study and pull books off the shelves. Harvey knew what his books contained. For once, Valeska was right. He needed to think of a solution not found on a printed page, as blasphemous as such a notion seemed. He needed a fresh way of looking at the whole problem.

"Agatha," Harvey muttered to himself. "I should talk to Agatha Crane." If anyone had a new idea, it would be the scientist who never feared to experiment. Nobody understood better how to use science to investigate and even control the impossible entities encountered in Arkham. If this was not a day for spells found in books, perhaps it was a day to use Agatha's methods.

CHAPTER EIGHTEEN

Minnie found her promise to Doyle about quickly finding the probable bootlegger Sol was perhaps too optimistic. Nor was she making much headway on the missing dynamite.

Everyone at Schoffner's General Store claimed that they hadn't seen Sol for hours. Furthermore, nobody knew anything about a fourteenth boat carrying away crates of dynamite. Everyone did agree that the dynamite had been loaded before dawn on the Rivertown waterfront. Later a pier washed away in the rising waters of the Miskatonic. Other than some oddball professor falling off a dock, nothing peculiar had happened. It decidedly was not a dunked professor that she wanted, but Minnie pretended to take their comments seriously. She knew if she pushed too hard for answers, she would be met with a wall of silence.

One old man had been excited to learn that she was a reporter, but he wanted to tell her a story about his wife. Minnie put off Mr Barnaby as gently as she could, giving him her card and promising to meet with him another day. She needed to stay focused on the dynamite, that was the story that Doyle sent her out to find.

Finally, Minnie wandered outside, apparently taking pictures as she had earlier in the day. Except Minnie didn't click the shutter. Why waste film on empty streets? The rain had slacked off again, and the people were largely gone. A few young men loitered near one corner, idly smoking and chatting among themselves. She judged them about Sol's age. One or two looked vaguely familiar. Had they been part of the rescue last night at the Black Cave? Minnie shrugged. She would learn nothing by staring at them.

Slipping the Speed Graphic back into its waterproof bag, Minnie advanced upon the group. She fished out her notebook and pencil. "Hello," she said, "I am Minnie Klein. I write for the *Arkham Advertiser*. Can I ask you a few questions?"

The four men backed up a little, apparently startled by being approached by a woman with a notebook and a camera bag.

"We don't know where Sol is," said the biggest man. Only to be punched in the ribs by a smaller comrade.

"Joey, you idiot, you don't volunteer information," the little one said. "Ain't you learned nothing? Wait until they ask you."

"What?" said big Joey and it sounded more like a plaintive "wo-at" when he said it. "She's not a cop. She's the reporter that Sol took into the Black Cave. The one we saw last night when we saved the puppies. Sol met her again this morning when he was moving the stuff to a new hiding place."

"Joey!" all three men exclaimed. The smallest one clapped his hand over his eyes and shook his head in despair.

Minnie bit back a smile. "I thought I recognized you," she said to the talkative Joey. "You helped rescue all those dogs yesterday." She tried to sound as admiring as possible, suspecting that praising puppies was the way to Joey's heart.

"Yes, miss," Joey said with a shy smile. "Those puppies didn't deserve to be stuck in the cave. They could have drowned. That'd be awful."

"Yes, it would have been terrible," Minnie agreed, not mentioning that she and Rex could have drowned too. Obviously rescuing the dogs ranked above rescuing a pair of reporters for Joey. "I would love to see the dogs again. To take their pictures for the newspaper. That would help us reunite them with their owners."

"Ah, that would be swell," Joey said. "They are good dogs. You can tell they came from nice homes. I can take you to them. We put the dogs in the stables. It is just down Peabody Avenue, near the graveyard."

"Joey!" exclaimed his friend.

"What?" said Joey. "The place is clean. You know, all the other stuff is gone. There's only the brooms, the bags, and the dogs now. She won't see anything else."

The little man sighed and said to Minnie, "Do you need any new workers at the *Advertiser*? Joey is my cousin. I swear he is a decent guy. Can lift heavy boxes all day long. He's just not so good at keeping his mouth shut."

"Marko, you worry too much," Joey said as he started down Peabody Avenue. "Miss Klein is a nice lady. She is writing a story about the dogs to help them."

"Yeah, sure," said the doubting Marko, but he trailed after them. The other two men turned back toward Schoffner's with comments that they needed to move the rest of the boxes.

"Mr Schoffner is shifting all of his stock to his second floor," Joey explained.

"I noticed the shelves looked bare when I was inside," Minnie said.

"Yep, we moved most of it upstairs," said Joey, then he paused and stared at his cousin Marko. "Aren't you going to object to me telling her about that?" he said with heavy emphasis.

"No, Joey," replied his cousin. "I don't care if you tell her where you put Schoffner's cans of beans. Sol doesn't care if you talk about the beans. It's the other jobs you are supposed to be quiet about."

Minnie kept her mouth shut, figuring she would learn more from their arguing, including the location of the elusive Sol.

But Joey just reached over and knocked Marko's cap so it slid forward and covered his face. "You're a funny guy, Marko," he said.

"Big galoot," Marko replied, punching Joey's shoulder and straightening out his cap.

Joey shrugged but didn't seem offended.

Minnie waited but the pair seemed to have settled their differences through this exchange. Hopefully she would find out more when they reached the gang's warehouse, where they had stashed the dogs and sometimes kept their smuggled goods.

They picked up their pace past the Christchurch Cemetery with its crooked gravestones. Minnie knew the cemetery was considered one of the oldest parts of Arkham. They ran a story every Halloween on "The Graveyard" as it was popularly called. Some claimed the place once stretched all the way down to the river but greedy men claimed the land for their stately homes. What happened to the graves was a matter of some debate, but Minnie always suspected the sort who stole land from a cemetery would not balk at building houses on top of old bones.

The homes fell into disrepair long ago, giving way to the crumbling tenements and warehouses filling the district now. One of the newspaper's Halloween stories even claimed the cemetery was now haunted by a monstrous dog, intent on avenging the desecration of the graveyard by earlier Arkham residents.

Even passing by the place in broad daylight, Minnie felt a bit uneasy. She had camped out there at midnight once, intent on photographing whatever toppled some of the new grave markers and left claw marks in the damp earth. She had been run out of the place by the caretaker, Leonard Coburn. She did not want to meet him again, although Coburn was probably too busy today to worry about a stray photographer in his graveyard.

"That's a bad place," Joey said, looking over the fence at the tangled weeds and bushes which marked the oldest edges of the cemetery. "Which is probably why everyone leaves our warehouse alone."

"It's not really our warehouse, Joey," Marko said, apparently resigned to his cousin's talkative nature.

"We have been squatting there for the last few months," Joey said. "Sol found the spot for us. He knows every place in Rivertown. This one works very well for our business. Especially for the dogs. Oh, and other stuff, which is not there now, I swear."

With a sigh, Marko added, "Miss Klein, we would very much appreciate it if you did not list the address in your story."

"Call me Minnie," she replied. "I promise I will not publish any information that you do not want shared with the general public." If she spotted Sol there, she would have to think of a way to raise the topic of the dynamite. She doubted the helpful Joey or his now polite cousin Marko were behind the thefts.

But Minnie still thought Sol was the most likely person to know about the early morning disappearance of the crates. And where the dynamite could be found now, especially if he was a person who knew every place in Rivertown. Actual photos of the stolen dynamite would certainly cement front page placement of her story. If she could convince Sol to help her.

"But what about the dogs? How will people know where to find them if she does not publish the address?" Joey asked.

Marko's mouth fell open. Before he could stammer out a reply, Minnie interjected, "We could give Schoffner's phone number. Tell people to call there to retrieve their pets."

"Schoffner's going to love that," Marko muttered.

Joey smiled. "That's great, Minnie," he said. "They can call there and we can take the dogs to them."

"Joey, we can't be taking dogs all over town," Marko objected.

"Why not?" Joey asked. "We make deliveries every day. Dogs will be easier to handle than barrels of beer."

"Joey! You don't talk about the beer in front of a reporter," Marko shouted. "Why did I ever ask Sol to hire you!"

Before the two could fall into arguing again, Minnie added, "There will probably be rewards for the dogs. People usually give something if you bring their pet to them." Then, considering that she was talking to a pair of lesser criminals, she added, "But no demands for ransom. If I hear anything like that is happening, I will write about the beer."

"We wouldn't kidnap a doggie or keep it from its owner," Joey sputtered, offended by this slur.

Marko patted his cousin on his shoulder. Then he turned to Minnie and stuck out his hand. "It's a deal. Joey and I will take the dogs back to their owners, no ransom demands, if you don't tell anyone where this place is or mention things like barrels of beer."

"Deal!" Minnie said, sticking out her own hand and giving Marko a good shake. "Now let's go take some pictures of puppies."

The fence of the Christchurch Cemetery gave an odd jog just before the road ran up to French Hill. In the lot created by the turning of the fence, a moldering house of considerable age stood surrounded by a yard given over to weeds. Ivy engulfed the structure, shading from a yellowish green to a bloody red. A pine tree lay across its sagging broken roof, the obvious relic of some past storm. Shattered windows, with only jagged teeth of glass protruding from the sills, and a boarded up door faced the street. The stairs leading to the front porch had pulled away from the structure, leaving a considerable gap for anyone who wanted to enter. The entire building looked as if the next windstorm would collapse it into a pile of kindling.

Between the derelict house and the graveyard fence was a sturdy two-story brick stable, obviously built in the days when a family needed to have a carriage, horses, and somebody to take care of them. The big barn doors opened right onto a wide drive leading to the street. Unlike the yard, the gravel of the driveway was clear of weeds. The windows on the second floor looked whole and clean. Minnie squinted up. Definitely clean and lace curtains hanging behind the windows. Lace which stirred as if some hand had drawn it back for a moment to spy upon the street.

"What is this place?" she asked.

"The family went away when the house fell in," Joey said. "But they rented out the stables. Various people have used it. There's an apartment upstairs too."

Abandoning his earlier inhibitions about talking to the reporter, Marko said with relish, "They say the last owner was eaten by the graveyard ghoul because his grandfather stole the land from the cemetery. There was a story by Virgil Gray about it in *Tales from Nevermore.*"

Minnie refrained from pointing out that Virgil Gray wrote fiction. Also, that everyone knew the cemetery was haunted by a giant dog, not a ghoul. Then she heard dogs barking in the stables.

She started toward the barn doors but Joey waved her around the corner to a small side door. From under a broken flowerpot, he fetched a big iron key. "Don't tell anyone about this," he said. "It's a secret hiding place."

"I won't," Minnie promised.

Marko sighed but said nothing to his cousin.

"The place sold recently," Joey said. "So Sol says we'll be leaving soon. Probably once we get the dogs out of here."

Inside, six horse stalls occupied one side while the other side was a broad open area, probably where the carriage was once stored. Stairs leading to the floor above ran along the back wall and some type of small office or tack room had been built underneath. A yipping came from the horse stalls.

Minnie walked over. Each stall was filled with dogs, mostly young puppies but a few older dogs as well. Fresh hay had been scattered across the floor of each stall and piles of burlap sacks provided improvised beds for the dogs. Water dishes and what looked like the remnants of butcher bones also occupied each stall.

"We did the best that we could," Joey said, leaning over

the door of a stall to scratch between the ears of a madly wagging collie. "But they need to go home."

"They certainly do," Minnie said, looking over the collection of dogs rescued from the Black Cave. She pulled the Speed Graphic out of its bag, cooing to the dogs and whistling to make them turn toward her. She took photo after photo, because cute puppy pictures were always welcome in the *Arkham Advertiser*. Even Doyle acknowledged a good dog story sold newspapers. They could splash the photos across the back page until all the dogs were claimed by owners.

Once she was sure that she had gotten a picture of every dog, Minnie turned to examine the open carriage space. A pile of brooms filled most of the area, along with stacks of burlap sacks. But in the very front, nearest the barn doors, were three large crates marked dynamite.

More than a little surprised that it had been so easy to find the missing explosives, she lifted her camera.

Then a voice she knew called out, "Now, Minnie, please don't take a picture of those boxes."

Minnie whirled around. Halfway up or halfway down the stairs, Sol sat on a step. He had obviously been watching her photograph the dogs. Uncrossing his legs, Sol stood up and sauntered down the stairs. For the first time since she met him, she saw his face grow cold and stern. In a stomach-dropping moment, she realized that Sol wasn't playing at being a bootlegger and gangster. He was one, and the leader of a Rivertown gang. Being caught with a few kegs of beer could probably be resolved with a fine. Being caught with stolen dynamite, that would mean serious prison time.

Marko and Joey shuffled to one side. Joey shrugged apologetically to Minnie. "I thought the stuff was moved earlier today," he said, looking at the crates of dynamite. "Guess I misunderstood. We shouldn't have shown you this place."

Marko looked resigned. "Sorry, Sol, we thought it was only the dogs left," he said.

Sol shook his head. "The truck never showed up. Guess the driver got caught down river. Some of the roads flooded after the blasts went off. So I called our buyer and they are looking for another driver."

Minnie edged toward the barn doors, thinking it might be best to go straight out and down the street. Sol waved at her to stop.

"I don't mind taking you around the Black Cave," Sol said to her, ignoring the other two. "Don't mind you taking pictures of the dogs, either. But those crates need to remain a secret. So no pictures and you need to stay here until I'm sure the crates are gone. Then you can go home and write about the dogs. Now hand over your camera. I will keep it safe for you until you can go."

Sol stuck out a hand. Obviously, he thought if he took the camera, he would earn Minnie's cooperation. After all, he had seen how desperate she had been to retrieve it from the Black Cave.

"Come on," he said. "Give it here. You wouldn't want to lose your only picture of the monster of the Black Cave."

Glad that she had already developed that picture but reluctant to lose the Speed Graphic again, Minnie considered her options. The door wasn't far away. She was fast. She could head over the fence and into the graveyard. It would take them some time to catch her, if they could catch her. Or she could try to talk her way out of this and save her last pair of decent shoes.

Just as she opened her mouth, someone pounded on the barn doors. "You in there, Sol?" a man yelled. "I have come for the brooms."

CHAPTER NINETEEN

Harvey lifted the phone's receiver and spoke reluctantly into it. He regarded this endeavor as an action akin to shouting into a void. One never knew who or what may respond. Nevertheless, time was slipping away. By sunset he must meet with Augusta Palmer on the bridge. It was already well past noon according to the softly ticking skeleton clock on the hall table. "Hello, operator," Harvey said. "Can you connect me with Agatha Crane?"

A woman's voice said, "Do you have a number for the party that you are trying to reach?"

Harvey tried to remember if he had ever called Agatha before. Most probably not. They often met somewhere by accident because Agatha was pursuing an obscure point of research at Miskatonic University. Not infrequently Harvey spotted her moving purposefully through the stacks of the Orne Library when he made his own visits there. Every now and then Agatha sent him a letter, asking for elucidation on a point of arcane history.

"No, I do not have a number," Harvey said, wondering why the operator would ask him for it. Wouldn't the have volunteered the information if he had it? Instead, he obviously only had a name and that was why he had requested to be connected to the person so named. Really, the phone company made this calling business more complicated than it should be.

"Then do you have an address for the party you want?" the operator asked him.

Harvey refrained from saying that he didn't want a party, he wanted a parapsychologist.

"Of course I have an address," he responded. "We correspond frequently." Well, not as frequently as they used to. Agatha's interests were wide ranging but lately she had been strangely silent about her current pursuits. If he considered the matter carefully, it must have been six months or more since he had heard from her. Still, Agatha must be in Arkham. After all, she had a husband here and she would not abandon Wilbur.

"If you could give me the address, sir," the operator said.

"I don't have her address with me. It is in my address book," Harvey explained, "which is in my study. The phone is in the hall." Because he hadn't wanted the silly thing in his study disturbing him, but he did not tell the operator why the phone was in the hall.

"Yes, sir," said the operator, whose patient tone never varied. Harvey was rather impressed by her calm. "Perhaps you could fetch your address book and give me the address of the party desired?"

"Will you be here when I come back?" Harvey asked, not willing to start the whole calling procedure over again.

"If you do not hang up, I will be here," the operator promised.

Harvey fetched his address book and read the required information to the operator.

"I have a number for a Wilbur Crane," she said.

"Yes, the number is probably the same," Harvey said, relieved the answer had been found so quickly. "He is Agatha's husband." It would make sense Wilbur had the telephone in his name. Wilbur was a businessman, although what exactly he did, Harvey could not recall. Nothing unusual or connected with the occult or academia. Which meant that they usually discussed the weather when they happened to meet. Wilbur did like to garden, and had given Harvey some sound advice on pruning his roses.

"Putting you through to Wilbur Crane," the operator announced.

The phone rang and a man answered. "Hello, hello, is that you, Aggie?" he said.

"Wilbur," Harvey replied, recognizing the voice. Besides, who else would be talking about an Aggie? "It's Harvey Walters, Professor Walters. We've met. Is Agatha there?"

Which, the minute he asked, Harvey knew was unlikely. Not if Wilbur was expecting his wife to be calling him.

"No," said Wilbur. The annoyance of the phone was that Harvey couldn't see the person speaking. Did Wilbur sound worried or was that just the crackle of the line impacting his voice?

"Agatha went out earlier today, despite all the warnings about flooding," Wilbur continued, who apparently was worried enough that he would discuss his business with a relative stranger.

"Surely you need not be concerned about the river," Harvey said, recalling the Cranes lived some distance away from the most endangered areas.

"We're perfectly safe here," Wilbur said, with an emphasis on the last word. "Which is why I wanted Agatha to stay home today. She's only been back in Arkham for a few weeks."

"I hadn't realized Agatha had been gone," Harvey said, feeling a bit foolish. He seemed to be losing track of people that he would have said were a part of his everyday life. First Armitage and now Agatha. Since he had retired to this house, he failed to keep up with so many people.

"Oh yes, Agatha has been traveling recently. She caught the most terrible cold in San Francisco. I blame the fog there. She should be in bed resting. But you know what she is like, the minute an idea pops into her head, she must go off and investigate. I should hang up. She might be trying to call." Wilbur's fretting was more obvious now.

"Do you know where she went? Did she go to the university?" Harvey asked. Agatha had numerous connections on campus. Harvey might be able to find her in person if she was there. Which would be easier than trying to phone their mutual acquaintances.

"I don't think so," Wilbur said. "She might have gone looking for some emporium or other. She mentioned wanting to find it again before the day was over. I don't like her traveling around town on her own. They say the storm is going to start up again."

"Yes," said Harvey, trying to think what type of emporium would attract Agatha's attention. She wasn't a woman prone to shopping, as far as he knew, unless it was for the latest test tube or some electrical gadget.

People began streaming out of his dining room, still chattering about their ideas to help Arkham with small actions. Most were carrying dishes back to the kitchen although the teacher, Sally, headed up the central stairs. Presumably she wanted to check on April and her friend. Or perhaps fetch their lunch dishes downstairs for Mrs Fox to wash.

"I must get off the phone," Wilbur said again, reclaiming Harvey's attention. "Agatha might call."

"Yes, of course," Harvey said, disappointed that he had been unable to speak to Agatha. She had seemed his best chance for a new idea to combat the shadow conjured up by Augusta Palmer. "If Agatha returns home before sunset, could you have her call me? I have an important question to ask her." Then, considering he might be out of the house in those final hours before the confrontation on the bridge, Harvey added, "If I am not here, she can leave a message with my housekeeper, Mrs Fox."

"So what is your question?" Wilbur said. "You know Agatha, she will try to answer you. If she comes home in time." His voice shook a little but then Wilbur continued stoutly on. "Of course she will be back. Agatha always comes home."

"When Agatha returns, and we know she will return," Harvey said, as much to reassure himself as Wilbur, "please ask her how I can dispel an enormous shadow."

"I would shine a very large light on it," Wilbur answered almost reflexively, "but I'm not the scientist."

"But you are a genius!" Harvey said, turning Wilbur's suggestion over in his head. Light! It was almost too simple an answer. But a very good idea. "That's exactly what I should do. But still have Agatha call me if you can. She might have opinions about what type of light dwould work best."

"If you insist," Wilbur replied. Then he hung up the phone.

Lefty returned from the kitchen. Waiting until Harvey disconnected himself from the phone, he said, "I'm heading to Rivertown to pick up those brooms."

"I don't suppose you know anyone who has the equipment to produce a bright light?" Harvey said, considering ways that he could have such a light shine on the Thomas Ward Bridge.

Lefty looked puzzled. "You mean a spotlight?"

"Maybe." Harvey thought for a minute. "Or a brilliant flash of light, possibly accompanied by a loud bang." Old texts might not be the complete answer, but Harvey did recall one of his Chinese manuscripts speaking of the effectiveness of gun powder in driving away demons. Fireworks could be easier to procure than a klieg light.

"Firecrackers might work," Harvey said out loud. "But who would have fireworks in Arkham?"

Lefty scratched his chin. "Boom-boom Mulligan. He likes all kinds of explosives. Makes his own, if rumors are true."

"Where would I find Mr Mulligan?" Harvey asked. Because now he had a glimmer of a plan. It was not as complete as he would like, but still it was a start. A series of actions, some very loud and bright, might well help reduce the oncoming miasma of madness and despair for Arkham.

At the same time, Harvey could not dispel his own suspicion that he was about to perform the largest act of whistling past a graveyard ever attempted in New England.

CHAPTER TWENTY

As Lefty told Harvey, he did not know Boom-boom Mulligan personally. But he knew people who worked with him, including Sol in Rivertown. Sol owed him a few favors as well, as he explained to Harvey when they pulled up in front of the stables where Sol had moved the dogs last night.

Lefty tipped off Sol when the owners called the garbage company to clean out the stables, including hauling off the brooms and bags left there by their last paying tenant. In return, Sol promised to remove any contraband from the premises before Lefty's company cleared the place. Then Lefty made sure to shift the schedules around so the garbage company would not show up until after Sol said it was safe to do so. The unexpected addition of the dogs was a bit of a headscratcher, but Sol thought they could claim that they were being good Samaritans by moving the animals into the stalls if anyone complained.

Luckily, the stables were adjacent to "The Graveyard." The dead would not be disturbed by the dogs' barking. Lefty was fairly sure that all of Sol's shuffling of his contraband over the last few days meant the stables were clear of anything illegal.

If there were still a few kegs of beer around, Harvey would not make trouble, as Harvey assured Lefty when they drove up the gravel drive.

"Now we can use the brooms, so I'll clear them out. Tell the company that it was what I was working on today, too," Lefty said to Harvey as he climbed out of the truck and banged on the barn doors. "You in there, Sol?" he yelled. "I have come for the brooms."

When he did not hear an answer, Lefty hauled on the barn doors. As expected, Sol had left them unlocked. He usually did, as nobody bothered the place. Everyone knew it was the Drowned Rats' current headquarters.

What Lefty had not expected was the group staring at him when he slid the door open. He spotted Sol in the back of the stables along with Joey and Marko, both members of the Drowned Rats. Facing them was a young woman dressed in a man's trench coat and fedora. She carried a large camera in her hands and looked vaguely familiar. Lefty thought he might have seen her around Northside. Which meant she might be one of April's friends from the *Arkham Advertiser*. He often gave April rides to and from the newspaper offices, and she tended to point out people she knew.

Something about everyone's stance signaled trouble. Lefty had walked into the middle of numerous bar fights in his drinking days. While he wasn't sure if the young lady was about to swing her camera at Sol's head, he wouldn't put it past her. Her narrowed eyes and flushed cheeks indicated that she was very angry. Which surprised Lefty, as he knew the Drowned Rats were fairly harmless.

They might shift booze up and down the river, but the Drowned Rats were often characterized as "good boys" by old ladies like Mawmaw. They all had family in Rivertown, including sisters, cousins, and other female relatives who felt safe calling on any of the Drowned Rats when they needed help. Sol acted the flirt, but everyone knew he was devoted to his girlfriend Genevieve. Lefty would have said they were all stand up guys who would have your back in a bar fight and not bother your sister.

So why was this young woman facing down this particular trio?

Hard on his heels, Harvey walked into the stables and exclaimed, "Dynamite! It certainly might be an advantageous alternative to fireworks. Although potentially more lethal. I need to consider the ramifications."

Which was when Lefty noticed the large crates marked as explosives and knew Sol had not cleared out all his contraband yet. Also, why he was looking so peeved at Lefty's arrival. Still didn't explain the young woman with a camera but it might be the dynamite, rather than the Drowned Rats, which caused her looks of disapproval.

"Sorry, Sol," Lefty said, hoping to ease the hostility crackling through the room. "I did knock. But I wasn't expecting anything more than the brooms and puppies. And maybe Joey." Everyone had noticed how much Joey liked the dogs. He had been the one to personally carry them into the stalls, ignoring yips, nips, and a little peeing by the most frightened pups.

Sol frowned. Like all of them, he had been up most of the night, helping clear as much as he could away from the river. For the first time since the storm began, Lefty could see the exhaustion pulling down the younger man's shoulders.

"First a nosy reporter, now the professor who falls off piers," Sol said. "This has not been a good day."

The young woman in the middle of the stables stuffed her

camera into a large leather bag. "I would object to the nosy, as I have kept quiet about your business," she said to Sol. "But you cannot expect to steal dynamite and get away with it."

"Actually, that's exactly what I expected to do," Sol retorted. "Everyone was supposed to be too busy with the flood to notice it had gone missing. Except it hasn't flooded yet!" He sounded particularly upset about the lack of water lapping around them.

Which Lefty understood. They had spent all night working as quickly as they could to take the most vulnerable out of Rivertown and sandbag as many homes and businesses as possible. Then nothing drastic happened. A few piers washed away. Piers collapsed every now and then. A bad storm, perhaps, but not the terrifying one that the newspapers had predicted. The rain had even stopped.

It wasn't fair or even rational to be disappointed that a disaster hadn't happened. But it did leave Lefty with a strange sense of foreboding. He was definitely no sibyl, but he believed every word uttered by Mrs Alba at lunch. At the time, it felt as if the old lady's predictions were what he expected to happen since he woke up in the front seat of Pequod this morning.

Like the monstrous shadow which rose behind Augusta Palmer at the hospital, Lefty's feelings of dread had not diminished even as the immediate threat of flooding faded away. The day still thrummed with terrible possibilities, an unseen but uneasy vibration under his skin. Outside, the wind picked up and rattled through the graveyard next door, carrying with it a scent of mold and decay. Inside he could feel the tension rising, Sol's hands opening and closing unconsciously into tight fists. The two other Drowned Rats felt it too, he could tell, shuffling back from their leader.

"The dynamite pays off some old debts," Sol blurted out, as if the wrongness permeating the day was too much to bear in silence. "I can settle this quickly and safely if all of you stop interfering."

His voice rose, cracking on the final syllables. Sol was acting nothing like the daredevil young man that Lefty thought he knew. Instead, this Sol seemed ready to splinter apart, struggling to regain control of the situation.

Without saying another word, the young woman turned on her heel and sprinted out the door, flying past Lefty as if pursued by the ghoul of the graveyard. With a shout, Sol raced after her, but Lefty shifted his bulk and blocked him. Grabbing Sol's shoulder, he spun the Drowned Rats' leader around and pushed him back against the boxes of dynamite.

He did trust Sol to make the right choices eventually, but Lefty could see the young man was on the verge of making some awful mistakes. Perhaps because of the terrible day that they were all having. And Lefty wasn't going to let him threaten one of April's friends. Or any young lady for that matter.

"Gently," shouted Harvey. "We do not want to set anything off."

The other two Drowned Rats seemed stunned by the sudden turn of events. But then they surged forward, either to free Sol from Lefty's grip or pursue the woman now running swiftly down the road.

They came to a stuttering stop when faced by Harvey brandishing what had to be the smallest handgun that Lefty had ever seen. Despite the oddity of his gun, Harvey seemed very comfortable in pointing it at Joey and Marko.

"Please, gentlemen," said Harvey. "I would rather not fire off a shot so close to the dynamite or the dogs."

Joey moaned a bit, probably due to fear for the dogs rather than himself, and Marko kept his mouth shut.

Convinced Harvey had the upper hand of those two, Lefty turned his attention to Sol. "What's wrong with you?" he said, suddenly angry that this young man that he liked had acted so badly. "You have never threatened women before. Or been a thief. Not stuff like this." Shaking Sol a little, he continued, "This is dynamite. It could kill someone. A lot of people."

"I had no choice," Sol said, pulling himself out of Lefty's grip. His shoulders slumped. "You know how it has been. The O'Bannions and the Sheldons busting each other's operations, fighting back and forth. Last two runs we made, we didn't get paid. Now I owe our suppliers and they aren't nice men, no matter what they say about Canadians."

"You didn't tell us," Marko said. "You paid us the same as always."

Sol shrugged. "I had a little extra saved. I was going to take Genevieve on a proper trip to somewhere nice in Boston," he said. Lefty thought he sounded a bit embarrassed to be admitting this.

"Genevieve won't take a trip to Boston with you," Marko said. "Not unless you are married."

"Yeah, well, maybe I had plans," said Sol, now turning a brilliant red. "Not that it is any of your business."

Marko looked stunned and Joey confused. "But we had boxes of whiskey in the Black Cave," Joey said. "The last shipment for the O'Bannions."

"Which they hadn't paid us for," Sol said. "So I tried to sell some of the O'Bannions' whiskey to the Sheldons, just to make some quick cash earlier this week. Then the whiskey turned out to be colored gin. Both sides started gunning for me, the O'Bannions because they never got the booze and the Sheldons because they did." He sounded particularly offended by this turn of events. "I hocked the ring that I bought for Genevieve and paid them both. But now I'm skint. A big dollop of dough would buy off our boys in Canada. Also get Genny's ring out of the pawnbroker's window."

Harvey gave a little chuckle. "Am I to understand that you stole the dynamite in order to facilitate a proposal?" he asked.

"Sounds like he did it to square up his debts with some Northern rumrunners," Lefty said, not willing to let Sol off the hook yet. Genevieve was a friend of April's and a very nice young lady from what he had seen. If she had been his daughter, he wouldn't have approved of her marrying a guy in debt to some of Arkham's most notorious gangs and their booze suppliers.

"Bit of both," Sol admitted with his old bravado. "But I would have straightened it all out. If we hadn't had this storm. So I listened when some dame offered me serious money for the mayor's dynamite. Hard to say no to moolah being waved in your face."

"When did this happen?" Lefty asked with a little less heat. Money made men stupid. He knew guys caught up in various baseball scandals, all revolving around betting and promises of easy cash. The world hadn't forgotten the infamous Black Sox. And if anyone thought baseball was clean of fixers and gamblers simply because eight men had been banned forever, then they didn't know human nature.

So Lefty dropped his fists and let Sol tell his tale. But he didn't drop his stern look. As sympathetic as he might be toward Sol, the man had made a mess of things. He might even have to mention the whole scheme to Mrs Alba, who would definitely make Sol tread a straighter and narrower path.

"Early this morning," Sol said, "we went down to the docks to load the boats. Legit work, just doing our civic duty. Kind of like what I am planning to do once Genevieve and I are spliced. There's more work coming to the docks every day. What they need are good foremen to run the crews. I could supervise, easy money."

Lefty shook his head. He didn't know if Sol could make the jump from small time bootlegger to wharf supervisor. But if anyone possessed enough ambition or drive, it might be this young man – if he did not end up in prison for robbing City Hall of their dynamite.

"Then a woman offered to buy some of the dynamite from you?" Harvey asked.

Sol nodded. "She said she needed a few crates and was willing to pay handsomely. That's what she called it, handsomely, and she flashed all these rolls of greenbacks in her purse."

"So how did you do it?" Lefty asked. The crates were big. Surely someone on the mayor's crew would have noticed them wandering down the street with the Drowned Rats.

"Borrowed a boat," Sol said. "The piers were bucking up and down, rain was blowing sideways, and we just slid Marko's uncle's boat next to the others. We loaded it the same as all the rest. Nobody noticed. Thirteen boats, fourteen boats, hard to tell what's going on when the river is raging under you in the dark."

"You are a very clever if rather dishonest young man," Harvey said, letting the hand holding his pistol drop a little. He did not pocket the gun, however, and cast a warning eye at the other two Drowned Rats. "Have you considered furthering your education? The dean keeps saying we need more entrepreneurial students at Miskatonic University."

"Don't encourage him," Lefty said. "Or you'll have bootleg rum stored in the basement of the student union."

"Who says we don't store it on campus already?" Sol retorted. "Students drink, same as everyone else." He also seemed more relaxed as he chatted with Harvey.

The strangeness of the encounter seemed to recede. Lefty felt his own tension decrease as Harvey continued to talk. Outside the wind rattled the barn doors and blew cold fingers inside, but it no longer felt laden with the old fury of the graveyard.

"Possibly students lack sobriety," Harvey said, "but do consider university as an alternative to prison. The food is about the same, the classes almost as dull as forced labor, but the final prospect is far pleasanter."

"You trying to talk me out of being a crook?" Sol asked. "What about the other Drowned Rats?"

Marko and Joey shook their heads at the question. "We are not college types," Marko said. Obviously life outside of Rivertown had not occurred to them.

"If they have half your talent for business dealings, they will do very well. Or, perhaps, some have an affinity for sports? The dean would love to field a decent football team in the fall," Harvey said with such sincerity that Lefty could not tell if he was joking or completely serious. Or, being Harvey Walters, maybe both. The old man did like to tease.

Sol shrugged. "Nobody in my family ever bothered with college," he said. "It's good work on the docks."

"Consider it," Harvey said. "It's not all dusty old men thumbing through crumbling manuscripts." Then he gestured at the dynamite with his pistol. "How about we purchase these explosives from you and remove the crates from this location?"

"What would a professor like you do with the dynamite?" Sol said. "Blow the dust off the books?"

Harvey smiled. "I want to galvanize the entire municipality and wake Arkham from its nightmares. There is a malaise crawling through the city which will seriously impede any attempts to survive the coming night."

The other three men scratched their heads at Harvey's overly academic warning of doom.

"Maybe some smaller words?" Lefty suggested.

"Sorry," Harvey said. "Let us simply say that there will be overwhelming sorrow when a certain entity enters the city's boundaries. We need to distract the population, if not actually cheer them up, in order to have any success at all."

"You're not talking about the flooding," Sol said, with narrowed eyes. "You're talking about things like the monster in the river."

"Something even bigger than that," Harvey said.

Sol considered his proposition for a minute or two, but then he said, "No. I tried double-crossing the O'Bannions. It didn't go well. The lady paid for her dynamite so I have to deliver it to her."

"Perhaps you could give us the name of your buyer and we could try persuading her to part with the dynamite?" Harvey said. "Do you know what she needs it for?"

"Nah," said Sol. "She wasn't the chatty type, if you take my meaning. And she had a couple of big goons with her to discourage long conversations. I can't give you her name as she didn't tell me. Which is not unusual for doing such type of business."

Having a feeling that he would regret the offer, but wanting to make it all the same, Lefty suggested, "Why don't we use my truck to deliver the dynamite? Then maybe Harvey can persuade the lady to give up part of her shipment. There's nobody better at talking people into things."

"Thought you didn't want company property used for bad dealings," Sol said in a peeved tone. He'd wanted to borrow Pequod once or twice for his business, but Lefty had always turned Sol down. Lefty's excuse had been the truck needed to be locked up at night in the company's yard.

"It's a strange day," Lefty said. "Harvey is right. It's better to get this stuff out of here before the cops show up." He had always liked the Drowned Rats and knew they did a fair amount of good around Rivertown. They weren't like the O'Bannions or the Sheldons. The boys kept away from the violent stuff, other than the occasional punch up. The dynamite heist was a stupid move, but he thought Mrs Alba would ensure Sol never pulled such a stunt again.

Sol nodded. "The buyer's been having a problem finding transportation for the stuff. I can call and tell her that I found a truck and ask for directions. I do have a phone number although it's just some office downtown."

"We will take the brooms and the bags too," Lefty said. "I need those for one of the professor's plans. Let's load Pequod and get out of here." If the woman who ran away was an *Arkham Advertiser* reporter, she was sure to return, possibly with the police.

Lefty grabbed an armful of brooms. The others came behind him, carrying the dynamite, except for Harvey. The professor wandered across the stable to chat with the dogs in their stalls. Heavy lifting did not seem to interest him.

But the four men loaded Pequod quickly, pulling the tarp in the back tight around the crates of dynamite to disguise the boxes from view. The brooms and burlap bags they piled on top of the tarp to further disguise the load. By the time Lefty stepped back, Pequod looked normal. A garbage truck piled high with junk. That some of the junk could blow them sky high was well hidden.

"That looks fine," Harvey said as he examined Pequod.

"Let's add the last of the brooms and bags," Lefty said, wanting to clear out the stables as he had promised. This way, he was doing company work with Pequod even if detouring a bit with dynamite.

"Now all we need to do is meet your buyer and see if we can persuade her to give up some of the dynamite," Harvey said to Sol as they walked back into the stables.

"Actually, I need every stick for my own endeavors," said a woman's voice behind them.

The men whipped around to see an amused woman standing in the big doorway leading to the drive. She looked to be around Harvey's age, with pale blonde hair mostly covered by a stylish hat. Blue gloves covered the hands holding an impressive handgun, much larger than the one Harvey was still holding. Behind her, Lefty could see a long black car parked in the driveway. A couple of large men followed the woman into the stables. The type of men that Lefty would describe as goons, if asked. They also held impressively large Lugers in their fists.

"Valeska!" Harvey cried. Lefty recognized the name of the woman that Harvey had gone to see earlier in the day.

"Good afternoon, Walters," she said. "I was not expecting to find you here." Then she gestured with her handgun. "Put your peashooter away."

Lefty moved to help Harvey, although he wasn't sure what he could do against three armed and dangerous individuals.

Sol and the others also advanced. Harvey must have realized three large guns to his small one were lousy odds. He signaled Lefty and the Drowned Rats to halt and pocketed his pistol. In their stalls, the dogs whined and barked, as if aware of this new disturbance.

"Is this your dynamite?" Harvey asked the lady.

"Yes," she said, gesturing with her gun toward Pequod outside. "I am delighted to find the dynamite loaded in such a convenient vehicle for us."

"Your convenience was not my first consideration," Harvey said. Sol started to open his mouth and then snapped it shut when one of the goons lifted his gun a little higher.

"Valeska, this is foolishness," Harvey said. "You gain nothing by shooting us."

She shrugged. "It could be a longtime ambition of mine to bring about your demise, Walters. You have caused me no end of trouble over the years."

Lefty shifted a bit closer to Harvey. The lady didn't look like she meant to open fire, but he thought he could knock Harvey out of the way if she did. As to whether he could punch out a woman, he didn't know. But her gun suggested that she might have the advantage. Which should make him feel a little better about tackling her to the ground.

As if guessing his thoughts, Harvey laid a hand on his shoulder. "Let's see if we can resolve this peacefully," he said.

The woman smiled at them all. "How about I make this a better deal for everyone?" she said, reaching one hand into her purse and pulling out a roll of greenbacks just as Sol had described. She threw it to Sol. "A bonus. For the loan of the truck," she said.

"Wait!" Lefty said. "That's not his truck."

But the woman paid no attention to him. "Reginald, if you

would be so kind." One of the large men turned on his heel and strode out of the stable. Through the open barn door, Lefty saw him climb into Pequod's cab.

Lefty growled and moved to stop him, only to find himself staring into the round barrel of the other man's gun. Lefty flung up his hands and stepped back.

"I did not think dynamite was your style, Valeska," Harvey said. "A little crude for you."

"Needs must when the devil drives, as you would say. And the devil is almost here. Thank you again for solving our transportation problem. I prefer not to have explosives in my vehicle," Valeska said as she retreated out the door. "We will leave the truck near the church for you to retrieve. A pleasure doing business with you, gentlemen. Walters, don't forget your appointment at the Thomas Ward Bridge. It is absolutely essential that you be there."

The other man with her slammed the barn doors shut. With a shout, Sol and Lefty jumped forward and dragged the doors open, but it was too late.

A stunned Lefty watched as his truck went rattling down the road without him. Although he thought he had seen the unimaginable earlier when a shadow of a monster engulfed the hospital, it did not hold a candle to losing his beloved truck. He could not believe what had just happened.

"Harvey," Lefty shouted. "Did your lady friend steal Pequod?"

"Yes," replied Harvey, sounding peeved. "With the umbrella still under the seat. So how does Valeska expect me to keep the appointment without the umbrella for Augusta Palmer? How does she even know I'm supposed to be on the bridge? And what does the woman want with dynamite?"

CHAPTER TWENTY-ONE

Minnie was absolutely furious at herself. How could she have turned tail and run from what might be the major story of the day?

Panting slightly as she leaned against a gravestone in the Christchurch Cemetery, Minnie considered her options. Nobody seemed to have followed her down the road. To foil anyone chasing her, she ducked through the fence railings and took a path which led deeper into the graveyard. Only to realize that there was no pursuit, which was simply maddening.

At least she didn't hear anyone crashing through the overgrown bushes which bordered the fence. Sol might be able to move quickly and quietly, but she was sure that she would have heard Joey and Marko blundering down the path.

Minnie reviewed her situation. She had some very nice pictures of dogs and absolutely nothing to prove that she had found the dynamite. When she returned to the *Arkham Advertiser* and faced Doyle's barrage of questions, Minnie was well aware that all she could say was, "Yes, I found all the boxes and now I have lost them. No, boss, I didn't get a picture." Because by the time they roused the police, Sol would have cleared out the stables. All they would find would be a bunch of brooms, some burlap bags, and far too many dogs to count. Minnie could almost hear Sol's smooth-tongued explanation that she had mistaken crates of Schoffner's beans for dynamite. She wouldn't put it past him to fetch crates of beans and canned corn from Schoffner to make his lies plausible.

Minnie ground her teeth and scuffed her feet through the wet leaves mounded over whatever grave was below. The storm had done some damage in the graveyard. Tree branches lay across many graves. The earlier rain turned the grass into a soggy mess. The grave before her dipped distressingly in the middle as if underground water was hollowing it out. She kicked the leaves again and heard something go pinging off into the distance to land with a wet plop in the bushes.

Doyle should have kept Edgar on the dynamite story. He probably would have done a better job – and that was the most depressing thought to ever cross Minnie's mind on a thoroughly frustrating day.

Ever since she staggered out of St Mary's Hospital, Minnie felt this was the day that she would finally secure her gigantic scoop. The big story that they all chased at the *Arkham Advertiser*, the one that none of them admitted to wanting but they all desired, the absolute and undeniable proof that Arkham was not like other cities. To finally show the world that Arkham contained unexplainable terrors hiding beneath its quaint history and New England charms. Except those terrors would no longer be unknowable challenges, because they, the stalwart truth seekers of the *Arkham Advertiser*, would expose these shadows and then...

"And then what?" Minnie asked herself as she stared at the gravestone of Jabez Rance, who died in 1790, age forty-six. *Far from his loved ones, beneath this stone lies Jabez Rance, in the prime of manhood gone* read the inscription. No further words clarified who those loved ones were or why Jabez had been buried far away from them.

Did they not know, whoever selected this inscription, the questions that it would stir for future generations? Or did they not care, because they knew as soon as the answer was found, another question would spring up? That today's groundbreaking story would become tomorrow's forgotten newspaper, lying soggy on some hospital chair?

Minnie pulled Doyle's hat off her hair and ran her fingers through her bob, as if the action alone would make her thoughts more optimistic. She'd faced setbacks over the years, what reporter hadn't? But today seemed unusually depressing. The failure to capture even one decent picture in the Black Cave weighed on her, as did her disappointment over the earlier pictures in her rescued Speed Graphic.

Then this dynamite story popped up, as good stories had a tendency to do, and that seemed like a solid bet for front page placement. It wasn't mysterious monsters but it did have the potential to go bang. Minnie groaned a little at her own puns. But the headlines practically wrote themselves.

And what had she done? Failed to get the picture! What would Doyle say? Minnie winced. She could just hear what Doyle would say but it wasn't nearly as bad as her own internal recriminations.

The doubts started well before this morning, when her dreams began to be filled with fish exploding and bloody guts raining down on her. She had woken in her bed convinced that Arkham's secrets could shower down on her in a similar manner and it wouldn't matter. Nothing would change. Not in any substantial way. They could print absolute proof that all the rumors were true and nobody would pay any attention.

Nightmares, that's what those depressing thoughts were, Minnie told herself. Only nightmares brought on by too many nights spent chasing whispers about places like the Christchurch Cemetery.

She rotated Doyle's old hat in her hands, caressing the worn press card still stuck firmly in the hatband. Where had Doyle flashed this faded bit of cardboard in pursuit of a story? Where would it take her?

"Not back to the office," she muttered, pushing away from Rance's gravestone. She turned, heading toward the stables where the dynamite was hidden. If she hurried, she might catch them moving the boxes. She began to plan how she could grab the photo that she needed.

Minnie jammed Doyle's hat tight on her head and went as fast as possible along the damp paths, even striding straight across graves to get back to her story.

When she reached the stretch of cemetery fence closest to the stable, Minnie spotted the men loading a big old truck parked in the gravel driveway. The driver certainly did her a favor by distracting Sol in the few minutes that she needed to escape. She wondered if he had been expecting to find the dynamite or if he really had been there to pick up the brooms.

Minnie pushed as gently as possible through the damp bushes, crouching on the very edge of the property behind a very prickly holly. She had a good view of the truck but not inside the stables. So she wasn't too sure who was there. She assumed Sol and his friends since they had not run after her. The driver must still be there as the truck was parked outside. Hadn't someone else come on the truck with him? She had been concentrating on Sol, trying to figure out a way to retain her camera and talk him into telling her more about the dynamite heist, although the latter was probably a bit of a delusion. If Sol was the one who stole the dynamite, he would not want the whole tale splashed across the front pages. Unless she could make him an anonymous source, which Doyle would not like. He frowned on anonymous sources in general although everyone had to use one every now and then. Minnie decided she would not protect Sol if he meant to use the dynamite to harm anyone. In that case, he deserved to be caught by the police.

But what if Sol had taken the dynamite to help prevent the flooding in Rivertown? Wouldn't that make him something of a Robin Hood? A man trying to help folks out? Like Nova Malone? When were the bootleggers criminals and when were they heroes? It was complicated and a question that she, Rex, and Darrell debated over many a lunch.

Because they all knew that it was the reporters who turned petty crooks into interesting characters in the newspaper stories. But were they right to do so?

Luckily, before she could tie herself into philosophical knots beneath a holly bush, Joey came out of the stable with a couple of crates. He set them gently down in the back of the truck. Then Sol and Marko joined him, pulling a big tarp across all the boxes.

Minnie hissed in frustration. From where she knelt, the only picture that she could take would look like a big old garbage truck piled high with nothing in particular. The men went back inside and then came out again. Sol, Joey, and Marko carried brooms and burlap bags which they slung into the truck, some of it landing on top of the tarp and the rest jammed up in the front part of the truck bed.

The truck driver, an older man in a sou'wester, loaded brooms as well. He dropped them into the truck a little more carefully than the others, placing the brooms around the crates hidden under the tarp. Then everyone went back into the stables, where they were frustratingly hidden from view.

Minnie considered her options as water dripped off the holly and down the back of her neck. She needed to get closer to the dynamite, Minnie decided, and take some absolutely irrefutable photos of the cargo, then take off before Sol spotted her. Once she had the photographs, she could bargain with Sol for his side of the story. That seemed fair, Minnie decided. No judgments, no taking sides, until she knew all the facts.

Before Minnie could move closer, a long black car drove up and parked directly behind the truck. Perking up at the addition of new people, Minnie pulled her smaller Kodak out of her coat pocket. Snapping away, she caught pictures of an elegant, older woman brandishing a very large gun. The woman glanced inside the truck bed. Minnie guessed the tarp did not fool her. The slight smirk on her face told Minnie that the woman was very aware of the dynamite concealed under the canvas covering. Then the old lady called a few words through the open window of her car and entered the stables. Two more men got out of her car, also carrying big guns, and followed her inside.

Wild to hear what they were saying, Minnie crept out from under the holly and sprinted the short distance to the truck. To her frustration, she could not make out what was being said or even see into the stables from where she hid behind the vehicle. She considered creeping around the truck for a better view. Then she looked up. Slats of wood formed the walls of the truck bed but it was open to the sky.

Anticipating everyone inside the stables was busy watching each other and not looking out the door, Minnie jumped up and grabbed the edge of the truck. Kicking and scrambling in a way that lacked elegance but went faster than she expected, Minnie propelled herself up the side. Ignoring the sound of ripping cloth, other than to hope it was her dress and not Darrell's trench coat, she slid over the side into the truck bed. Minnie squirmed under the tarp. Then she slid across the bed so she could peer out between the slats. From this angle, she could see Sol, Joey, Marko, the truck's driver, and an old man in a tweed suit facing the elegant old lady and her two henchmen.

The old man had a little gun in his hand but dropped it into his suit pocket. Minnie took a closer look at him, certain that she had seen him around Miskatonic University. Walters, Harvey Walters, that was his name. And what was he doing with Sol and a load of stolen dynamite? More importantly, why was this woman taking it away from them, because it was obvious that the dynamite was now being transferred into her blue gloved hands. From the unhappy faces surrounding her, Minnie also guessed that Sol and his friends had not expected this turn of events. This story was getting better and more complicated by the minute. Doyle would love it, if only she could make it back to the *Advertiser* with all the facts.

The woman said, "Thank you for your help." One of the goons strode over to the truck. Minnie ducked under the tarp, holding her breath. She felt being caught by these people would be worse than facing down Sol. The truck rocked as someone climbed into the cab. Then the engine started up.

Minnie swore and then she shrugged. Well, at least she would find out where the dynamite was going. And on the way, maybe she could figure out a way to escape being caught with it before they unloaded the truck.

Chapter Twenty-Two

Harvey never considered the inconvenience of travel by bus until he decided to pursue Valeska in one. It was not like taking a cab or even being driven by a friend. Buses meandered, Harvey observed, stopping and starting as well as going in odd loops toward a specific destination. However, when they had departed the stables, there were no taxis available. And Harvey's friend with a car, specifically a garbage truck, had just had his vehicle stolen. So they took a city bus running in the same probable direction as Lefty's truck.

"When we arrive," Harvey said to his companions, "let me do the talking."

"Doesn't seem like the lady paid much attention to you before," Lefty grumbled. "How are you sure that we are going in the right direction?"

Lefty filled up the seat next to Harvey. Behind them sat Sol and his friend Marko. The large Joey had been left to watch over the dogs, which the other two thought would be a better task for him.

After Valeska's minion drove Pequod off with Valeska's

car following close behind it, Sol and Marko sprinted down the road with Lefty lumbering after them. The trio came back to report they had seen Valeska's car turn west when she reached the end of the cemetery fence. Whether she went north toward the bridges or south away from the river, they did not know. Both were possible from the next corner. Harvey flipped a mental coin and guessed south. Valeska once owned property near the Historical Society. He thought she might be heading there.

"Valeska said she would leave your truck near the church," Harvey said to Lefty. "She probably meant South Church."

"Why not Christchurch? It's closer," Lefty said, naming the church sitting on the north end of the cemetery.

"The bus started there and we didn't see your truck," Harvey pointed out, very gently, as he knew how upset his friend was. After being unable to find a taxi, Sol led them to a bus stop close to Christchurch. The first bus to come by was heading south, which clinched the decision for Harvey. If the only transportation was taking them near to South Church, then that was where they should start their search.

However, he had not expected the bus to zig or zag so much through the largely residential Southside neighborhood. The close-knit houses on each side of the street looked prosperous if not particularly ornate. Wide steps led up to deep porches of handsome bungalows. The two-story homes sported gambrel roofs, a nice callback to the long ago Dutch influence in the region.

Unlike Rivertown, no abandoned houses or rough warehouses marred Southside's neat streets. A few corner stores provided discreet evidence of commerce but mostly these sported signs advertising the spaces as dentist or doctor offices. There was no sign of sandbagging of any establishment, probably because it was so much farther from the river.

As they meandered toward South Church, the few people already on the bus reached their destination and departed. Almost all carried bags or suitcases. Harvey supposed that the passengers were removing themselves from the riverside neighborhoods to be as far from the river as a person could be in Arkham. Nobody boarded the bus in Southside, so the riders dwindled to Harvey and his companions. Obviously, nobody wanted to head toward the river on the return journey.

According to the driver, when the bus reached South Church, it would turn around and run back to downtown Arkham, crossing the Erwin Bridge. There would be approximately a ten minute delay before the bus commenced its return route. Harvey pointed out to Lefty that this would give them plenty of time to search for Pequod. If they could not find the truck, then they could return to Rivertown and start the hunt again.

Lefty frowned and shook his head. "A lot of back and forth," he said. "And the afternoon is already half gone."

"I am acutely aware of the passage of time," Harvey replied, checking his watch again. "But the sibyls think the moment on the Thomas Ward Bridge is fixed. Which means we should recover the umbrella before sunset so I can make the appointment."

After his initial surprise at Valeska stealing the truck and the umbrella, to say nothing of the dynamite (which might have been useful too), Harvey pondered probabilities and predictions. He contemplated his fate, and the fate of Arkham, as the bus trundled very slowly down Garrison Street.

If Mrs Alba was correct, the umbrella could not be truly lost. It would return to him in time for the meeting, perhaps in an unexpected way, but it would be found. Since the umbrella was still secured beneath the seat in Pequod's cab, it seemed most likely that the truck would be recovered as well. Especially since Augusta had seen Pequod in her vision of the future.

This aspect of predicting the outcome of a prediction, he tried to explain to Lefty but the big man was less than enthusiastic.

"So you are saying that because the meeting is supposed to happen, Pequod will just be wherever we look for it?" Lefty asked.

"Basically, yes," Harvey replied.

"Then why didn't we look around Christchurch and save ourselves a long bus ride?" Lefty retorted.

While he considered a rational rejoinder to this illogical statement, Harvey became aware of Sol and Marko whispering behind him. The men tried to be discreet, but Harvey's hearing was excellent.

"What are you going to do?" Marko asked. "The dame paid you for the dynamite. You planning to give the money back?"

A long pause, then a soft "Maybe" from Sol's side of the seat.

"But what about Genevieve? What about your trip to Boston?"

"Forget about it," Sol said, sounding depressed. "Crazy ideas, all of them. Going to Boston? Finding a real job on the docks? Not for the likes of us."

Marko sounded surprised and a touch worried. "What's wrong?" he asked his friend. "You're the one that said the Drowned Rats could do anything, be anyone."

"Guess I am an idiot," Sol said. "I don't know. It's this day. It's dragging on forever. I made a terrible mistake. What if the lady with the gun kills somebody with the dynamite?"

Harvey twisted in his seat to address the two young men. "Valeska very rarely shoots people. She prefers to curse them instead. I certainly never knew her to explode anything," he said with as much conviction as possible, although it had been many years since he worked directly with Valeska. But he had heard reports about her, various rumors circulated by other occultists venturing further afield in pursuit of arcane knowledge than the safe confines of the Orne Library. He was almost certain that none of those stories involved dynamite.

"This day will not last forever," he said to Sol, in the same voice that he once used to reassure students that exams would end and freedom would be found outside the classroom.

"It may end in unnatural phenomena clouding our minds and obfuscating our senses. This seems to have begun already," Harvey continued, recognizing at the same time as a speech of encouragement that his words lacked a certain zest. But Sol was right. It was a depressing day, trapped on a city bus, searching for a dangerous woman now possessed of far too much explosive power, while three more frightening women awaited him at an apparently preordained appointment.

The women would be accompanied by the gigantic shadow of an Ancient One whose coming was drawing closer and closer. He would have to make do with a green umbrella and a garbage truck. Harvey speculated on these unfair odds. He tried to ignore the prediction of his demise accompanied by a small plaque at the university, but it intruded into his thoughts. Really, they should put up a statue. Harvey shook off his disappointment about his memorial. The looming appointment on the Thomas Ward Bridge must be kept according to the sibyls, but would it simply add to the terrors of the day? Or could he use it to save his friends? And when would this bus ever stop turning and twisting through the streets?

"Professor?" Lefty asked.

Harvey sighed in response. If only Lefty had stayed with his vehicle instead of loading it with brooms, he might have prevented Valeska's goon from driving off with it. Although what he could have done against the pistols pointed at him, Harvey certainly couldn't say. Fight them off with a broom like poor Willoughby?

With that irrational thought, Harvey's frustration with the bus and its meandering route through nowhere in particular nearly boiled over. Then, just as unpredictably, all his feelings disappeared as if swallowed down some immense and unfathomable big throat, a mere morsel of spiritual frustration to feed a formerly dead god.

The bus slammed to a stop. Lefty snapped out his big arm and prevented Harvey from falling off his seat. Behind him, Harvey could hear gasps and then exclamations from Sol and Marko.

"Sorry, folks," the driver called to the four men. "Can't think what happened. Nearly dropped off there. Not getting enough sleep. Hit the brake wrong. Next stop is your stop, South Church."

"How intriguing," said Harvey, thoroughly snapped out of the irrational gloom which had settled over him by experiencing a phenomenon that he recognized. "Such emissions will certainly cause a few psychic migraines around town. Be thankful, gentlemen, that we are not as sensitive as some to manifestations of unfathomable power."

"Professor? What was that?" Lefty asked, rubbing his face as if he had been slapped or punched.

A glance over his shoulder showed Harvey that Sol and Marko looked equally shaken.

"Cthulhu appears to have breached some ocean in our world," Harvey said, pulling out his pocket watch and checking the time again. As soon as he spoke the name, the three men with him looked both ill and intrigued, a frightening combination for a man who once tried to talk his students out of combing ancient texts for mere mentions of the Ancient One.

"What is Kulu?" Sol stumbled over the name.

Harvey didn't correct Sol's terrible pronunciation. The actual naming of the entity brought it closer, and he had been foolish in the extreme to break his own vow on a city bus of all places. Except the Ancient One was nearly upon them and all attempts at hiding from its influence were now as futile as mice trying to escape the hunting notice of an owl gliding overhead. The mice might believe they were safe in the field, but they existed only to nourish the owl.

Actually, the more he thought about it, the oncoming threat to their sanity was more like Robert Burns' terrible plow, something which didn't need the mice to survive, but overran their house and destroyed all their plans with no pity or awareness of the mice at all.

Except Burns cared enough to soliloquize in a chilly field in Scotland about the fate of a field mouse. Would Cthulhu sound such poetry through the cosmos if Arkham became a burned and wrecked shell in its wake? Absolutely not! So it was up to Harvey to make a plan that did not go awry, no matter his confinement to a hard wooden bus seat. He did not need to be in his comfortable study, with his best carpet slippers on his feet, and smoking his favorite pipe, to be able to use his knowledge of entities found in books best left unopened by the unwary.

In response to Sol's question, Harvey said, "The Ancient One exudes a fog of depression, angst, and general lassitude to paralyze the more psychically sensitive among us, often driving them deep into dreams of horrors. The nightmare plague, if you will, which has fallen on Arkham. It will, like all plagues, become worse before it runs its course."

What he did not add was the strength of this latest wave of depression indicated the Ancient One was very close to Arkham, practically on its borders. The closer Cthulhu drew to the city, the worse the terror would become, until everyone succumbed to the numbness and despair which rolled off the Ancient One like fog swept onto the mainland from the ocean. Except this miasma would cloud people's minds rather than reduce visibility on the river. However, it would make it just as likely for terrible accidents to happen.

"South Church!" yelled the bus driver. "We're here. Everyone needs to leave the bus."

"What if we want to go back to Rivertown?" Marko asked as he passed the driver.

"You climb back on the bus," the driver said. "But not until quarter after. I get my break. It is in the rules."

"And where do you take your break?" Harvey asked as he joined his friends on the sidewalk outside South Church.

"Inside the bus. But without any passengers," the driver said as he snapped the doors closed with a bang.

"So we are here," Lefty said, looking up and down the street. "I don't see my truck." If Harvey did not know his friend was a better man, he would have said Lefty sounded smug to have been proven right about the lack of truck at the end of the bus route.

Other than the city bus, there were no vehicles on the road. The big, old stone church was clear to see, its tower rising above all other buildings on the street. Absolutely no trucks were parked by it. Harvey knew a feeling of disappointment which had nothing to do with the emanations of Cthulhu. He had expected to find Pequod here. He was sure that was how the prophecies worked. Obviously, he would need to rethink his paper on the infallibility of sibyls.

Marko and Sol went around the church. They reported no sign of Pequod or Valeska. Lefty made a similar search up and down the street, as if Pequod would be found parked behind a bush on someone's tidy lawn. Harvey sat on the bus stop bench and thought about what he could do next. Just go to the Thomas Ward Bridge and expect the umbrella to magically appear?

That wasn't a plan, Harvey decided. That was simply resigning oneself to one's fate. Which had never appealed to Harvey as a strategy. Besides, he was fairly sure that he needed dynamite or fireworks if he wanted to drive off Augusta's monstrous shadow. Acutely aware he needed to accomplish this expulsion of the shadow before Cthulhu arrived, Harvey considered how else they could hunt for Pequod. Obviously random traveling by bus was not the solution that was required.

Harvey also desired time to prepare for his confrontation with Augusta, because once Cthulhu was actually in Arkham, the amount of effort needed to fight Augusta or anything larger than a mouse would be enormous. Like going up a mountain while carrying a hundred-pound sack of pure depression.

"Guess we should climb back on the bus," Marko said. The driver still had the doors closed and a check of their watches showed the man still had five minutes break time remaining.

"I thought your truck would be here," Harvey said to Lefty, because he had raised hopes falsely through his own misunderstanding of the situation.

"I know," Lefty said with a sigh. "I believed you, even though it didn't make much sense. But the day's been like that. Things aren't turning out so good today. Although the flood hasn't happened either. It's a weird day."

"Instability of the immediate future along with general ennui might also be counted as a manifestation of the Ancient One's aura," Harvey said, but without much snap to it. Honestly, he anticipated more to come from this bus trip. He expected answers.

A raucous toot of a car horn startled all of them. A small green car hurtled down the road toward the men, squealing to a halt just behind the city bus. The driver cranked down her window and called, "Professor Walters, there you are! You have to hurry!"

To his amazement, Harvey recognized the voice of his housekeeper. Mrs Fox gazed at him from the driver's seat. Next to her was a tiny old lady all swathed in black shawls. Harvey was delighted to see Mrs Fox arrive with transportation, although he had absolutely no idea how she came to be in this part of Arkham.

"We found him, auntie," Mrs Fox addressed her companion.

"About time," muttered the little old lady. "Why was he wandering about on a bus in Southside?"

"I don't know, auntie," Mrs Fox said, sounding as if this conversation was taking place for the third or fourth time. "But we found him."

"Well, good," the old lady said. "Let's go. We will not have much time."

"Is this your great-aunt?" Harvey said, addressing both women through the open car window. "Another sibyl, I believe."

The old lady turned her rheumy, almost blind eyes in his direction. "My name is Lucasta Esposito," she said. "You should be under the Thomas Ward Bridge."

"Yes, I know," Harvey said, "but we lost the umbrella and Lefty's truck." Mrs Fox gave a small gasp of concern at the latter part of the statement. "But I am sure we will find both soon," he added to reassure her.

"It will be *under* the Thomas Ward Bridge," her great-aunt said very slowly and distinctly. "Along with many boxes of dynamite. You will need to fetch the truck away before they blow up the bridge."

CHAPTER TWENTY-THREE

Lefty sat squashed in the back seat of Mrs Fox's car, Sol on his right side, Harvey on his left. Marko took the bus back to Rivertown because Mrs Fox's car was a small car. They might have fit him on the front bench seat, but Mrs Fox's great-aunt gave Marko a glare and refused to move over. Even more disturbingly, the great-aunt winked at Lefty.

Now Mrs Fox drove straight through Southside, taking the shortest route to the Thomas Ward Bridge. Lefty admired her driving, but then he admired most everything about her. But on this ride, he did not spend as much time staring at the back of her head as he would have liked, his thoughts being tangled up in what Harvey said about some great fog blanketing all of Arkham. A fog created by a creature with a name, which he had heard once or twice but still could never get to stick in his head. It sounded so much like the creatures described in *Tales from Nevermore*, but more unsettling.

Because Harvey wasn't creating a story to scare the readers, not like Virgil Gray. Harvey was telling what he believed to be the absolute truth. Everything that Lefty had seen over the past few days only reinforced his belief in the professor's strange knowledge of horrific creatures. But how that knowledge could save them from this fog, let alone the creature causing it, Lefty could not even begin to guess. It was like the impending flood. A person could do everything possible to avoid the worst damage, including dynamiting the river banks, but nobody had a way to stop a flood. Not that he had ever heard of.

Harvey also spent a lot of time talking about the future during their bus ride. As far as Lefty could tell, parts of the future were set. There would be a flood. There would be a monster. But how exactly it would impact everyone, that seemed to be much less certain. As a man who had gone up in the world and fallen back down, Lefty wondered where the next few hours would leave him.

Oddly, at this point, he glanced at the back of Mrs Fox's lovely head and thought, *perhaps I will survive this too.*

They were almost back to where they had started, racing along the road past the graveyard. Christchurch Cemetery was a weird old place, but it had always been there. Lefty liked the parts of the city which stayed the same. Seemed so much had been changing recently and he wished it would not. He had an uneasy feeling that Arkham was going to change even more in the coming days.

"Professor," Lefty said, thinking maybe Harvey should start sharing the plan that he kept saying he was working on. In his experience, teams worked better if they knew what the coach was thinking.

"Call me Harvey," said Harvey.

Lefty smiled. "Kind of a comfort to call you professor. Like you have all the answers."

"I wish I did," said Harvey, looking out the window at the gravestones flashing by. "I thought I did. But what if I am wrong? I had a student once, Thomas Willoughby, and I gave him terrible advice. I told him to face his fears."

"I gave bad advice to a friend," Lefty said and felt Sol stir on his other side. The young man seemed as lost in his thoughts as the rest of them. He wasn't sure if Sol was listening, but he knew he had Harvey's attention. "I told him to crowd the plate."

"Crowd the plate?" Harvey asked.

"Makes it easier to hit some pitches," Lefty said. "Makes the pitchers nervous too. So they throw you an easy one. But it didn't work."

"I am still not sure…" Harvey said, but Sol caught on.

"Pitcher didn't back down?" Sol asked, turning from his contemplation of his reflection in the car window. Like all the young men in Rivertown, he always wanted to hear Lefty's baseball stories. He shared some around Schoffner's potbelly stove, the kind to give young men daydreams. The ones that gave him nightmares, Lefty kept to himself until today.

"Nope. The pitcher got riled up instead," Lefty said with a sigh. This was his worst memory but something about today made it important to share. Those graves flashing past the window made him want to tell this story before he was dead and buried. Also, if he told it to the back of Mrs Fox's head, he would never have to tell it to her face. But she would know what had happened and how sorry he still was. "Carl Mays never backed down. He threw a spitball right at Ray. Maybe he didn't mean to hit him in the head, maybe he did. Didn't matter. He killed him, sure as if he shot him."

"You knew Ray Chapman?" Sol asked, recognizing the story even if Harvey looked puzzled.

"Yeah, I played in Cleveland. My last year, and I was

mostly benched. But Ray and I kept talking about how we would handle Mays if we came up against him. Should have kept my mouth shut," Lefty concluded. "He was a young man, had a wife expecting a baby, and dead so quick."

In his mind, Lefty could still see Ray after he collapsed and then revived, brushing off the questions even as the umpire screamed for a doctor and his teammates carried him back to the dugout. Ray died the following day. Being on a winning team, even a team which took the World Series title that year, meant nothing because of the empty spot on the bench. The black armband that Lefty wore over his uniform still resided in the bottom of his trunk.

"A tragedy," Harvey said as Sol explained the whole horrible game to him. It had been written up in all the newspapers, and everyone had an opinion on whether Mays threw deliberately or not at Chapman's head. Lefty didn't care. He just wished the day had ended differently.

"Yeah," Lefty said, "and then I crawled all the way to the bottom of a bottle to try to forget it. But that doesn't work either."

Harvey seemed puzzled. "What doesn't work?"

"Pretending you are dead," Lefty said. It took him several years to figure this out. He was never sure if he was absolutely right. But he knew the answer wasn't being numb to everything going on around him. The answer, however painful, could be found in living his life, hoping for better, for doing better, as well as he could. "Wish I had all the big words that you do, professor. But I think we cannot escape the past or the future. We just have to do something now. Preferably something that helps people."

Harvey nodded. "Willoughby would have liked you," he said. "He was sports mad. But a scholar too. I let him read far too much. He studied texts that I should have kept locked away from my students and he became obsessed with finding evidence that the Ancient One existed."

"Did he?" Lefty asked. He couldn't imagine why anyone would want to see such a thing. Especially if it was anything like the shadow which crawled up the wall behind Augusta Palmer. And that was just a shadow, not the actual monster according to Harvey.

"He did. It ate him. But not before he attacked it with a broom," Harvey said. "The more I consider Willoughby's fate, for which I blame myself to no small extent, I must acknowledge his actions were effective in some ways."

"I thought you said he was eaten?" Lefty asked. The whole story was strange, and not terribly reassuring when he considered they were working on a way to attack the shadow creature summoned by Augusta Palmer. If this was Harvey's version of a pep talk, he was much worse at it than any baseball coach.

"Most certainly," Harvey said. "But if Willoughby had not turned and attacked the creature, the two men with him would not have escaped. They also would have died that day. The sheer shock of Willoughby's actions gave them the impetus to flee the scene."

"So perhaps telling Willoughby to face his fears was not the worst advice?"

"Perhaps telling your friend to crowd the plate would have worked well on another day," Harvey said gently, and the way he said it actually did comfort Lefty. "We can never know. We can only try our best."

The car came to an abrupt halt on a street full of moldering warehouses. They had arrived back in Rivertown.

Mrs Fox said, without turning her head, "If you are done

discussing the past, we need to worry about the future. My aunt saw the dynamite being loaded on a green-and-white boat."

Her prosaic but also kind tone convinced Lefty that he should take Mrs Fox to dinner and dancing someplace fancy, like the dining room at the Excelsior Hotel, if they survived the day. At which point, her tiny great-aunt turned her head and looked directly at him. She winked again and smiled. Which, in its own peculiar way, was much better than any pep talk.

Harvey and Sol exited on opposite sides of the car. As Lefty slid toward the car door, Lucasta Esposito said to him, "Jump when he tells you to jump if you want to dance at the Excelsior."

Mrs Fox blushed and shushed her aunt. Then she also turned to Lefty and said, "I hear the band at the Diamond Dog is even better than the Excelsior. I have always wanted to go."

As usual, all the words dried up in Lefty's throat but he managed an affirmative mumble. Then he hurried after the professor and Sol.

The warehouses so close to the river were packed tightly together. From his regular route of garbage collection, Lefty knew most of these warehouses ended in piers sticking out in the Miskatonic River. Double-sided sliding doors allowed trucks to be driven directly into the warehouses for the unloading or loading of merchandise brought down the river. But those doors could also be closed, as these ones were, hiding whatever freight was inside there. Which, of course, was why Sol and his gang knew these havens of bootlegged merchandise so well.

"You can get to the river through there," said Sol, pointing at a narrow, shadowed alley running alongside one dingy warehouse.

As he followed Harvey and Sol down the grimy alley, Lefty's thoughts were no longer on Pequod or its load of dynamite. The earlier depression of the day also vanished from his mind. Even the rumbling of thunder, the flash of lightning, and the sudden downpour of rain did not distract him from his thoughts about the relative merits of the Excelsior and the Diamond Dog as expressed by Mrs Fox.

So Lefty plowed into Harvey's back when the professor came to an abrupt stop. The long warehouse which formed one side of the alley ended in a pier. Still intact, despite the water lapping over the boards, the pier swayed in the river. A green-and-white tugboat was anchored to the pier by a barnacle-laden hawser. Heavy rope wrapped around the edges of the hull, protecting the tug from being battered against the pier.

Lefty knew tugs like this as they nightly hauled the garbage barges down the river to the ocean, although the company contracted to Arkham Sanitation favored a gray-and-black trim on their wooden tugs. Behind the tug was a small barge laden with very familiar crates of explosives. A burly man in a heavy sweater and oilskins lifted a crate from the dock and set it on the barge. A tall, elegant woman dressed in a long coat and blue gloves oversaw the operation.

In front of Lefty, Harvey straightened his shoulders and called out, "Valeska, what exactly are you planning to do with those explosives?"

With a shrug, Valeska turned around and replied, "I plan to use this dynamite to blow up the Thomas Ward Bridge, Walters."

"But I am meeting Augusta Palmer there," Harvey said.

Two big men appeared around the corner of the warehouse. Lefty and Sol put up their fists. The men put up their guns. Lefty growled but he stepped back. Sol spat but also stood aside. Through the open doors of the warehouse, Lefty spotted Pequod. The truck looked empty of everything except the brooms and bags. The tarp was crumpled in a corner of the warehouse floor. Lefty did not know how they could retrieve the truck, but he hoped Harvey had a plan.

Because if Harvey didn't have a plan, Lefty knew he would do something stupid, like grab his truck and ram it through a wall. He was not leaving this warehouse without Pequod.

"Yes, I know about your appointment, Walters," Valeska said, drawing a gun out of her leather purse and aiming it at Harvey. "You must be on the bridge at sunset so Augusta will be there too. Then we will blow it up."

CHAPTER TWENTY-FOUR

Harvey knew he occasionally annoyed people. He was not unfamiliar with ducking punches or thrown objects, or even diving for cover when the shooting started. Actually, considering the number of things thrown at him from fists to bullets, perhaps he should amend his assessment to "frequently annoyed people." But Harvey thought this was the first time anyone had threatened to blow him up. Sacrificing him had been suggested once or twice in the past, but only involving long ceremonial daggers with jeweled handles. Dynamite was such a crude way to end a man's life.

Harvey also considered that Valeska should not look so peeved. After all, she must have expected him to object to such a plan. Although it might be the rain sluicing down which caused her aggrieved expression. The downpour certainly crushed her hat onto her sleek head as well as causing the roof gutters to overflow, sending splashes of muddy water over the group trapped in the alley.

"Your meddling adds unnecessary complications, Walters," Valeska complained while keeping her Luger aimed at Harvey's midriff. "If you simply did as I asked, you would not have known about the dynamite and voiced no objections. The bridge would have exploded at sunset and removed a number of dangers from Arkham."

"As well as myself," Harvey huffed. "Why do you think such an explosion improves the situation?" In other words, was this a personal attack against himself? What had he done to deserve such an action? Or was this Valeska's new *modus operandi*? Did dangerous women abandon occult curses for dynamite as they grew older?

"The destruction of the Palmers removes one threat. Once Augusta is gone, her shadow will be gone as well, thus eliminating a second threat," Valeska said as if Harvey would not have already deduced the obvious. "Thirdly, there are other things stirring in the river which have been attracted to Arkham. The shadow acts as a lure for them as well. Without it here, the river monsters may well move on."

"Yes, but if the shadow is no longer attached to Augusta, then it will merely return to Cthulhu," Harvey said, as all gloves were off and if he did attract the attention of a certain Ancient One, it might give his friends time to escape. Lefty and Sol were cornered by the warehouse wall by one of Valeska's minions holding another large Luger.

Which did distract Harvey for a moment wondering why Valeska was favoring a German make of pistol these days. What exactly had Valeska brought back in her luggage from Europe?

"True," Valeska responded to Harvey's comment about Cthulhu. "But if the shadow is not roaming freely through the city, the Ancient One may ignore more of Arkham and pass on by. The spawn preceding the Ancient One should also be drawn out of Arkham's waterways by its return to deep waters."

"Wait," Harvey said. "You think there are Star Spawn in the river?"

"Possibly," Valeska said. "Although the reports are not clear. But Michael McGlen's description of what snatched his partner off this very pier sounds much like those entities."

"Valeska, have you been dealing with bootleggers?" Harvey knew McGlen, as the man had come to see him, willing to trade a rather fine whiskey for information. He hadn't considered McGlen's search would bring him into Valeska's orbit. However, if the gangster was serious about knowing "the beasts" (as he had called it) which lurked in the depths of the Miskatonic River, Valeska was not the worst source of information.

"McGlen paid for information with an object that I desired," Valeska said. "I am a business woman."

"I have no objection trading information for whiskey," Harvey said very truthfully.

"Whiskey?" Valeska almost snorted. "I received a Portuguese port bottled more than forty years ago."

"I didn't know the O'Bannions dealt in such liquors," Harvey said to distract Valeska while trying to ascertain exactly where everyone would be when the shooting inevitably started. Valeska's minion backed Lefty and Sol up the ramp to the riverside doorway of the warehouse. Behind them, he could see the outline of Pequod. From Lefty's longing looks at his truck, it was obvious that securing the truck must be part of their escape. Sol simply looked depressed by the turn of events. Being a bit of a romantic, Harvey disliked the idea of a thwarted engagement and resolved to get Sol home again to court his Genevieve.

"Walters, if you are calculating some spell to persuade me to abandon my plans, be aware that I am well armored against magical influences of all types," Valeska snapped at him.

"Actually, I was considering engagements of the diamond ring variety," Harvey responded and smirked a little when Valeska's jaw dropped.

It appeared all of the dynamite had been loaded on the barge. Valeska's other minion pushed the empty handcart up the pier and onto the ramp connecting the dock to the warehouse. The captain of the tug stepped out of the cabin, examined the people facing off over drawn guns, and shrugged.

"Ready to leave?" he shouted to Valeska. "We need to finish this soon. The river's rising fast."

"You are being paid enough to wait," Valeska called back. "I need to persuade this nice gentleman to keep an important appointment." To Harvey, she said, "Meet Augusta or I'll shoot your friends."

"Crude, Valeska, very crude for you," Harvey responded as he calculated the odds of escaping without a bullet hole appearing in someone.

The bearded captain gave a sour look at the whole group. "Not paid enough to lose my tug," he said but ducked back into the cabin. Obviously, Harvey could not count on him for any form of rescue but he considered the tug as an avenue of escape. Could he persuade the captain to take off without Valeska? But a tug tied to a barge full of dynamite still tied to a pier probably would not be the best route. Off the pier, up the ramp, and into the warehouse to liberate the truck still seemed the best route to freedom.

Except that left Valeska in control of the dynamite and the Thomas Ward Bridge in danger.

"So you are taking the dynamite via the river to fasten to

the undersides of the bridge?" Harvey asked as he stalled for more time. "Is such a journey with explosives wise, given the condition of the river?" The water was now obviously higher than this morning.

Valeska nodded. "Reginald gained some experience during the war destroying bridges. He will go on the barge and fasten the detonators and explosives. All the bridges will be destroyed at sunset, but I was going to have the Ward explode first."

"Now wait a minute!" Harvey exclaimed as Valeska's words sank in. "You are going to blow up all the bridges?"

"Running water serves as an effective barrier. You know the recommendations of the old texts," Valeska said. "Also, dynamiting the bridges will cut the city in half, perhaps protecting more people." Valeska sounded almost smug about this part of her plan.

"Valeska, we are not talking about turning back Tam o' Shanter's witches! The Ancient One, Star Spawn, and all the rest will not be deterred by running water. They are aquatic!" Harvey could not believe Valeska's scheme was so illogical. She generally created a much more crafty plan of action.

"The other bridges are more for civic reasons," Valeska admitted. "It keeps certain elements confined to certain neighborhoods."

"So you are saying the south end of the city doesn't want the north end invading it," Harvey said, trying to think who would have the wealth or the motive to advocate such a drastic change to Arkham's infrastructure.

"Or the reverse." Valeska shrugged. "I did not inquire. After we acquired the detonators, from a source that I will not reveal to you, Reginald was approached to expand our plan of destruction. Honestly, I only meant to blow up one bridge to remove the annoying Palmer sisters from Arkham."

"And me!"

"Purely collateral damage," Valeska assured him.

"I am not mollified," Harvey said. "Nor am I going to help you do this." Out of the corner of his eye, he thought he saw a shadow moving in the warehouse doorway. Lefty and Sol were now a few steps inside the warehouse as their guard shifted himself out of the range of the overflowing gutters. Which left only two Lugers pointing at him, held by the explosives expert Reginald and Valeska.

He knew Valeska was a deadly shot but if he dived toward Reginald, would she hold off for a moment or two simply to avoid shooting her own minion? Most days, probably not. But today Valeska needed Reginald to blow up those bridges. So it was as good a plan as any.

Harvey drew a breath and readied himself for the leap. Suddenly every sound disappeared, from the creaking ropes straining to hold the boat and barge in place, the pounding of the rain upon the wooden pier, and the rushing of the river. Harvey felt suspended in a dim bubble of a moment, just waiting for the pop.

A shadow stretched across the pier, a dreadful shadow of wings, talons, and the impossibly tentacled head.

"Did you truly expect to stop me with your pathetic plan?" asked Augusta Palmer as she walked out of the alley and onto the pier.

CHAPTER TWENTY-FIVE

When the truck stopped, Minnie's luck improved. The driver switched off the engine, left the cab with a slam of the door, and then walked across what sounded like an empty space with wooden floors. Curled under the tarp, Minnie tensed, waiting to see if the driver would circle around to the back. But the footsteps kept moving away from her. She heard another door creak open and then slam shut.

For a second or two, she remained frozen under the tarp. "If he's waiting for you, he already knows you are here," Minnie told herself firmly. She lifted the tarp and peered out. The truck was parked inside a large warehouse devoid of any goods. A few loose boxes and a pile of tarps similar to the one in the truck were piled in one corner.

In a flash, Minnie clambered over the sides of the truck. It seemed harder getting out than getting in, but she made it without any loud noises or ripping another piece of clothing. She tugged Doyle's hat into place, then sped across the floor as quickly and as quietly as she could to get away from the truck and its load of dynamite. A large open doorway let in light, wind, and rain as it faced the rushing Miskatonic River.

At the opposite end of the warehouse were a pair of closed barn doors. That was probably what she heard slamming earlier.

Although tempted by the open doorway, Minnie wanted to figure out where the driver had gone and, hopefully, avoid running into him. As she had already found out, people who stole dynamite took a dim view of reporters.

From the river behind her came a melancholy tooting of a tugboat's horn as Minnie stood on tiptoes to peer out the grimy warehouse window. She wasn't exactly sure where she was, but the general look of the street suggested that she had returned to Rivertown. Although her view was limited through the rain-streaked dirty glass, she did not spot anyone moving on the street. Minnie crept to the barn doors to try them. Frustratingly, the doors were locked and she could find no mechanism to release them. She checked the window but it was painted shut. Which left the far too easy open door on the opposite end of the warehouse. Could it be as simple as walking away after all the events of the day?

Of course, she would stay until she had the answers and pictures that she needed. But it wouldn't hurt to have her escape route secured as well.

Not wanting to take any chances, Minnie slid along the wall, keeping to the shadows, while trying to see if anyone stood outside the warehouse on the Miskatonic side.

As soon as she came even with the open doorway, she could see three people standing on the pier. The elegant old lady wearing blue gloves clutched the large handbag. Two big men with hard faces moved down the pier to meet a tugboat pulling a small barge. As the tug came level with the pier, a burly, bearded captain popped out of the cabin to throw ropes to the waiting men. The tug and barge secured, he jumped off the boat and strode down the dock to meet with the woman.

Minnie could not hear what they were saying but she saw the woman point to the warehouse.

Like a mouse frightened by a cat, Minnie created a hiding place in the corner. Guessing the men would head for the dynamite, she ducked behind the boxes and pulled the tarp over her head. It reeked of tar, like it came off a boat. Minnie fought to keep from sneezing as the men unloaded the truck. She had a bad moment when the truck's tarp came sailing through the air to land near her.

Boxes of dynamite were loaded onto hand trucks and pushed out of the warehouse. The wheels squeaked on one hand truck. Minnie tracked the position of the men by their footsteps and persistent rattle of the hand trucks' wheels. When the first load went down the ramp, she dared to peek out around the boxes. She strove to store all the details in her head, wanting to keep her hands free for her camera.

As quietly as possible, Minnie slid the Kodak from her pocket. She would have preferred to use the Speed Graphic, but its noisy shutter might give her away immediately. She thought she could dare a shot or two with the Kodak.

Eventually the men stopped walking back and forth. Minnie decided it was safe to risk a closer look at the action outside. One hand truck stood alone at the top of the ramp down to the pier, but the men were gone. Minnie squeezed her way around the rubbish, hearing the sound of raised voices.

Minnie crept closer to the door so she could see what was going on. Flattening herself against the wall, she shifted to an angle which would give her the best view out of the door while leaving her largely hidden from anyone on the pier. She readied the Kodak.

Outside, the rain was coming down harder. The old woman with blue gloves was brandishing a very large gun in the direction of a white-whiskered gentleman in a tweed suit. With a start, Minnie realized it was Harvey Walters, the darling of the newspaper reporters whenever they needed a learned quote about occult history. Immediately the headline "Miskatonic University Professor Confronts Dynamite Thieves" sprang into her head. Could she snap a picture of Walters before anyone noticed her?

Footsteps rang on the ramp again as three men moved up the ramp, shifting out of the rain to stand just inside the doorway in front of the handcart. Minnie immediately recognized Sol and the large working man in overalls who had stopped Sol from chasing after her. The third was one of the men who had unloaded the truck. This dubious character held a gun on the other two. Minnie wondered how Sol and the other man ended up here. Had they chased the truck all the way to the river? Why was Professor Walters mixed up in all this? Where was the boat going with the dynamite? Too many questions and not enough facts, as Doyle would say. Minnie shifted closer, hoping to hear what was being said outside. When she moved, Sol turned his head and stared directly at her. He looked as startled as she felt. Luckily the shouting on the pier distracted the other two. The tug also let out an impatient whistle.

Minnie raised her eyebrows. Sol mouthed the words, "I am sorry." And he honestly looked sorry. Minnie had never been one to hold a grudge, especially with a source for a good news story. She mouthed back at Sol, "What can I do?" Apparently, he had seen enough silent movies to translate her exaggerated question.

Sol jerked his head at the hand truck almost directly

behind the man with the gun. The gesture reminded her of one made by Rex when they had been trapped in a fight at the Clover Club. That time she used a bar cart to disable his opponent.

Minnie did not hesitate. She jumped from her corner and shoved the hand truck hard against the knees of the man with the gun. He toppled over in surprise, rolling down the ramp to land with a thump on the pier.

"Minnie!" shouted Sol, darting toward her. "Get away from the door. They have guns."

"Saw that," she said, looking out on the pier with her camera raised. Now she might as well take the picture. No use trying to be stealthy after sending a man sprawling down the ramp. Then she had a lot of questions for Sol. Seeing as she had just saved him, she thought she could finally secure some answers.

"Pequod!" the man in overalls yelled, heading toward the truck parked in the center of the garage. His lumbering run through the warehouse caused the boards to bounce under Minnie's feet.

Then, as if all the air rushed out of the room, there was a moment of perfect silence. As strange as it was, Minnie took advantage of this moment to place herself in the doorway. Nobody paid any attention to the man groaning at the bottom of the ramp. Instead, everyone concentrated on another woman now standing near Professor Walters. She was tall and stout but something about her reminded Minnie of Columbia, the *Arkham Advertiser*'s office manager. For some inexplicable reason, the woman made Minnie think of two women standing on the steps of St Mary's Hospital. Minnie felt unusually queasy and her headache came roaring back. Why would a resemblance to Columbia frighten her so?

Shaking off her feelings, Minnie raised her camera for the best possible picture of the tug, the barge, and the dynamite. Through the center of her viewfinder she saw a shadowy monster spin out of thin air like a blot of ink crossed with a tornado. It was most definitely the creature which appeared in the Black Cave, but even larger and more imposing.

With her own yell of surprise and fear at the monster's reappearance, Minnie dropped the Kodak. Swearing, she scrambled after her camera as Sol and his friend also cried out in sudden terror. The shadow with tentacles, wings, and clawed arms spread across the dock, slowly engulfing even the tugboat and its barge full of dynamite.

CHAPTER TWENTY-SIX

Harvey heard a yell and a thump from the warehouse, but his attention was focused on the shadow of Cthulhu looming over them all. A wave of fear, fierce as the river flowing under the pier, crashed over him and presumably all within range of the shadow. A sense of dread coupled with a far more unwelcome feeling of helplessness threatened to overwhelm his sense of preservation.

Augusta Palmer smiled as the people facing her retreated from the growing shadow, now as large as an elephant and still expanding into a creature too vast to comprehend. It flowed over the tugboat. The captain inside the cabin must have sensed or seen it, because the tug's horn wailed the maritime warning usually used in heavy fog.

Her sisters stepped into the alley running alongside the warehouse, but they allowed Augusta to advance onto the pier by herself. Their brother Ira stood a step or two behind Columbia and Barbara. As Harvey had observed during their encounter at the hospital, Augusta commanded their every movement as coldly as she directed the shadow stretching before them. As Ira shrank behind his sisters, Columbia and Barbara let Augusta speak for all of them.

The rain streamed down the ungodly angles of the shadow as if it was solid matter. Except Harvey could see through its swirly substance. He felt as if he was staring into a night sky, a sky remarkably devoid of stars and other celestial bodies, an endless well of bone-chilling nothing. It was both real and unreal, a distillation of the Dreamlands' impossibilities where Augusta had found it. The rain outlined what should not exist in Arkham but was horrifyingly present. A thousand waterfalls fell from the bat-like wings and monstrous talons to splash upon the pier, the tugboat, and the barge full of dynamite.

"Did you think I would not predict this moment?" Augusta said to Valeska. "That I would let you interfere with my plans? Using dynamite? How pathetically unoriginal. I expected more from the great Valeska Stange."

"I work with the materials available to me," Valeska said, stony faced as she confronted the shadow now grown past the size of a house. It spilled over the pier and spread through the river, adding a hideous stain to the water.

Harvey resented the maelstrom of crushing emotions broadcast from the shadow. But he was profoundly grateful that the feelings of dread and despair were only fragments cast by a simulacrum made out of the discarded dreams of an awakened god. If the actual Ancient One had risen from the river, he doubted that he would still be capable of running away. Ignoring Valeska and her Luger for the larger threat looming over them, Harvey sped for the warehouse and his friends.

Valeska's companion Reginald decided to fight rather than flee. The big man began shooting at the very center of the shadow. No doubt the bullets struck, but no damage was done. Harvey could have told him that bullets do not destroy shadows, however, Harvey saved his breath for running.

Reginald emptied the Luger into the shadow's belly as it scooped him up in one taloned hand. It drew the man into the air, closer and closer to its impossibly tentacled head. The man continued firing as his face distended into one gigantic scream. Then a shrieking Reginald was flung over Harvey's head, cleared the barge, and splashed down into the Miskatonic. The man flailed to the surface but the swift running river swept him away.

As Harvey raced from the shadow, Valeska swung her Luger toward Augusta Palmer with a blistering recitation of Latin curses. Harvey was impressed. He was having a hard time keeping a few good American oaths running through his mind. But like Valeska, he knew anger could boil away the fear and despair for a moment or two. In his case, it might give him time to take cover inside the warehouse. The less he could see of the shadow, the better.

Besides, if he was very lucky, Valeska would eliminate his Augusta problem. Even though various prophecies indicated Augusta would survive until their sunset appointment. Which meant Augusta might eliminate Valeska, which would be a pity, because he liked Valeska, even when she was planning his murder.

Diving through the open doorway of the warehouse, Harvey collided with Sol. The young man seemed paralyzed with fear, staring out at the tentacled shadow slowly rising to blot out the sky. Harvey apologized as he punched Sol upon the chest. As he expected, the young man was solid enough to take no hurt from the blow, but it startled him into clutching at Harvey.

"What is that?" Sol asked, now looking directly at Harvey for answers. "Why is it here?"

"A nightmare cast by Augusta Palmer upon us all," Harvey answered, disentangling himself from Sol. "We need to put as much distance between it and us as possible."

Shaking out his aching fist, Harvey surveyed the warehouse for an exit that would not send him back into the battle between Valeska and Augusta. When such a pair of dangerous women were armed with guns and magic, a prudent man withdrew from the scene. He had never been one to believe in the folderol of the weaker sex.

Outside, Valeska's voice rose to shrieking levels, most unlike her, as she spat at Augusta: "Stay away from my dynamite!"

"Ira" – Augusta's voice was equally clear although perhaps magically amplified by the shadow – "cut the barge loose."

Unable to resist, Harvey peeked through the warehouse door to see Ira Palmer shambling across the dock. The man seemed to be unaware that he was wading through a monstrous shadow as he carried out his sister's orders. First he undid the line holding the barge tight against the dock. Then Ira awkwardly jumped onto the barge and began to untie the rope connecting it to the tug.

"Ira," Augusta shouted, "come back here."

Perhaps Ira was not as unaware as he appeared, Harvey considered. It looked to him as if the young man was making a foolish attempt at escape. With a familiar twinge of regret, Harvey remembered the plea to "save me" that he had not answered earlier. Just because somebody annoyed him by rearranging his books, that should not mean that he be abandoned to his maleficent sisters.

On the other hand, Harvey had no idea how he could have saved Ira then, or how to help him now.

The shadow took a swipe at Ira's hunched body as the man frantically struggled with the knots. Ira ducked, flattening himself against the boxes of dynamite, as the claws passed over his bandaged head.

The barge swung into the river, pulling on the tug through their shared line. The tugboat let out another blast from the whistle. The captain took one wide-eyed look at the enormous shadow looming over him as he uncoupled his boat from the pier and dived back into the cabin. The thrum of the tugboat's engine increased as it headed toward the center of the river, still towing the barge and Ira behind it.

Both Valeska and Augusta shouted "Stop!" as Ira completed unhitching the barge. The tugboat steamed away down river as the barge began to spin in circles. Even as the shadow began to engulf it, something else rose from the river.

A great rounded back emerged from the waves and then submerged below the barge. Unlike the shadow, this creature shimmered with a bioluminescent light so it was visible even as it dived, a glowing bubble beneath the Miskatonic's murky surface. This seemed to slow the shadow's reach for the barge. Or perhaps the shadow was indifferent to the light, the barge, and the now screamed commands of Augusta. Similar to the encounter at the hospital, the shadow lost interest in the proceedings, stretching out its wings and taking to the sky.

Thick tentacles broke through the surface of the water. The tentacles coiled around the barge, squeezing it and the unfortunate Ira. The creature's oddly fluid anatomy shifted and contracted. Above the rush of the river, Harvey heard a wet sucking sound as it began to drag the barge into the depths of the Miskatonic.

"It could be a Star Spawn," Harvey observed to himself as absolutely no one was paying attention to him. Everyone's terrified attention was riveted on the barge, which cracked in half, spilling the crates of dynamite into the water. He did notice Augusta and her sisters looked more annoyed than terrified and Valeska simply looked furious at losing the dynamite. But the remaining goon was almost pea green with fear. Harvey's companions in the warehouse looked shocked. The young woman with the camera raised her Kodak with shaking hands as she strove to take a picture.

Ira disappeared beneath the surface, his white bandaged head clearly visible for a moment and then gone. Harvey hoped wherever the river took Ira, it would be a better place. The young man had been an annoying, thieving assistant who attempted to be a dog sacrificer in his basement, but destruction by a Star Spawn was a wicked way to go and far too reminiscent of poor Willoughby's fate.

With a shriek probably prompted by the loss of the dynamite rather than Ira, Valeska turned the Luger on Augusta. Ira's sister gave no more reaction to his drowning than a slight frown upon her features. But she was swift to react to Valeska's attack.

Before Valeska could squeeze the trigger, Augusta stepped closer to the other woman and felled her with a roundhouse punch to the stomach. The Luger spun away down the pier, skidding almost its entire length before dropping into the river.

"Now would be an excellent time for us to leave," Harvey told Sol. The young woman with a camera plastered to her face was clicking madly at the action happening outside the warehouse. The name Minnie Klein slid into Harvey's head as he recalled an inquiry or two from her in the past.

"As much as I hate to impede the press, we should go," Harvey said to the reporter from the *Arkham Advertiser*. She looked startled at his comment. He gently pulled her away from the door and out of the line of fire in case Valeska's other goon recovered enough to remember he still had a Luger.

Valeska reeled back from Augusta's punch and hauled off with a left upper cut to the jaw that made Harvey wince. He remembered debates at Miskatonic University about whether the questionable circus attractions featuring lady boxers were real fights, including the contentious claims that women who boxed could never be called ladies. He also recalled when Valeska demonstrated her own pugilistic abilities on one or two of the more foolish freshmen.

Once again Harvey thought of a younger version of himself who might have made some attempt to rescue Valeska, despite her recent plan to blow him sky high with the city's bridges. Now his older and obviously wiser self counseled him that the person most likely to save Valeska was Valeska. He hoped he was right. Because it seemed that he was fated to meet Augusta and her shadow again on the Thomas Ward Bridge.

Although he could hope that Valeska left Augusta a little winded and easier to defeat.

A horn sounded behind them. Lefty leaned out the window of Pequod and called, "Come on."

They scrambled for the truck. Harvey swung open the passenger side door and said, "After you" to Minnie.

"I will ride in the back. It is easier to take photos," Minnie said as she swarmed up the side of the truck with an agility that made Harvey sigh. "Besides, I need to ask Sol some questions."

Sol shrugged and swung himself into the back of the truck as well. Harvey thankfully took the passenger seat which required no acrobatics at all.

"You think the ramp will hold?" Harvey asked Lefty, assuming that was how he intended to leave the warehouse. There didn't seem to be any other opening. But the ramp was barely the width of the truck and driving down it would land them squarely on the pier and in the middle of the ongoing fight between Valeska and Augusta.

Although the view was now more obscured, it appeared Augusta and Valeska were still trading body blows. However, Valeska's downed henchman was staggering to his feet. Harvey supposed Valeska would use him to shield herself from Augusta. So he was not surprised to see Valeska grab her minion and throw him directly at Augusta. When the two went down in an awkward tangle, Valeska sprinted for the alley and her car.

Harvey was impressed and pleased at Valeska's fast escape. The woman might have planned to blow him up, but that did not negate more than fifty years of friendship. There were very few people left in the world who Harvey had known as long as Valeska. He would prefer not to survive her demise as well.

"Not going down the ramp," Lefty told Harvey as he gunned the motor and swung the gears of the truck into reverse. "Going out on the street side and then swinging by Mrs Fox to make sure she and her aunt know what happened."

"If her aunt is as good a sibyl as I think, they already know," Harvey said. He twisted in the seat to peer through the small window in the back of the cab to observe the barn doors coming rapidly closer. The closed barn doors. "Shouldn't we open…" he started to say, but his voice was drowned out by the shattering of wood and flying shards from the now nonexistent barn doors.

Pequod bounced onto the street with an almost jaunty air.

"Are the two in the back still with us?" Lefty said as he yanked the wheel around and barreled down the street.

Harvey checked through the window on their passengers.

A weak wave went up from Sol while Minnie still seemed to be clicking away with an even larger camera. "Jumping Jehoshaphat, does the woman carry multiple cameras?" Harvey asked, impressed by her fortitude.

"Don't know," Lefty grunted. "Where is Mrs Fox?"

Harvey twisted again to face front. They were now careening down the street where Mrs Fox had stopped to let them out. But now the street ahead of them was empty of cars, including Mrs Fox. The glint of water caught Harvey's eye. The falling rain no longer struck the pavement. Instead, it created ripples on a sheet of water stretching from building to building.

"Is the river over the road?" Harvey asked.

"Yeah," Lefty said. "The flooding is here. Rivertown is going under water." He pumped his foot down and the truck leaped forward with a growl, sending crests of water rising on either side of them. "I'm heading for higher ground."

"Good idea," said Harvey. They were free but they also needed to prepare for meeting Augusta again. Flooding in Rivertown, the rise of the monster in the Miskatonic, and the growing size of Augusta's hideous shadow could only mean the Ancient One was very close indeed. Harvey checked his pocket watch. Mere hours now until sunset. He needed to return to his original plan and prepare a surprise for Augusta Palmer which would alert the entire city to their danger and inspire them to fight it at the same time.

"Now where does Mr Boom-boom Mulligan live?" Harvey asked. "And how quickly can we enlist his services?"

CHAPTER TWENTY-SEVEN

Lefty could not believe that Harvey still wanted to find Boom-boom Mulligan. He sincerely regretted ever telling the professor that there was a seller of fireworks in Arkham. But Harvey insisted he needed fireworks.

"Mulligan's place is clear across the city, up in Northside," Lefty said as they drove away from the warehouse and whatever it was that pulled down the barge in the Miskatonic. The last half hour was still a jumbled mess of emotions and the overwhelming feeling that he could not have seen what he just saw. So Lefty tried to concentrate on Harvey's request because thinking about monsters led to worrying about Mrs Fox. Would her aunt have warned her? Probably. Certainly. But why hadn't they waited on the street for the rest of them to return?

He thought he knew where Boom-boom was, but Lefty rarely drove the Northside garbage routes. He remembered one or two stories about a still live firecracker being mixed in Boom-boom's garbage and going off in the incinerator. After that, the regular driver for the route spoke to Boom-boom and things went better. Nobody wanted to lose their garbage service, so threatening to stop pickups was a pretty effective way to make customers behave.

"We need those fireworks," Harvey repeated. "The more the better."

"You think firecrackers will work on the shadow?" Lefty asked, the screams of the man tossed into the river by the thing echoing in his head. The terror of it, and the creature rising from the river, created a sour taste in his mouth that made him long for a beer.

But a worse fear continued chewing at his heart. He still hadn't spotted Mrs Fox's car. Lefty thought she might have moved a little ways away from the warehouse with the rising water, but he was worried about her stalling out. Some of the puddles that he was driving through were deep. Pequod rode high, like most trucks, and he was clearing the water so far. But Mrs Fox's car was a Chevrolet and sat closer to the road.

"There she is!" Harvey said, pointing out the window.

To his relief, Lefty saw Mrs Fox parked in front of an apartment building. The back door of her car was open to the sidewalk, and a family was struggling to fit themselves and some boxes into her backseat.

Lefty pulled over. Climbing down from the cab, he helped the father shove a damp cardboard box onto the lap of a squirming little girl.

"Here's your Teddy," the man said to her. "Hold on tight. You need to protect Teddy."

Through the flap of the box, Lefty could see a battered stuffed bear which appeared to have survived numerous disasters including losing one eye. The child sniffled but nodded firmly and clutched her box close to her chest. Teddy obviously had a fierce protector.

"I am glad you are here," Mrs Fox said so calmly that all of Lefty's earlier fears vanished. She had that effect on him. "There's another group still inside. I'm going to drop these people off at the student union. They have friends there. Then I will take Auntie back to the professor's house. She wants to speak to Mrs Alba."

He smiled at Mrs Fox, wanting to tell her that he was glad too. She was safe and that lessened many of the horrors of the day. Lefty wondered if she had witnessed the shadow conjured up by Augusta Palmer or the strange monster dragging down the barge. Or had her aunt directed them away from the scene before it happened?

Lefty did not know how to ask Mrs Fox about whether or not she had seen monsters. But he did feel comfortable talking about the flood water now visibly trickling into the streets. Lefty eyed the road. "Be careful. Go over French Hill, it's higher ground before you head to the university."

Just a few blocks south of the river, the storm drains still seemed to be doing their work in this part of Rivertown. The water was only a shimmer across the road, but he knew it could turn treacherously deep in areas where the land dipped.

"Auntie says it will be dry enough for us to make it through," Mrs Fox said. "I trust her visions. But it's a good suggestion to take them across French Hill." She smiled at him.

Relieved, Lefty promised to load the truck with whoever was left. "Go tell the people inside to bring what they can. I will take them out of Rivertown," he said. Mrs Fox nodded and headed into the apartment building.

Harvey climbed out of the truck to join them. Over his head, he held the green umbrella.

"Do you think that is wise, professor?" Lefty asked.

The umbrella still gave him shudders, made worse by the knowledge that Augusta Palmer wanted it for her own crooked reasons.

"While I doubt your truck will be purloined again," Harvey said, "I will not make the mistake of leaving it behind for any random thief to steal."

Given that Harvey used a couple dozen words to say what Lefty could have said in three or four, he figured the professor was feeling better. Lefty found he could ask Harvey the questions that he dared not put to Mrs Fox.

"Didn't it bother you? Seeing those things?" he asked. "Watching those men drown?"

Harvey sighed. "Sadly, it no longer frightens me enough. You are a man who has labored all his life. How would you describe your hands? Soft? Gentle?"

Lefty turned over his meaty palms, looking at the calluses and scars left by swinging a bat and later lifting hundreds of garbage bins to dump them in Pequod. He flexed his fingers, feeling the ache deep in the knuckles which came with middle age. "Guess I have hard hands," he said.

"Of course you do. And you should be proud of your calloused hands. They mark you as a working man, and that's a title to be proud of, just as another man might be proud to be called a teacher," Harvey said. He turned over his own hands, which had their own nicks and scars as well as slightly swollen knuckles, the sign of a man who had lived through too many New England winters.

"My hands may be softer than yours," Harvey said, "but my mind is sadly far more hardened. Too many encounters with phenomena which cannot be rationally explained. Too many colleagues lost to unreasonable horrors. And, yes, reading too many books full of forbidden knowledge.

Over the years, the mind creates its own barriers to the fear pervading it, and the soul becomes detached from the grief. I do not have an immunity to the terrors, but a certain tolerance much higher than others. My friend, Carolyn, is writing a fascinating article upon the subject which absolutely no reputable medical journal will publish."

"So you are saying it does bother you, but not as much as it bothers me?" Lefty asked.

"I am saying that I would gladly trade my soul for one far less jaded," Harvey said, "if I could once again weep at the death of a stranger. Value your tender heart, my friend, as the treasure that it is."

"I don't know," Lefty said. "I think I would rather live in an Arkham without monsters."

"I doubt we can achieve the impossible," Harvey said with a twinkle that invited Lefty to smile despite the rain pouring down and the horrific events of the day. "But I hope we can encourage a few monsters to leave us alone. Perhaps we can inspire others to strive against the shadows cast by people like Augusta Palmer. That's all I ever wanted, to give my students the knowledge necessary to stand strong against the terrors. Unfortunately, Willoughby took my words too literally and failed to strengthen his own soul. Still, I am proud of him. My greatest regret is that so few remember Willoughby's example today."

As they waited for Mrs Fox and the others to return, Lefty heard Sol say to the *Arkham Advertiser* reporter, "I told you everything! I don't know nothing else."

Lefty grabbed the step stool out of the cab that he used to help people in and out of the truck during the early morning evacuation. Standing on it, he looked over the back at the sodden pair.

"We are going to take the people in this building," he said. "Do you want to stay with them? We will probably go across the river, because the professor has business there. The flooding shouldn't be so bad in Northside." At least he hoped this would be true.

The young lady swung herself out of the truck, using Lefty's step stool and helping hand with a nod of gratitude. "I have to return to the *Arkham Advertiser*," she said. "I have a story to write. I'm Minnie Klein, by the way."

"I know…" Lefty started to say but Minnie's attention had turned to Sol, who was calling her name as he climbed out of the truck.

"Don't use my name," Sol grumbled as he hopped down to the road. "Minnie, I mean it. I need to live here." When she frowned at him, Sol threw up his hands. "No threats. I am sorry about threatening you. I should never have tried to take away your camera."

"I won't use your name, I promise," Minnie said with a satisfied nod at his response. "I will describe you as a concerned citizen of Rivertown who led me to the stolen dynamite. Which you did, in a way. I won't mention you stole it the first time or somebody stole the dynamite from you. I will simply say the stolen dynamite was taken by barge from Rivertown and lost in the Miskatonic. I have photos to prove that happened. The rest is too confusing, especially if I want Doyle to concentrate on the river monster. My editor does not like stories about creatures with tentacles, but he will have to print this one." She grinned and straightened the sopping wet hat on her head. "Rex will be so sorry that he missed the monster in the river. This will beat any story he finds at the hospital."

Lefty was impressed with how quickly Minnie had

recovered from the disasters that they had witnessed. He was a little disturbed by her attitude as well. Two men drowned in the river, as far as he could tell, but perhaps witnessing it through the lens of her camera had made the scene more unreal for her. Or perhaps the impact of the scene would come later.

He knew guys who soldiered through disasters without turning a hair, only to be weeping over their beer months later as they realized what they had witnessed. The horrors of Arkham hit everyone a little differently. Or, perhaps like Harvey, she had built up some calluses of the mind to help herself cope.

"You are a strange woman, Minnie Klein," Sol said, echoing Lefty's thoughts, "but I owe you several favors. Anytime you need help from the Drowned Rats, let me know." Then he turned to Lefty. "I am staying in Rivertown. The Drowned Rats have boats already stored in high places. We will move out anyone who is left. We planned to meet at the stables. Joey and Marko will definitely be there. Joey would never abandon the dogs."

"Do you think the dogs will be safe?" Minnie asked.

Sol threw up his hands. "Everybody keeps fussing about the dogs. The dogs will be fine. If not, we will move them again. But that end of the cemetery doesn't flood as much as the north end. The ground slopes up."

"Good luck," she said. "Give my love to Joey and tell him that I will run the story about the lost dogs as soon as I can."

A small group streamed out of the doors of the apartment building, a mix of young and old carrying boxes, bags, and a few battered suitcases. Mrs Fox pointed them toward Pequod. Minnie snapped a couple of pictures but then dropped her camera to help a young lady whose suitcase burst open and spilled its contents on the wet sidewalk. Minnie bundled various lacy items out of sight while joking with the embarrassed lass. Lefty took the suitcase from Minnie and swung it into the back of the truck. Minnie gave the owner a consoling hug. After the young woman climbed into Pequod, Minnie waved to her, raising her hands above her head in a gesture of triumph and encouragement. Lefty decided that the reporter's soul was not so calloused after all.

Harvey gallantly held his umbrella over heads while Sol and Lefty helped people into Pequod. Finally, all the people from the apartment building were loaded. Mrs Fox moved up and down the street, knocking on doors and calling out. Lefty reached into Pequod and sounded the deep horn a few times to bring out any stragglers, but nobody else appeared.

Mrs Fox returned to her car. She carefully turned it in the direction of French Hill, a longer way back to Miskatonic University and the professor's house, but hopefully a route which would stay above the flood. The water was definitely inching up as Lefty checked the side streets leading down to the river. But everyone seemed to have cleared out. He waved one last goodbye to Mrs Fox and her passengers.

"Time to leave," he declared to his friends as Mrs Fox drove away.

Sol nodded. "I'll walk to the stables from here."

"Before you go, does Mulligan still have his fireworks stored near the Curiositie Shoppe?" Lefty asked Sol. As Lefty remembered the stories, Mulligan's place was close to it. Which was why nobody liked picking up garbage on that route. Mulligan's trash might explode once in a while, but even stranger things were found in the rubbish of the Curiositie Shoppe.

"Boom-boom?" Sol scratched his head. "He is on West

Derby Street, but you have to circle around to the back of the building to find the door." He spoke with the confidence of a young man who had made illicit deliveries to the location. Nothing like a bootlegger for finding out where people were in Arkham.

"That's near the *Advertiser*," Minnie exclaimed.

Lefty nodded. "I can drop you off at the *Advertiser* and take the professor to Boom-boom's. But we need to find a good place for these people." The back of Pequod was once again nearly full but they could probably take a few more if they spotted anyone needing a lift. Lefty had a feeling this would be his last trip through Rivertown before the neighborhood was lost to the rising waters.

"The Palace Movie Theater would be closest," Sol said. "Straight down Peabody and across the bridge."

Lefty nodded. The Palace was much closer to their destination than following Mrs Fox to Miskatonic University and the student union. Going to the movie theater would take them north across the river, which might mean less problems than the Rivertown roads as well. The early morning newspaper article, and all the talk in Schoffner's General Store, predicted the worst flooding would be along River Street.

Minnie agreed too. "The Palace is one of the designated Safety Stations and not far out of the way. But who is Boom-boom Mulligan?"

"A man who hopefully possesses the necessary fireworks to drive off a certain shadow," Harvey said as he climbed back into Pequod's cab.

Lefty almost laughed at Minnie's surprised expression. "Why don't you ride up front in the cab?" Lefty suggested. "You can ask the professor all your questions. He loves to talk."

Minnie looked at the passengers huddled under the tarp in the back of the truck, obviously torn between wanting to know more about Boom-boom and wanting to question the people fleeing Rivertown.

"I will ride with you as far as the Palace," she decided. "I can find a cab or a bus to the *Advertiser*. But I need to talk to the people sheltering there. So we have the complete story."

Sol gave them a wave as he headed to the stables. Minnie climbed up into the cab on the passenger side while Harvey slid obligingly to the center of the bench. The umbrella had disappeared so he must have stowed it under the seat again. Lefty resumed his usual spot behind the wheel.

"We'll take everyone to the Palace and then go to Boom-boom's place," he told Harvey.

"Oh, very good," Harvey said. Then he turned to Minnie. "I thought of a particular way that the *Advertiser* can help with our efforts. Do you think you could add a story to the evening newspaper?"

Minnie shrugged and looked at her wristwatch. "It will be tight," she said. "Doyle is working on the evening edition now. But I plan to type up one more story on the rescue efforts and how people are coping with the flooding. We always hold some space open until the very last minute on a news day like today."

"But are you not writing an article about the stolen dynamite?" Harvey asked.

"I will," Minnie said, "but I still need to call City Hall, and try to get a few quotes from them, and check the facts against whatever Edgar found out. So it may be a day or two before that story comes out. And I have a few others too."

"How do you manage to pursue so many stories concurrently?" Harvey asked with genuine interest.

Minnie shrugged. "That's just what reporters do. We always have multiple leads to investigate. That's what I love about my job. So many new things to learn, so many questions to ask, and so many stories to tell about Arkham. I wouldn't have it any other way. But how can I help you, professor? What story do you want us to tell tonight?"

"Please tell the citizens of Arkham to head for the roofs of tall buildings," Harvey said, "and look toward the Thomas Ward Bridge at sunset."

As Minnie and Harvey discussed Harvey's idea, Lefty drove carefully down Peabody. The water was definitely higher when they neared the river, but then they crested a slight rise up to the bridge. Now Pequod's tires rolled along wet streets but did not send fountains of water up on either side of the truck. Lefty increased his speed, anxious to reach the bridge as quickly as possible. As they crossed, great yellow-brown waves churned below, colored more by the debris carried from farther up the river than the leaden sky above. But the Miskatonic still rushed beneath the bridge, not yet up to the high flood marks painted to warn boats below and travelers above that the bridge was unsafe to use.

Halfway across, they saw a group of people struggling to walk against the wind and rain. Lefty stopped Pequod and hopped out. "Need a ride?" he yelled. "We are heading to the Palace."

Below his feet, the river rolled with a thunderous rumble that he felt as much as heard. The island which normally divided the Miskatonic into two channels was almost lost beneath the swirling waters. Looking up river, Lefty spotted the outline of a roof disappearing beneath the waves. With a sinking heart, Lefty knew this was a sign of houses swept away. Somebody had lost their home to the flood.

"Please!" a woman said, leading an old man toward the truck. "We were going to take a bus, but none showed up."

"The bus stop is under water," the man told Lefty. Another couple trailed behind him, hanging on to each other and trying to pull a cat on a leash closer. The cat looked furious. After a couple of futile tugs on the leash, the young lady scooped the cat up and clutched it to her chest.

"Can you take us with Matilda?" she asked. "We can't leave Matilda behind." Matilda hissed at Lefty.

"There's room for everyone," Lefty promised as he lifted them into the back of the truck. People rearranged their blankets to cover the newcomers. One brave soul even tried to pet Matilda, although the cat spit and swiped an angry paw at the world gone very wrong for small cats and their owners.

Harvey and Minnie poked their heads out of the cab. "Need help?" Minnie called. Lefty shook his head and waved them out of the rain. When he got back into the cab and started up Pequod, Minnie was saying to Harvey, "I can add your suggestion to go higher to the newspaper's general advice about evacuation. But not everyone will see the newspaper."

"But many people will. If they see it at the Palace, Miskatonic University, and every place that people have gathered to avoid the flood, they can act," Harvey said. "If you take extra newspapers to the Safety Stations, it will be enough to spread the word."

"It's possible," Minnie said. "We will need drivers to distribute them."

"You could call my company," Lefty said. "Ask for the garbage trucks. Tell them it is their civic duty." One of the big bosses liked being praised for doing "civic duties" and would probably approve the trucks for such use.

"And the cabbies of Arkham." Minnie bounced on the seat a little as she ticked off ways to increase distribution of the newspaper through the city. "We can ask the taxi offices to send them. Doyle talks about how they did that when the Armistice was declared, to get the news to everyone as quickly as possible."

"This is even more important than the end of the War in Europe," Harvey said. "This is about the fight for the soul of Arkham. Tell people to head for the roofs and look to the sky." Then, as they continued over a bridge that was still intact and now safe from dynamite, he asked Minnie what she thought about his plan for saving Arkham.

"It is the strangest idea that I have ever heard, and that's saying something considering how many years I have been a reporter in Arkham," Minnie declared. "But if you think it will help, I will do it. I will have to leave out all the occult jargon and dead gods for now. Doyle is more likely to print it today if I say a Miskatonic University professor advises people to climb to the roofs of taller buildings to escape the flood. We can add a line about keeping your eyes on the Thomas Ward Bridge to reckon the height of the flood."

"That will do splendidly," Harvey said.

"But I want to know more," Minnie said. "Because after this is over, I'm writing up a monster story that Doyle can't refute. All about the shadow, and the creature in the river, and how we are living in the New England town with the most secrets. I'm sure Rex and Darrell will have contributions as well. If we all pool what we know, we will have a humdinger of an article."

Lefty kept his eyes on the road but he heard everything that they discussed. One thing he noticed, although Minnie didn't ask about it, was that Harvey's explanations for his plan did not include what would happen to Harvey. Lefty could not figure out how the professor would escape Augusta's wrath if he carried out his idea.

Lefty remembered the screaming man tossed into the Miskatonic by the shadow and feared Harvey Walter's fate would be the same.

Chapter Twenty-Eight

Harvey found Boom-boom Mulligan's lair rather intriguing. After they had unloaded all of Pequod's passengers at the Palace, including the very charming *Arkham Advertiser* reporter who promised to write up his suggestions, it took only a matter of minutes to cross Northside to find the nondescript building housing Mr Mulligan. Lefty parked his truck in an alley and led Harvey around to the back of the building where he thumped on a plain wooden door.

"Mulligan! Open up!" Lefty shouted through the door.

"Who do you work for?" a voice yelled back.

Lefty shot a puzzled glance at Harvey and then shouted, "Arkham Sanitation!"

"There's nothing in the trash that explodes!" a voice said. "Promise!"

"Open up," said Lefty, pounding the door again. "I am not here about the garbage."

"You do not need to shout." The door swung open, revealing a short, thin man dressed in overalls similar to the larger Lefty.

"Mr Mulligan?" Harvey asked, raising his hat to the other

man while keeping a firm grip on the green umbrella. He had no intention of leaving it behind before the fateful meeting with Augusta Palmer and her sisters.

"You don't look like you work for the garbage company," the man said.

"He doesn't, I do," Lefty explained. "The professor needs your help, Boom-boom."

Boom-boom gave a nervous glance up and down the alley. "You better come in. I don't want to be standing out here all day."

Past the nondescript metal door, an even more anonymous corridor led to the large open space. The air smelled like chemicals, mixed with saltpeter and sulfur if Harvey trusted his nose. One end of the room held a long, scarred table. A fascinating array of items such as spools of wire and crimping tools were spread across the table. Pinned to the wall above it was a slightly scorched blueprint for an elaborate pyrotechnic display. Even from where he stood, Harvey could see the chart contained notations for a sequence of explosive charges and a neat column of calculations for the timing of the display.

"Mixing anything in particular, Boom-boom?" Lefty asked as they passed the table.

"Not today," Boom-boom replied. "I don't feel lucky. And it's not a good idea to build fireworks if you are nervous." When he gestured at the table, Harvey realized that Boom-boom was missing a number of fingers.

The man caught Harvey's glance and spread out his hands to display two stumps on the right hand and one on the left. "I still have seven fingers, including both thumbs," Boom-boom said. "That's enough to do what I need to do."

"How many toes?" Lefty muttered.

"Those don't count," Boom-boom said. "And I don't count them."

Farther in the room were a stack of crates marked with brilliant paper labels, promising blossoms of chrysanthemum and showers of dragon's fire. Also stenciled in red paint on every crate were warnings of danger.

"You seem to have a goodly number of fireworks already here," Harvey said. "These are the types meant to go up in the air and create large explosions of light?"

"Some of the very best," Boom-boom said. "Got a new shipment from Singapore a few days ago. But not enough for both of my customers, which is causing me some upset in the stomach." He rubbed his middle to emphasize.

"What's wrong?" Lefty asked.

"The Tick-tock Club wants to do a dance party with fireworks, and so does the Clover," Boom-boom said, mentioning two of the most popular speakeasies in Arkham. "A very exclusive type of affair with the fireworks set to go off at midnight. I blame this mess on Nova Malone."

"The woman in Kingsport?" Lefty asked. "The one in the newspapers?"

"Yeah, that's her. She had the idea for a dance with fireworks in July, very popular it turned out. Now the Tick-tock and the Clover are wild to do the same thing, but even bigger. But I sold most of my fireworks to Miss Malone. I don't have enough to make everyone happy. Because if their displays aren't bigger than the Diamond Dog's, I am going to hear about it!" Boom-boom grumbled. "Luckily, with all this rain, they both decided to put off their dances until later in the fall. You wouldn't believe it was still summer, it's been so cold and wet."

"Summer?" Harvey said. He was startled by the thought,

but Boom-boom was right. They hadn't reached the autumn equinox yet. Over the past few days, it had been so cold that it felt like autumn. Even the trees had started turning color on his street. Unseasonably early, Harvey now realized. Was this yet another sign of Cthulhu's approach?

Whatever the reason, it did give them one advantage. Harvey clicked open his pocket watch. They had nearly three hours until sunset. More than enough time for the *Arkham Advertiser* to print its evening edition while he put the final touches on his plan. Including acquiring all these lovely boxes of fireworks.

Another contraption caught Harvey's eye. In a corner as far away as possible from the fireworks was a fascinating construction of a pair of metal cylinders in a canvas backpack. A long hose and metal nozzle similar to a fireman's hose ran from the backpack to the floor. "What is this?" Harvey asked.

Boom-boom sidled over and petted the thing as if it was a favorite dog. "A *flammenwerfer*," he said proudly. "I bought it from a guy in Texas. He brought it back from Germany after the war ended."

"A what?" Lefty said, looking at the thing as if it might explode in their faces.

Which, as Harvey quickly translated from Boom-boom's German (surprisingly good), was not an unlikely occurrence. "It's a flamethrower," he said to Lefty. "But I thought they were much larger."

"Most of the German flamethrowers were big," Boom-boom said. "Needed a four man crew at least to use the *Kleif*. The Texan couldn't fit anything like that into his trunk. But he found this and took it back to the ranch to clear the sagebrush. Well, that's what he said. I think he just liked shooting flames out in the field. But the fire got away from him and, well, long story short, the wife insisted he sell it. Isn't it beautiful?" Boom-boom petted the pyrotechnical marvel again.

"It is wonderful," Harvey agreed, "and exactly what we need. How much to sell me the flamethrower and all the fireworks?"

Boom-boom looked distressed. "Everything? But what do I tell the club owners?"

Harvey fished the pouch of diamonds out from under his shirt. He was happy that he had remembered to take it with him. He poured a couple of sparkling gems into his hand. "This should be enough to cover all your stock and more," he said to Boom-boom. "Promise them both all the fireworks they want."

"You don't know what they are like," Boom-boom said, licking his lips and staring at the diamonds glittering on Harvey's outstretched palm. "Very territorial. They cut up rough about me selling to Nova Malone."

"Then tell them the dynamite thief stole your fireworks," Harvey said, reaching out and pressing the diamonds into Boom-boom's four-fingered right hand. "They can't blame you for losing fireworks to the thief, not when he or she already stole the mayor's dynamite."

"Really?" Boom-boom said. "Not all of the dynamite went down the river? Some of it is still around town?"

"Don't bother looking for it," Lefty said. "The last of the dynamite is at the bottom of the Miskatonic."

"Too bad," said Boom-boom, but he pocketed the diamonds. "Who is going to operate the flamethrower?"

"I will have the privilege," Harvey said before Lefty could make any foolish remarks. It was his plan and the risks should be his alone. Unfortunately, some of the danger would fall on his friend, but Harvey wanted to do as much as he could to protect Lefty.

Boom-boom looked doubtful. "It is supposed to be a one-man operation but it has a kick," he said. "You need strong arms."

"I am sturdier than I look," Harvey lied.

Boom-boom shook his head. "The flamethrower is likely to knock you over and set you on fire," he said. "Even the Texan had a hard time holding it and he was a very big man."

"Are you still planning to put everything on the truck?" Lefty said with a sigh. He hadn't liked this part of the plan. Harvey truly regretted the probable fate of Pequod, but it would be better to lose a machine than a person.

"Unfortunately, I can think of no alternative," Harvey answered.

"Oh, you have a truck?" Boom-boom exclaimed. "That makes a difference. How big is it?"

"It's my garbage truck," Lefty said. "We parked it outside."

"I've built a brace for this," Boom-boom said. "We can add that and it should hold the nozzle steady. But what are you going to do with the fireworks?"

"Put them in the truck too," Harvey admitted.

"That doesn't sound too smart," Boom-boom said, shuffling through the items on his worktable for a notepad and pencil. "You better tell me exactly what you want to do. I can figure out how to load everything so you don't blow yourself up before you get to wherever you are going. I'll even throw in the brace for the flamethrower. I won't need it now."

"What an excellent idea," Harvey said as he began to outline his plan to the inventive Mr Boom-boom Mulligan.

CHAPTER TWENTY-NINE

Minnie found Harvey Walters' address in the city directory. It was nearly an hour until sunset, but the evening edition was done and out on the streets. She took some pride in this slim and hasty version of the *Arkham Advertiser*, even though the pages were few. They had done it, put a newspaper together with the best and latest information for the city.

Darrell made it back in time to update the information on Kingsport's efforts to keep their town safe, along with descriptions of couples dancing away the rainy hours at the Diamond Dog. Rex's story about the fire at the hospital and how the brave nurses quickly extinguished it filled the back page. Even Edgar contributed a short story about the lost dynamite with promises of more revelations to come, just as she dictated to him. Wait until she turned in the sequel to Doyle along with pictures of the river monster swallowing all of it along with the guy in a head bandage!

"What are you working on now?" Doyle asked, leaning over her desk.

"Finding an address," Minnie said, although Doyle could clearly see the open pages of the battered city directory. "I want to take a copy of the newspaper to the professor for his reaction."

"I thought he was going to the Thomas Ward Bridge?" Doyle said.

"Not for another hour," Minnie said. "I should have time to meet him and snag a quote before he leaves." Also, she hoped she could talk herself onto the truck for the professor's meeting with Augusta Palmer. She still didn't understand how the shadow worked or exactly what it was, or how it was related to the creature in the river, but this could be a chance to button up her story.

Doyle checked the clock on the newsroom wall. "You will never make it," he said. "Not across town and back to the bridge. You are planning to be at the bridge, aren't you?"

"Of course," Minnie said, sliding the Speed Graphic into its waterproof case. She had changed out the film. The roll taken earlier was locked in her lowest desk drawer. Once she developed those pictures, Doyle would have to accept her monster story, but she didn't want to discuss it. Not yet. Not until she made sure the photographs looked better than the ones taken in the Black Cave.

"Risky," Doyle said, but apparently he wasn't talking about the bridge. "Cabs are hard to find and most of the buses are running emergency routes, trying to shift people to the shelters as quickly as they can. You need a car, Klein, to make it to the professor's house and back to the bridge in time. And how do you even know he is at home?"

"I don't," Minnie said. "I tried calling his phone number but the operator said the line was busy. Someone must be there, though, because they are talking on the phone."

Doyle nodded. "You need a car," he said again. "Grab your hat. I will take you."

Surprised, Minnie exclaimed, "You are going to leave the office?"

"I don't live here," Doyle huffed. "And I own a car. If Walters isn't at home, we can still make it to the bridge by sunset."

"Thanks, boss," Minnie said as she reached for the battered fedora propped on the corner of the desk. Doyle's big hand came down and snatched the hat up.

He jammed his fedora on his head and straightened the wilting press card in the hatband. "Find your own hat," he said. "I'm wearing mine."

"Looks good on you," Minnie said as she grabbed her now dry cloche from the peg on the wall. Her torn coat still felt damp to the touch and its time steaming above the radiator had not improved the smell. Minnie looked around the room but Darrell was off downstairs to doublecheck his facts in the morgue. He hadn't noticed his trench coat had gone missing for a few hours so she supposed it was fine to wear it for one more trip across town. Besides, she had all of her notebooks, pencils, and the Kodak still stashed in its pockets.

"Don't dawdle," Doyle said as he strode to the door. "We have a story to chase down."

Still bemused to see her boss moving out of the newsroom (really the whole staff suspected he slept in his office), Minnie trotted after him. Doyle's car turned out to be a battered old Ford parked behind the *Arkham Advertiser*. Like most Fords, it was black and completely nondescript. Not a bad car for tailing someone, Minnie thought. Inside the car was surprisingly clean with nothing personal left on the seats. Doyle fished his keys out of his pocket. He started it and popped the car into gear.

"Give me the address again," he said. Minnie recited the street address from memory and Doyle nodded. "That's close to Miskatonic University," he observed. "Keep your eyes on the river when we go over the bridge. I wouldn't mind a photo or two now and then later, to show how the water levels change."

"Are you telling me how to do my job?" Minnie asked as she readied the Speed Graphic.

"Don't need to tell you how to be a reporter, and a good one too," Doyle said. "Just want you to know what I need for tomorrow's newspaper." Which, from Doyle, was such high praise that Minnie felt a little better about the entire day as well as more certain that this time he would print her story about a monster with tentacles attacking barges in the Miskatonic.

As they crossed the Thomas Ward, they spotted people walking across all the bridges, heading north away from Rivertown. The unnamed island in the middle of the river was now completely covered by water. Doyle stopped his car. Minnie got out and took photos of the exodus as Doyle questioned the people walking past them.

Watching him standing in the rain, jotting notes down on a pad that he took from his own pocket, Minnie grinned to see her often cantankerous editor transformed into a reporter. The folks surrounding Doyle told tales of flood water up to the first floor of the houses and apartment buildings in Rivertown.

Minnie leaned over the railing of the bridge to snap the muddy water flowing past. It was still below the high water marks painted to warn ships that the necessary clearance was gone. Beneath her feet, the bridge deck vibrated with the force of the river and wind hitting it. She leaned out a little further, trying to capture the perfect photograph to testify to the force of the Miskatonic as the rain soaked her cloche hat again.

"Klein!" Doyle yelled. "If you fall, I am not jumping after you!" But the sound of his voice was worried, as if he thought he would have to go diving.

"Sorry, boss," Minnie said, swinging away from the river and snapping a couple of shots of the people heading across the bridge toward higher ground.

As the people gathered around their car and discussed where they could go, a city bus came rattling onto the bridge. The driver swung open the doors. "Get on!" he called. "I am heading to the train station. You can shelter there." People hurried to climb aboard, as much to have a certain destination as to get out of the rain.

When the loaded bus headed north, Minnie took a final picture of it pulling away. Doyle tucked his notebook back into his coat pocket. "I will give you my notes when we get back to the office," he said as they continued toward Harvey Walters' house.

"Thanks, boss," Minnie said. And then, remembering Doyle's gentle questions and concerned comments as people told him about losing their homes in Rivertown, she added, "For a hard-nosed editor, you are a pretty nice guy."

"Yeah, well, don't go telling the others," Doyle growled. "Those dopes would never turn anything in on time if they thought I was soft. And we still have deadlines, Klein, if we want to publish a newspaper tomorrow."

"So you think we will be printing tomorrow?" Minnie asked and tried to keep any anxiety out of her voice. The more she saw, the more she heard, the more she felt this was a flood that might sweep away everything in Arkham, especially if Harvey Walters' crazy plan did not work.

"As long as there's a city, there's a newspaper," Doyle said. "It takes more than a little water to stop us."

"About that," Minnie said, wondering if this was the time to mention the creature dragging the barge under the waves of the Miskatonic.

But Doyle came to a halt in front of the type of brick house favored by professors and professionals in Arkham. "We're here," he said. There was a long black car parked on the street as well as a smaller Chevrolet. Both automobiles looked familiar to Minnie.

As Minnie went up the walkway to knock, a woman opened the door. Pulling on her blue gloves, she addressed somebody behind her. "Keep them chanting," she said. "It may not work but Walters' ill-conceived plan needs your help."

Minnie blinked to see the woman who had commissioned the theft of the dynamite from Sol at Harvey Walters' house. Before she could open her mouth to ask any questions, a second woman appeared in the doorway. Minnie recognized Mrs Fox from their brief meeting in Rivertown.

"You could help too," Mrs Fox said to the first woman.

As the woman with blue gloves stepped around her, Minnie tried to decide whether to ask about the dynamite or the fist fight first.

"Close your mouth," the lady said to Minnie, ignoring the comment from Mrs Fox behind her. "Or you will drown like a silly turkey in this weather."

"Wait!" Minnie said as she spun on her heel to pursue her. She pushed past Doyle, who was raising his hat to Mrs Fox and introducing himself. "I have questions!"

"How very exciting for you," the woman said as she slid into her long black car. "You might even find some answers if you go to the Thomas Ward Bridge at sunset." The car started up with a roar and disappeared down the road.

Minnie ran back to the house. "Is Professor Walters here?" she asked Mrs Fox as the housekeeper conducted Minnie and Doyle into the house. "And do you know who that woman was?"

"The professor is not here. And yes, I know who she is," Mrs Fox said as she shut the door against the wind and rain. "Professor Walters never came home. I have not seen him since we left Rivertown." Somewhere in the house, the voices of women were raised in a moaning chant that shivered through the air. The sound grew louder and then softer, almost like singing from a distant choir but far more eerie.

Doyle shifted his feet, looking uncomfortable. Minnie was about to question Mrs Fox about the woman in the blue gloves, Harvey's possible location, and the sound reverberating through the house when she heard someone call her name. Looking up the stairs leading from the second floor into the entry, Minnie saw tiny April May clinging to a banister. Her friend, Nella, had an arm wound around April's waist as she helped her down the stairs.

"April!" Minnie exclaimed. "What are you doing here? How are you?"

"I am fine," April said in her soft voice. She was dressed in what looked like a borrowed quilted robe that trailed along the floor. One arm was bandaged and held tight across her chest by a sling. Minnie thought April looked terrible, with dark circles under her eyes, but she hugged her gently when she reached the final step. Even standing on a step, April was still shorter than Minnie. April felt as fragile as a bird in her arms.

"You should not be out of bed," Mrs Fox started as Doyle came to stand beside them.

"Good to see you," Doyle said, awkwardly patting April's uninjured shoulder. "Klein says you have quite a story to tell."

April smiled vaguely at Doyle but then held out a piece of paper to Mrs Fox. "This is what I saw in my dream," she said. "Mrs Alba said they need to hide this vision from Augusta Palmer."

"She should never have woken you up," Mrs Fox fussed. But she took the paper from April and gave a nod to Nella. "Take her into the kitchen. There's soup on the stove. See if you can persuade her to eat something."

"I have been eating and sleeping all day," April said in a surprisingly firm voice. Minnie had never heard her friend complain, but April sounded almost grumpy as Nella tried to steer her down the hall.

"Wait! What are you doing here?" Minnie had so many questions stirring inside that she thought she might explode in the hallway.

"Oh, the professor asked everyone from our boarding house to come here," April said. "Along with all the sibyls of Flotsam Street. Now they are trying to prevent Augusta Palmer from seeing a piece of the future."

Minnie was fairly sure that she had missed chunks of a story, but she latched on to the last statement. "Augusta Palmer can see the future?"

"Oh yes," Mrs Fox said. "That's why my great-aunt is leading her friends in the song of the sibyls, to prevent anyone from seeing the future. Valeska Stange came by to urge them to chant louder and harder. As if we need advice from a woman like her."

There were several questions that Minnie wanted to ask but the first one tumbling out of her mouth was "Song of the sibyls? What is that?"

"The most terrible song any sibyl can sing," Mrs Fox answered, "because it blinds the singer as well as anyone else with predictive powers. As long as it is sung in this city, nobody can know what will happen next."

"I had a dream," April said. "And they are sure that it is going to come true. So we are trying to hide it from the Palmers."

"What dream?" Minnie demanded, because it was the easiest question to ask. And somehow this felt even larger than stolen dynamite and monsters in the river. This was even bigger than landing on the front page. Somehow Minnie knew this was about saving the city.

"This dream," Mrs Fox said, handing the paper to Minnie. She saw a picture of a truck speeding across a bridge. April's drawing left the driver hidden in the cab, but standing tall in the back of the truck was Harvey Walters with his white whiskers flying. Over his head, stars burst and arcs of flame surrounded him.

"We are trying to hide the professor's plan from Augusta," Mrs Fox said. "It is the professor's best hope for success, according to the sibyls. So they are singing themselves blind to the future to conceal this moment from Augusta."

Doyle looked like he had as many questions as Minnie, as he peered at the drawing over her shoulder. Finally, he asked April, "Did you see this happen?"

"I dreamed about it," April replied. "And Mrs Alba says that it feels true."

"On the Thomas Ward Bridge?" Doyle asked. At April's nod, he turned to Minnie. "You said in your story that everyone should climb on the roofs and face toward the bridge."

"Yes," Minnie said. The professor had said to look to the sky for explosions to drive off the shadow – although she had left the shadow part out of the story. But she hadn't thought he meant to set off the explosions himself. While riding in the back of a speeding truck. How could that sweetly curious old man survive such a gambit? Was Harvey Walters going to gamble away his own life to save the city?

"Then why are we standing around here?" Doyle said, tipping his hat again to Mrs Fox and the wide-eyed Nella and April. "Miss May, take the time you need to recover. Then we will have to chat about you drawing for the newspaper. That is an excellent picture."

Doyle pulled the door open. "Klein, let's go! The biggest story of the day could be barreling across the bridge any minute now. We don't want to miss it!"

"On it!" Minnie said as she gave a quick wave to April and plunged back outside. She jogged down the walkway to Doyle's car. Behind them rose and fell the unworldly chant of the sibyls. Minnie could not help but wonder if their weird song could help Harvey Walters survive his own plan.

CHAPTER THIRTY

Crossing Arkham, Harvey found that the city outside the truck window was not the city slowly disappearing under a silvery curtain of rain. The city that he saw was the one he remembered. Every corner passed, every street traversed, brought back memories of buildings, businesses, and people no longer there. But if he closed his eyes for a moment, he could still see them, the light spilling from windows on the excited faces of Miskatonic University students enjoying a night on the town like the opening of *The Student Prince*. "Drink, drink, drink," Harvey hummed the popular song.

"Sorry, professor," Lefty said. "I don't have anything. But I could use a beer too."

"No," Harvey said. "I was thinking about how much this city has changed around me."

"Arkham?" Lefty said. "Seems to me it stays the same from year to year."

"No," Harvey said as they passed a storefront selling shoes. Once it had been a bookstore, a very good bookstore full of fantastic old books tucked into overflowing bookshelves. But the owner died and his children didn't want to sell books. So the place became a shoe store. Harvey liked the shoes that he bought there, but he missed the bookstore.

They passed the train station. In some ways, Lefty was right. The train station had sat there for many years without any obvious changes. Harvey had come and gone from Arkham so many times. He had seen off so many colleagues and friends there. Far too few of them had returned.

In his mind, Harvey could still see Willoughby standing on the platform surrounded by the gear of his expedition. The others were already aboard the train, but Willoughby had lingered to thank Harvey for finding him a place on his first archaeological dig. Harvey accepted the thanks and fought with his own instincts to grab the young man and haul him back to the safety of Miskatonic University. Like all professors, Harvey tried not to play favorites. But they all had preferences.

Willoughby became Harvey's secret favorite and his greatest worry. Because in Willoughby, he perceived all his own longing to understand the cosmic terrors which inspired the ancient texts and arcane ruins scattered around the world. But he also saw in Willoughby a far more empathic soul and a mind more attuned to sympathy and compassion for others. These were not the attributes of an archeologist or scholar who could survive a brush with the weirdest terrors lurking behind the hideous carvings of the temple to be explored. Nor did he think the organizers of this expedition understood or even appreciated his own warnings of how men's minds could grow clouded and crack with terror upon encountering even a trace of the Ancient One or its hideous Star Spawn.

But he allowed his own misgivings to be silenced by pride in the praise garnered by his student when the same organizers told him that Willoughby was exactly the right sort for the job. If only Harvey had questioned the job more or taken matters into his own far more capable hands. He might have saved Willoughby rather than dooming Willoughby to save others at the expense of his own life.

So he had waved Willoughby farewell at the train station so long ago, never guessing it would be a permanent goodbye.

This time, he would not make the same mistake. Harvey knew the best man for the job was himself. If anyone could pull off his plan, it would be him. If someone had to die in a blaze of flaming glory, Harvey Walters was indeed that man.

Still, he was sorry that there was nobody left to shake his hand and wish him luck, like he had done with Willoughby.

As if summoned by his musings, Harvey spotted Valeska waiting on the road leading to the bridge. He tapped Lefty's shoulder. "Stop," he said, nodding at Valeska standing by her car.

"Do you think that's smart?" Lefty asked. "She wanted to blow you up."

"Yes," Harvey admitted, "but this may be my last chance to talk with her."

Valeska nodded at him as he walked over to her car. She wore a maroon coat and a smart burgundy hat as well as a pair of brilliant blue gloves. Harvey was impressed that she had found time to change after the fight with Augusta Palmer. But that was Valeska's style, always elegant.

"Walters," she said, holding up a dripping newspaper between two fingers. Harvey recognized the evening edition of the *Arkham Advertiser*. "So this is your grand plan? Tell everyone to climb up to their roof?"

"Part of it," Harvey said. "I am glad you survived."

"She punched like a girl." Valeska's grin was savage. "Also, Oswald decided to be heroic and threw himself at her."

"How is Oswald?" Harvey asked.

"Gone, of course." Valeska shrugged. "Augusta may not have full control of that shadow yet, but it comes when she calls. And she calls very loudly when she is under attack. Luckily her sisters dragged her away before I had to make a drastic dive into the river. They seemed annoyed about the lost brother, and Augusta blamed the incident on you."

"I did not tell him to climb aboard a barge of dynamite," Harvey protested.

Valeska snorted. "Nobody said the Palmers were reasonable women. Augusta will destroy you and then use that silly umbrella to compel the shadow to create even more havoc."

"Perhaps," said Harvey, "but I am betting that I can dispel it before she can drown me. It's an interesting proposition, don't you think? Care to place a wager?"

"On one of your arcane gambles?" Valeska asked. "I am not so foolish as to bet against you, Walters. You may very well dispel the shadow. Of course, you most probably will end up in the river doing so. However, rather than wait around and see the outcome, I will concede defeat and pay your winnings now."

She flipped a coin to him. It looked like nothing that he had ever seen before, a trident embossed on one side and a dolphin on the other.

"Greek?" he asked, intrigued enough to question Valeska as the rain sluiced around him and the sky began to darken. The sun would soon go down.

Valeska stared at the bridge and did not meet his eyes. "According to legend, it's a favor of Poseidon," she said. "Sailors carried it to prevent drowning."

"Does it work?"

"Who knows? It was part of a sunken treasure that came to auction recently." Valeska opened the door of her car. "If you survive, you should leave Arkham. I am going as soon as I can collect a few artifacts from their hiding places. This city may be stomped to rubble by tomorrow morning."

"If I decide to stay?" Harvey asked, fairly certain that he would not have a choice after sunset.

"Isn't there a prediction that you will die in Arkham?" Valeska countered, which was not an answer.

"How do you know that the sibyls predicted my death?" Harvey asked, because he could play this game of answering questions with questions.

"Maybe I did not," Valeska said, determined to break the rules and stay mysterious until the end, demonstrating the most annoying and appealing part of her personality. "But now I do. Don't let a bunch of old women dictate your fate, Walters. Even me."

Harvey smiled and fingered the strange token now residing in his pocket. "I will miss you," he said to her.

"You shouldn't," Valeska retorted as she climbed into her car. "Enjoy life, Walters, for however long or short a time you have. I will be watching from the widow's walk on my roof. Be sure you give the city a good show."

CHAPTER THIRTY-ONE

Harvey returned to Pequod. In only a few minutes, they reached the closest end of the Thomas Ward Bridge. The drumming of rain upon the truck's metal roof felt like a pounding in his blood. A day of relentless water was coming to an end. Below the bridge, the Miskatonic roared past, numbing the ears to any other sound but that of destruction. "I should go," Harvey said to Lefty. The sun was definitely starting to set. He pulled the green umbrella from under the seat and held it on his lap.

"Seems there are a few more folks waiting to talk to you," Lefty said, pointing to the street in front of them.

Surprised, Harvey peered out the window. He recognized Sol and some of the Drowned Rats. Sol was standing on the running board of a large sedan.

"Is that a stick of dynamite that he is waving in his hand?" Harvey asked.

"Looks like it," Lefty said.

Harvey got out of the truck again and raised the umbrella over his head. As long as he had it, he might as well use it.

"Sol, what are you doing here?" he asked when he reached the car.

"Found this left behind in the stable," Sol said, pressing the dynamite into Harvey's free hand. "We saw the *Arkham Advertiser* and realized why you were talking about lights on the bridge. To scare away the shadow, only they didn't exactly say the shadow in the article."

"I suspect Miss Klein had a limited number of words in which to warn the population. It would be difficult to explain Augusta's manifestation in a short paragraph or two," Harvey said. As always, giving a little lecture made him feel better even though the chill of the rain soaked into parts left exposed by the umbrella.

"Then April and her friends started phoning everyone still on a working line," Sol continued. "Genevieve found me. Mrs Garcia sent a message that we were to help you. Mrs Alba too. And the other landladies of Flotsam Street. You don't say no to those ladies."

"No, I don't suppose you do," Harvey said, still a little bemused by this contingent of support from Rivertown.

"So, the boys and I, we brought a few noisemakers of our own," Sol said, pushing back his coat and showing off what looked like a Colt.

"I would very much appreciate it if you did not shoot anyone. Besides, bullets won't harm the shadow," Harvey reminded him.

Sol nodded. "They are just for the noise, same as your flash bangs. It will rattle them."

Harvey considered this amendment to his plan. It might help. But he still did not want to put anyone else in danger. "Go to the far end of the bridge," he advised. "And stay hidden until the Palmers go past. They will be looking for me. Wait until they are on the bridge and then stop them from fleeing south. But wait for my signal."

"Will do," Sol said. "What's your signal?"

"You will know when you see it," Harvey said.

Sol nodded and stuck out his hand. Harvey had to juggle the dynamite and the umbrella, but he managed to get a hand free to respond to the friendly gesture. The young man's grip was firm and warm. It reminded him enough of his final goodbye with Willoughby that Harvey had to tell himself not to be a sentimental old fool. But he said out loud, "Be careful. Stay alive. Make it home to Genevieve."

"Plan to see my gal soon. Good luck, professor," Sol said as he shook Harvey's hand. Then he waved his crew back to the waiting cars. They took off across the bridge at a speed that made Harvey smile.

"Still more coming," Lefty called to him. "You are a popular man, professor."

A black Ford rattled across the bridge and pulled up beside them. Minnie Klein leaned out the window. "Are you ready, professor?" she called. "Did you see our article?"

"I am ready. And thank you for the article," Harvey said. He glanced down the bridge. Sol and his friends were no longer visible, but three women were walking down the center of the road. Harvey carefully placed Sol's gift of dynamite in the truck bed. He would need it later.

"I believe my appointment is here. Stay back, Miss Klein, and do not draw their attention. These are dangerous women."

Harvey walked away from the truck and its flammable contents. He wanted the Palmers to ignore Lefty or Pequod. In their previous encounters, he had noticed Augusta focused on what she wanted and the other two kept their eyes on

Augusta. As he drew closer, he saw Augusta's attention was riveted on the umbrella held high over his head. They met halfway across the bridge.

"I saw that silly article. Telling people to go to the roofs for their safety," Augusta said to Harvey. "Do you really think that will save them from Cthulhu?"

Harvey tried not to wince at Augusta's casual use of the Ancient One's name. But he supposed that it did not matter anymore. The sun was going down and Cthulhu would arrive no matter what they did. Whether or not the city would survive, that he could influence over the next few minutes.

"Here is your umbrella," he said, handing it to Augusta without ceremony or explanations. The time for words was slipping away. For once in his life, he was going to act without lecturing his opponent on the nature of his plan.

True, the lectures had served as a warning to his opponents and a last attempt to give them time to escape the consequences of their actions. But the soulless gaze of Augusta, the sheer indifference of her expression as she grasped the very item that she had desired, made it clear that the shadow had consumed her soul. Any spark of humanity had flared out, leaving her as utterly removed from the concerns of ordinary people as Cthulhu itself.

The fact that Augusta did not even bother to gloat or exclaim to her sisters was telling enough. The burning ambition of Augusta Palmer to destroy the city that she loathed was the only emotion left in the sibyl. She raised the umbrella high and the shadow began to grow around them.

As always, Columbia and Barbara focused hungrily on Augusta, or perhaps on the wand held aloft in her hand. None of them paid any attention to Harvey.

Harvey turned and walked away, forcing himself to move

without haste to where Lefty waited for him in Pequod. Only when he reached the truck did Harvey dare to glance back. Columbia and Barbara remained where they had stopped on the bridge. Augusta stood a little apart from them, the shadow pouring out of her, wings stretching to the sky and the great tentacled head searching blindly for the next thing to destroy.

How lucky he planned to give it a target, Harvey thought. He stepped into the back of the truck and pulled off the tarpaulin covering the fireworks. The rain had stopped again as if in deference to the shadow stretching out across the bridge. The crates looked reassuringly dry. Harvey hefted up the flamethrower and aimed it across Pequod's cab. The rack rigged by Boom-boom held the flamethrower steady and would swivel in all directions,

Banging on the roof of the cab, he yelled to Lefty: "Let's go!"

An unhappy looking Lefty stuck his head out the window and said one last time, "Are you sure, professor? Are you ready for this?"

"We will all be fine!" Harvey promised him because he was fairly certain that Lefty would survive, as would parts of the city. As for his own fate, he only hoped that they would mark his passing with one of the large plaques. Although he really would have liked a statue. "Just drive and sing! Be ready to bail out." Then Harvey waved at the rooftops of Arkham. "Remember, people are watching! We need to give them a show."

"I can stay with you until the end!" Lefty yelled back.

"Don't!" Harvey said. Then he absolutely lied to his friend. "I can save myself but I can't save both of us. Trust me! One more gamble!"

Lefty revved the engine and turned the heavy truck around. Racing the motor, they barreled back across the Thomas Ward Bridge toward the Palmer sisters and their shadow monster.

Harvey lit up the flamethrower and shot an arc of fire into the sky. That was a signal nobody could miss.

"Take me out to the ball game!" he roared just as Lefty started singing in the cab. "Take me out with the crowd!" They had discussed this early. It was a song that they both knew and while neither of them were good singers, they could use it to time the explosions as Boom-boom suggested.

Across the rooftops of Arkham, Harvey could see them. Shapes of people fleeing the flood and turning their eyes toward the Thomas Ward Bridge.

From the opposite end of the bridge, he heard the pop-pop of guns. A car, its running boards crammed with Drowned Rats, drove toward them, neatly sandwiching the shadow and the Palmers between them.

Racing behind Pequod, just visible over his shoulder, was another black Ford. A bright flash lit the side of the car. Harvey spotted Minnie hanging out of one window firing off her camera. He hoped she caught the picture of the century.

The impossible shadow began to grow, slate blue against the silvery clouds, leaching its color from the Miskatonic River and the bridge itself. The stink of fear spread out from it, but the shouts and bangs seemed to drive back the worst of the emotion. Certainly, for him, the only feeling surging through his body was a great exhilaration to finally be fighting for Arkham against the shadow thrown over it. Harvey hoped this feeling of hope spread to the others charging against the Palmers as well as those watching. He was counting on it.

The bridge began to buck, oscillating wildly as if trying to throw them into the river. Lefty held the wheel steady and kept Pequod going straight for the belly of the beast. Harvey twisted the flamethrower so a long jet of fire aimed straight at its tentacled head. The shadow recoiled and in its retreat bloated to even greater size, surely visible now to the crowds lining the rooftops of Arkham, as was the flame that washed across it.

"Buy me some peanuts and Cracker Jack! I don't care if I never get back!" Harvey practically screamed.

Behind the shadow woven out from the dreams of Cthulhu, the Palmer sisters stared in amazement at the garbage truck hurtling toward them. For once, it seemed, Augusta had not predicted what was about to happen and it left them stunned. In this perfect moment of surprise, Harvey shot another bolt of flame across the monstrous bat wings of the shadow.

The shadow broke apart, and then came together, and then split again to become two shadows filling the bridge as they raced toward it. Now it was double-headed, quadruple-winged and yet somehow smaller. It did not cringe from the flamethrower but it wavered.

The bang-bang of the Drowned Rats distracted the Palmers, who were practically spinning in place. Augusta was visibly struggling to hang on to her wand and control the shadows now filling the bridge.

Gigantic hands plunged out of the tentacled swirling mass, as razor-sharp talons scored deep gouges into the asphalt and concrete, tearing up chunks of the roadbed and spinning those chunks toward Pequod. Lefty swerved around the oncoming boulders, hooting Pequod's horn.

Did the figures on the rooftops cheer? The thunder

boomed and lightning flashed, and the rain started up again. Still, Harvey thought he could hear shouts of defiance as they attacked the shadow of the monster descending on Arkham.

"Let me root, root, root for the home team!" Harvey never sounded better. He never felt better. Lefty was right. It was an uplifting song.

The shadows tipped back their tentacled heads. If they roared, they roared in the silence of a nightmare, a psychic echo rippling across the city. Below the bridge, the turbulent waters of the Miskatonic River churned with storm debris and crested over the flood marks.

Harvey locked the flamethrower on the two shadows and shot out another bolt. If they could stop Augusta from summoning more, they stood a chance. But Harvey could see her raising the wand high in the air, chanting as she spun it between her two hands. Tendrils of smoky shadow began to swirl around her.

In the bed of the rocking and weaving truck, Harvey sighted along the line of the flamethrower. Could he hit the umbrella and miss the woman? He swung the tip higher, aiming more for the shadow and hoping for a little luck. Another bolt of flame shot out. Augusta flinched and, as Harvey hoped, swung the umbrella to shield herself from the flame. The green canvas caught fire as Augusta staggered back.

If he had any breath left from his crazy singing, Harvey would have cheered. Instead, he concentrated on sending another bolt of flame high over the bridge.

Now the Palmer sisters broke. Columbia and Barbara whirled around and began to race for the far end of the bridge, abandoning their sister. Augusta screamed at them, tossing the flaming green umbrella to the ground. Snarling defiance at the world, she gestured to the two creatures already summoned, motioning them to attack Pequod.

Harvey reached into his pocket and pulled out the matches. He lit one and threw it over his shoulder, and then another and another, tossing them like falling stars into the bed of the truck and onto the fuses already prepared by Boom-boom. The dry paper and straw, soaked with kerosene, began to crackle and smoke.

"If they don't win it's a shame." Harvey's voice dropped a little, hoarse from singing so loudly in time with Lefty caterwauling in the driver's seat. But they had come to the most important line. Promises to keep and all that.

Behind him, fireworks began to sizzle and pop. Rockets burst out of the truck bed and filled the sky with blooms of light. The shadow creatures ducked as the fireworks whizzed overhead. They actually ducked! Harvey could have kissed Wilbur Crane, but he would leave that to Agatha. Brilliant manmade bursts of light filled the twilight sky, and the shadows shredded before it.

Harvey shot another bolt of fire at them. The two creatures melded into one double-headed monstrosity that definitely had holes appearing all over its body. Every burst of light and flame seemed to shred it into pieces. Or maybe it was the rising tide of hope that Harvey could feel in himself and those who watched.

Out of the corner of his eye, Harvey saw Augusta stagger back against the rail of the bridge, teetering over the stormy waters of the Miskatonic. Then she dropped over the edge, disappearing into the shadow that she had summoned.

"For it's one, two, three strikes you're out!" Harvey yelled. He pulled Sol's gift, the stick of dynamite, from where he had been holding it between his feet. Harvey lit it with his last match. With a throw that even Lefty would admire, Harvey flung the dynamite at the shadow. Below him, the driver's door sprang open. Lefty dived out of the cab, rolling away on the bridge as they had agreed.

Without a driver, Pequod skewed to the left. The truck hurtled toward the edge of the bridge. Driving straight through the tattering shadows still there, Pequod hit the railing and flipped over. The dynamite boomed behind him, shaking the bridge and the world. As Harvey flew through the air, he knew the sibyls had spoken truly.

This was his last gamble in Arkham. But, oh, what a way to go. He spun in space, falling into the disintegrating shadow monster. Above him, fireworks burst in glorious color, brightening the world.

As he dropped into the maelstrom of nothingness summoned by Augusta Palmer, Harvey spotted a broom spinning beside him. "Hope you approve, Willoughby," Harvey Walters said as he disappeared from Arkham, straight into the shadow cast from the dreams of Cthulhu.

CHAPTER THIRTY-TWO

Lefty stared at the roses. After surviving the confrontation on the Thomas Ward Bridge, he spent hours looking at Harvey's roses. Even though it was October, the roses were still blooming like it was summer.

He had also wasted a few days in the speakeasies, bending his elbow along with the rest of the stunned population of Arkham. And he wasn't happy about that. But friends hauled him out, and he was dry again. Lefty intended to stay dry for the rest of his life, so he wouldn't beat himself up for a lapse. He was getting better at forgiving himself for everything, even losing the professor.

Fortunately, there was plenty of work to keep him busy too. As always, repairing, mending, and cleaning helped settle his head and heart.

The storm and flood swept away entire blocks of Arkham. Fires had broken out all over the city. But, as everyone said over their beers, it could have been worse. He didn't know if it was the professor's fireworks show or just the inherent stubbornness of the people who lived in Arkham, but heroic acts happened throughout the city that night according to Minnie's stories in the *Arkham Advertiser*.

He owed a debt to the reporter. Minnie had hunted him down in his most miserable hour, and listened to his sorrow and his rage. Then she turned it into a beautiful tribute to Harvey Walters splashed all across the front page of the newspaper. Mrs Fox had clipped out the article and carefully framed it. It was hanging in the front hall of the house now.

The article called Harvey's actions an endeavor to set off warning flares when the Miskatonic exceeded all previous flood levels. Certainly, the destruction of the waters had spread further than originally predicted. But many successfully made it to higher ground or the rooftops of Arkham. The loss of life would have been far greater, according to a quote from the mayor, without the heroic sacrifice of Harvey Walters.

As for monstrous shadows, tentacles reaching out of the river to snatch a barge, and the even greater destruction that came later in the night, the *Arkham Advertiser* remained rather vague. Minnie's annoyance with her editor had been voiced loudly when she had joined them for one of Mrs Garcia's celebratory dinners after her house was reopened. April and Nella giggled as Minnie imitated her editor in a growly deep voice, "Facts, Klein, facts and pictures. Monsters stomping across the city must be proved with more than wild tales from a shocked populace and a few blurry photographs."

Both Minnie and April were back at work at the *Arkham Advertiser*, along with Nella, who had taken some type of secretarial job there following the disappearance of the office manager Columbia Goadby. They seemed to enjoy working together. During boarding house meals, with Minnie becoming as big a fan of Mrs Garcia's cooking as the rest of them, the gals often talked about new reporters coming on and possible expansions of the *Advertiser*'s coverage. Apparently, there was more news happening every day as the city rebuilt itself.

It was nice to see the girls recovering. The young ladies, as Mrs Fox reminded him when he slipped and called them girls, were the future of Arkham and a good future at that. He was simply glad that the shadows at the end of alleys were only shadows again and the Miskatonic had settled back into its place.

"I thought I would find you here," said Mrs Fox, wandering into the yard. As was her habit, she carried two mugs of coffee. She handed one to Lefty and sipped from the other.

"How is she?" Lefty asked about Mrs Fox's great-aunt as he did every day. Something had happened to all the sibyls during the storm which left them, according to Mrs Fox, blind to the future. Strangely, none of them seemed very bothered by this, other than a certain physical exhaustion. Mrs Alba even joked it was refreshing not to know what would happen next.

"Quiet," Mrs Fox replied. As the oldest sibyl in Arkham, her great-aunt had suffered the most. For days she had been barely strong enough to walk across a room. "She is sleeping more each day. But her dreams seem pleasant. How are the repairs coming?"

"Here or at Mrs Garcia's?" he asked.

"Here first."

"Pretty good. The roofers are done and there's no real damage in the attics," he said. "The basement is cleared. The boiler is working again. The carpenters will have your new laundry room framed out by the end of the week."

They had found Harvey's instructions. The house, and the

gold in his bedroom, belonged to Mrs Fox. She had put most of the gold somewhere (Lefty hadn't asked where) but used a little to make necessary repairs. Mrs Fox hadn't seemed surprised that Harvey had left her the house. She also wasn't inclined to do too much. Harvey's study was exactly as he left it and his bedroom remained closed and locked, although Mrs Fox cleaned it weekly. But she did move ahead with the removal of the laundry from the basement, apparently a change that she had long wanted.

"That's good news about the carpenters," she said. "How is Mrs Garcia?"

"Fine," Lefty replied. "We finished cleaning the basement. It was the last thing to be done." Most of his stuff had not survived, but most of his stuff had been second hand, scrounged from various customers. He still had his job. After a night of destruction by a storm, flood, and something that nobody in Arkham wanted to name, there was plenty of cleanup work. The Arkham Sanitation Company even shrugged at the loss of Pequod, listing it as destroyed in the flood. He had a new truck. It wasn't the same, but it ran well enough. He supposed that he would get used to it. Maybe even paint a name on the hood.

"You can stay here as long you like," Mrs Fox said. "I feel better having someone watching the house."

"Don't you want to move in?" he asked, because it was really her house and not Harvey's, even though evidence of the professor remained throughout the place. Mrs Fox was still living with her great-aunt. Lefty stayed with the rest of Mrs Garcia's boarders until everyone else had moved back to Flotsam Street. But his apartment in the basement had suffered the most damage and wasn't usable. Mrs Garcia urged him to help Mrs Fox with her repairs.

It felt strange to be living in the professor's house. Even though he'd only been in it for a few hours when Harvey had been there, Lefty kept expecting to hear the professor stomping down the stairs reciting lines from the *Rubaiyat* like that day. It must have been even worse for Mrs Fox. So he understood her reluctance to move. He was grateful for the bed and all the books. The professor's collection of novels was impressive but he stayed away from the stuff in the study. Eventually, Harvey's occult books would go to Miskatonic University's library, but another old professor named Armitage said he would prefer to keep the books locked up at the house for now.

"I am not ready to move in," Mrs Fox said as she sipped her coffee and contemplated the roses. "Not until we are sure. Besides, Auntie is more comfortable in her own home."

"I don't think he's coming back," Lefty said. It had taken him a long time to say it out loud and he still felt bad when he did say it.

The day after the storm, Sol and the Drowned Rats had searched the river both above and below the Thomas Ward Bridge. They had found far too many bodies. Some of the drowned were still waiting for identification at the city morgue. But of Harvey Walters in his second best suit, there was no sign.

"I will wait a little longer." Mrs Fox leaned against Lefty, her head resting on his shoulder. He put an arm around her waist. He would never have Harvey's skill with words, but he was learning how to talk with her. It was a small precious gift, one he was still stunned to realize that he had received in the aftermath of all that had happened.

"Laura," he said slowly and with wonder at having her first

name fall so easily from his lips. "Harvey would tell us to get on with it. Stop moping. But in more words."

She chuckled. "And then he would tell us to go eat a good breakfast, preferably with cornbread."

"Yes, he would," Lefty said.

Mrs Fox, Laura Fox, nodded. She reached out and plucked a white rose from the hedge. At breakfast, the rose rested on the kitchen table, gently placed where Harvey would have sat. They both saluted it with their coffee mugs as they discussed a future devoid of predictions and full of possibilities, just as Harvey would have wanted.

ACKNOWLEDGMENTS

Writing a book takes an invisible team behind the author, cheering her on and sometimes gently correcting her historical errors. As always, any foul ups belong to me and, possibly, Cthulhu. But the amazing Arkham Historian continues to tie fictional encounters to real dates... and puts up with a slight twisting of the timelines by me or Cthulhu with great civility.

For this adventure, I owe thanks to Rosie and her father for confirming that Pequod could look as described. My dear Oogaboo friends spent a Zoom meet-up discussing all their memories of garbage disposal in the latter half of the twentieth century, some of which I swiped for Lefty's job. Final conclusion: it varied by community. Usually garbage was burned, buried, or floated out to sea.

As for catastrophic floods in the United States, 1927 was a record year when the most famous of all was the Great Mississippi Flood. It inspired the Randy Newman song "Louisiana 1927." The flood actually impacted Missouri, Illinois, Kansas, Tennessee, Kentucky, Oklahoma, and Texas with the worst damage occurring in Arkansas, Louisiana, and Mississippi. An estimated 27,000 square miles were covered by floodwaters, killing many and displacing hundreds of thousands of people.

The National Museum of African American History and Culture displayed a remarkable collection of photos taken after the Mississippi flood on their website in 2024. This led me to clips of Bessie Smith singing "Back Water Blues," which she wrote in 1927, although the history of the song indicates it was written about another flood. I also highly recommend the PBS American Experience episode "Fatal Flood."

To protect New Orleans in April 1927, wealthy business-men decided to destroy certain levees with thirty tons of dynamite. This resulted in record flooding down river. So, Arkham being Arkham, I stole this questionable practice for the flood relief efforts depicted in this novel.

The quote about flamethrowers is real, and occurs in the late 1920s supplement for the *Encyclopedia Britannica* on my shelf. The author was critiquing the use of flamethrowers on the battlefields of Europe, but I prefer to think it is about fighting Cthulhu and friends.

The infamous spitball started to be outlawed from Major League Baseball in the 1920s (a number of pitchers were exempt from the rule changes and the last legitimate "spitballer" played in the 1930s). In 1920, Carl Mays killed Ray Chapman by cracking Chapman's skull with a pitch, possibly a spitball. Whether or not it was an accident was a matter of considerable debate at the time. In 1921, the "Black Sox" went on trial for colluding with gamblers to throw the 1919 World Series. The accused players were banned from the game for life. The song "Take Me Out to the Ball Game" was written in 1908 and is still sung during the seventh inning stretch at many games. My grandfather could sing all the verses when he was older than Harvey.

As always, a huge round of applause to the entire Aconyte team and our friends at Fantasy Flight Games for continuing to expand the world of *Arkham Horror*. It's been a joy to write two stories based on the Drowned City Expansion. The beautiful *Arkham Horror Role-Playing Game Core Rulebook* provided more fantastic descriptions of Cthulhu and influenced my depiction of the shadow. It also contains this message to players: "Reinforce the idea that hope makes the impossible possible. The fate of the world hangs in the balance."

For all those reading this book, please know you are appreciated too! May this adventure bring hope to you and others as well.

ABOUT THE AUTHOR

ROSEMARY JONES is the author of the *Arkham Horror* novels *Mask of Silver*, *The Deadly Grimoire*, *The Nightmare Quest of April May*, and *The Bootlegger's Dance*. She is an ardent collector of children's books, and a fan of talkies and silent movies. Her other works include *Wrecker of Engines* (Cobalt City 20th Anniversary edition), *Dungeons & Dragons' Forgotten Realms* novels, numerous novellas, short stories, and collaborations.

rosemaryjones.com // x.com/rosemaryjones

ARKHAM HORROR

**Prepare yourself for the terror
of the Drowned City!**

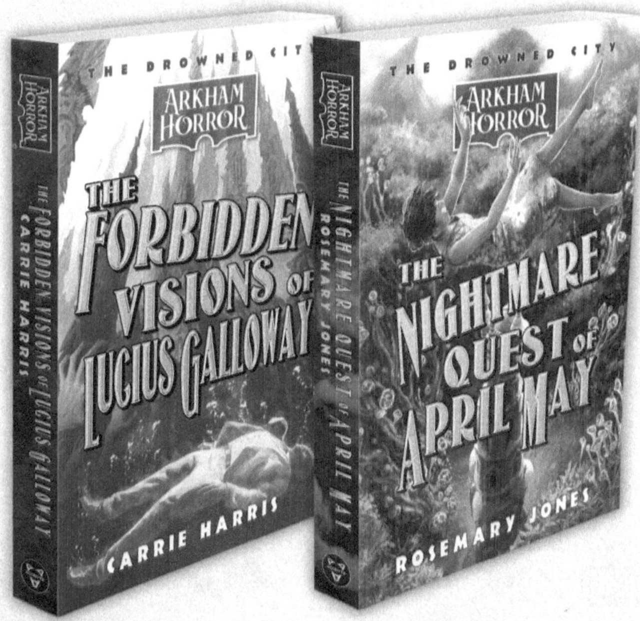

**Read the brand new prequel novels to the
Arkham Horror: The Card Game
The Drowned City expansion!**

**ACONYTEBOOKS.COM
ARKHAMHORROR.COM**

CHOOSE YOUR INVESTIGATOR.
CHOOSE YOUR PATH.
DECIDE YOUR FATE.

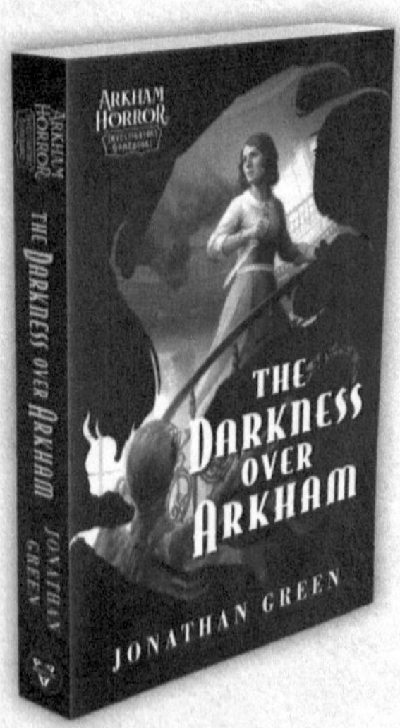

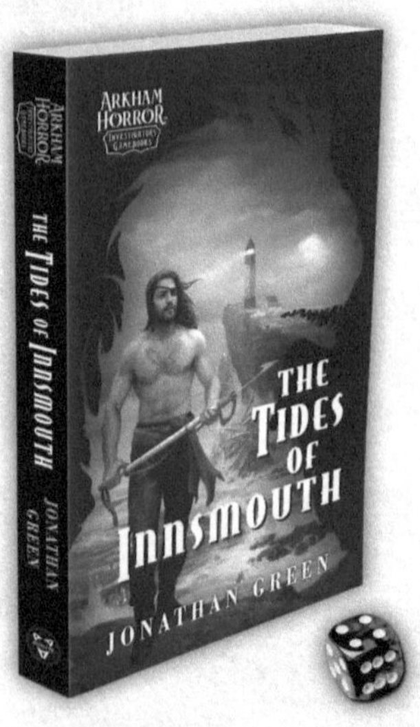

Take on the mantle of Investigator and explore the world of Arkham Horror in a whole new way as your choices change the story.

ACONYTEBOOKS.COM
ARKHAMHORROR.COM

Arkham Horror

Explore the terrors lurking in the dark heart of Arkham in uncanny tales of occult adventure.

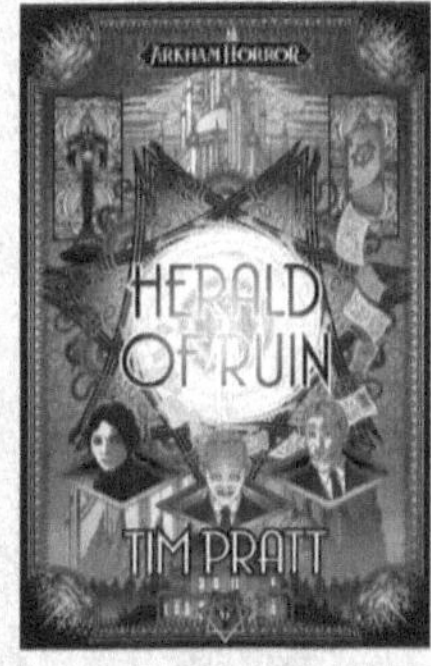

Eldritch omnibus editions available now in paperback & ebook.

ACONYTEBOOKS.COM
ARKHAMHORROR.COM

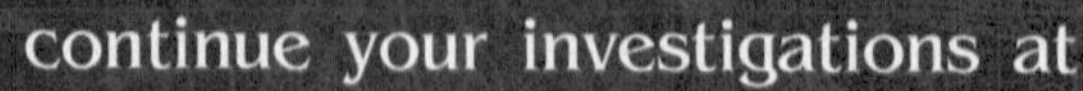

continue your investigations at

ArkhamHorror.com

Visit Arkham from the safety of your browser

Meet the Investigators, explore the lore, discover your next favourite game and find the latest news, all in one place

Latest Arkham news

NEWS · GAMES · STORIES
LORE · FEATURES · BONUS CONTENT

www.ingramcontent.com/pod-product-compliance
Lightning Source LLC
Chambersburg PA
CBHW030541190726
48283CB00006B/1970